Praise for *PROVIDEN*

"[A] terrific sci-fi thriller."　　　　　*—Publis*

"Something for everyone: space combat, interpersonal tension, and aliens, ultimately leading to a story about survival."　　*—Kirkus Reviews*

"A fast-paced, intelligent military space opera . . . Barry brings his skills of characterization and satire to the fore. . . . Barry delivers some stunning action sequences and provides a bittersweet resolution."　　*—The Guardian*

"*Providence* is an absolute treat. Pulls the trick of being both irrepressibly old-school sci-fi and creepingly relevant to the data-driven future."
　　—Austin Grossman, author of *Soon I Will Be Invincible*

"I could not put *Providence* down until I'd finished it in one thrilling sitting. This is science fiction at its best—a ship so believably alive and characters so determined, flawed, and compelling that you'll forget you're not also part of the crew."　　—Peng Shepherd, author of *The Book of M*

"Yet another example of [Barry's] ability to deliver big ideas in the form of breathlessly efficient sci-fi thrillers . . . As always, Barry excels at hitting the sweet spot between brainy and entertaining. A crackerjack thriller set deep in enemy territory."　　*—Shelf Awareness*

"Brain-bending adventure."　　　　　*—Newsweek*

"Max Barry has a true comic writer's pessimism, imprisoning his crew in a ship as indifferent and unreadable as any alien enemy. What must this ship think of its crew? Are they its children? Or an infection it must deal with? *Providence* is a light-hearted thriller with a superb dark, existential sting in its tail."　　*—London Times*

"Such a blast you almost overlook how clever it is."　　*—The Daily Mail*

"After all this myth and fantasy, time for some proper SF with aliens and futuristic hardware. Max Barry's *Providence* sees the four-strong crew of an AI-controlled spaceship shot into deep space to take part in a war against a reptilian extraterrestrial species nicknamed salamanders. Claustrophobia and isolation lead to tensions on board, while the ship itself, almost godlike in its indifference to the people within, pursues its mission regardless. The result is a quirky, character-driven commentary on the mechanisation of conflict and the sheer perversity of human nature." —*Financial Times* (UK)

Praise for *LEXICON*

"A dark, dystopic grabber . . . [an] ambitious, linguistics-minded work of futurism." —Janet Maslin, *The New York Times*

"An extremely slick and readable thriller . . . Barry's particular addition to the genre is a corrosive wit." —*The Washington Post*

"An extraordinarily fast, funny, cerebral thriller." —*Time*

"The words brilliant and exemplary aren't adequate enough to convey the amazing craft of *Lexicon*." —Associated Press

"Page-turner of the year . . . a smart, character-based thrill" —*Chicago Tribune*

"[Barry is] racing up alongside the likes of Neal Stephenson with this smart, compelling, action-packed thriller." —*Kirkus Reviews* (starred review)

"An absolutely first-rate, suspenseful thriller with convincing characters who invite readers' empathy and keep them turning pages until the satisfying conclusion." —*Booklist* (starred review)

Praise for *MACHINE MAN*

"Inspired . . . memorable, thought-provoking, sardonic and flat-out nerdy . . . *Machine Man* is the cyborg novel you've been waiting for." —io9.com

"Barry's razor-sharp authorial voice perfectly articulates Charlie's inner desires, and anyone who's worked with, studied as, or loved an engineer will appreciate the host of in-jokes that pepper the novel. With clever commentary on the military-industrial complex and the modern consumer's desires, Barry brings a nerdy sense of humor to an entirely believable premise no longer limited to the realm of science fiction. Darkly comic, genuinely tender, with more than a few great fight scenes, this is a triumph." —*Booklist*

"A smart, cynical book packed with both action and very geeky ideas . . . If you've never read anything by Max Barry, now's a great time to start."
—wired.com

"As in his previous novels, Barry takes scenarios that ought to be tragic and cannily reshapes them into smart, piercing comedy about contemporary workaday life. Here the target is both corporate greed and technological obsession, though this time the humor grows bleaker and more grotesque—Barry nervily explores how much of the body can be mechanized, right down to heartbeats and synapses."
—*Kirkus Reviews*

Praise for *COMPANY*

"Make(s) topics like outsourcing, mission statements, and H.R. come alive, breathe fire, and vomit all over your in-basket . . . Smart and fast paced."
—*The New York Times Book Review*

"Hilarious . . . Barry underscores his credentials as both satirist and saboteur. . . . *Company* is Mr. Barry's breakout book."
—*The New York Times*

"Barry's accomplished an impossible feat—he's written three books without succumbing to a sophomore slump. Insightful and devilish . . . If you're reading a management book right now, any management book, put it down and get this instead."
—*Forbes*

"Laugh-out-loud funny . . . Superbly observed."
—*The Washington Post*

"Biting, hilarious."
—*People*

"Establishes [Barry] as one of the keenest and shrewdest minds in corporate satire . . . Utterly original."
—*Entertainment Weekly*

"A raucous black comedy . . . Enters some sublimely Kafkaesque territory."
—*Kirkus Reviews* (starred review)

"As bitter as break-room coffee . . . Eviscerates modern management techniques."
—*Publisher's Weekly*

"Would do Evelyn Waugh proud . . . Management types will double over laughing."
—*The Economist*

TITLES BY MAX BARRY

PROVIDENCE

MAX BARRY

G. P. PUTNAM'S SONS
NEW YORK

PUTNAM
— EST. 1838 —

G. P. PUTNAM'S SONS
Publishers Since 1838
An imprint of Penguin Random House LLC
penguinrandomhouse.com

The Library of Congress has catalogued the G. P. Putnam's Sons
hardcover edition as follows:

Names: Barry, Max, 1973– author.
Title: Providence / Max Barry.
Description: New York: G. P. Putnam's Sons, [2020] |
Identifiers: LCCN 2019049937 (print) | LCCN 2019049938 (ebook) |
ISBN 9780593085172 (hardcover) | ISBN 9780593085189 (ebook)
Subjects: GSAFD: Science fiction.
Classification: LCC PS3552.A7424 P76 2020 (print) |
LCC PS3552.A7424 (ebook) | DDC 813/.54—dc23
LC record available at https://lccn.loc.gov/2019049937
LC ebook record available at https://lccn.loc.gov/2019049938

First G. P. Putnam's Sons hardcover edition / March 2020
First G. P. Putnam's Sons trade paperback edition / May 2021
G. P. Putnam's Sons trade paperback ISBN: 9780593085196

Printed in the United States of America
1st Printing

Book design by Nancy Resnick

For Freddy
They use the guns this time

Providence is wiser than you, and you may be confident it has suited all things better to your eternal good than you could do had you been left to your own option.

—JOHN FLAVEL

THE ENCOUNTER

At last it's time and you file in to watch the contact video. You've seen it before; everyone has. When you enter, you recognize the bulkheads, the fat tube lighting they used everywhere back then, even the black rubber coffee mug that sits atop a panel near the breach chamber's exterior door. But it's different. They said you had to see it for yourself to appreciate it, and they were right. When you turn your head, the picture is all around you. You can walk right into it. You could just about pick up that coffee mug and drink from it. This isn't like what you've seen before. It's like being there.

Up front are four white-suited figures. Since this is the contact video, you recognize them: Maladanto, White, Esperanza, and Bock. Just standing there, large as life. Someone beside you inhales. A wild compulsion rises in your throat: You should warn them! A man to your right even takes a step and clenches his hands. You knew what you'd be watching today but you weren't prepared for it to feel like this, like it's wrong to be here. And wrong not only because you know what's going to happen, and not even because there are four people who need your help and you can't give it, but wrong like you're intruding. They're about to experience the worst moment of their lives, and you've come to watch it.

Fabric suits, plastic helmets. Esperanza is holding a thin stick that functions a little like a cattle prod, and that's the best weapon they have. They're scientists, remember. They went into space to study bacterial growth. Then they picked up a hint of controlled propulsion in a place it didn't belong and there was no one else for millions of miles. They could have turned tail and run—they should have—but here they are. Side by side. With a cattle prod.

Their positioning is terrible. That's something you didn't appreciate from the standard video. At first glance, they're poised and ready. But with this much detail you can see everything that's waiting to go wrong. Esperanza is a half step back from where he should be, his weight on his right foot; he's going to get tangled up with Maladanto, it's as clear as day. Bock is supposed to be stationed by the interior door, but she's come too far forward. White is a mess of nerves. His eyes roam the chamber and—*aha!*—alight on that coffee cup. You can see his thought: *So that's where I left it.*

"Open it," says Maladanto.

Coral Beach's exterior breach door clacks and thumps and splits to reveal a depthless dark. Decompression ripples their suits. White's coffee mug falls off the shelf and rolls toward the void.

"Steady," says Maladanto. His voice is deep and rich and more intimate than you've heard it before. He's ex-Service, the only one of the crew with any military background. Used to fly shuttles, back when they needed human pilots. "We're making history today. Don't fuck it up."

Bock lifts a hand to wipe her brow. Actually draws the back of her hand across her faceplate. Then lowers her arm like she didn't even notice how crazy that was.

The wind dies. The doors open as far as they go and halt with a sound you can feel through your feet. It's hollow breathing and nothing else. For minutes, everyone holds position. The standard video skips this. You see the doors open, then contact. Because it's four people just standing there; what's to see? It turns out that White swallows repeatedly. He closes his eyes for ten seconds at a time. At one point, Bock says, under her breath, "*Shit*," so quietly it's barely a word. A tremor starts in her left leg, enough to wobble the suit fabric. You see these details and they matter.

Maladanto says, "Where are they?"

Up in the command station of this little plastic suitcase is de Veers, watching the monitors. He's the youngest of the five, and when Maladanto ordered him to take the helm, he protested, because he wanted to be down here in the breach chamber with them. But only briefly, because de Veers is irrepressibly good-natured, with a grin that never goes missing for long. He's going to die in about four minutes.

"From what I can figure, two starboard, one aft, one port, one below," says de Veers. "Don't think they've noticed that we opened the front door."

For three days, they've been tracking a half-mile-wide brown rock. All they know about it is it's full of holes and moving like it has some control over where it's going. Ten hours ago, it began to angle toward *Coral Beach*, as if noticing them for the first time. Sixty minutes ago, it exuded five small, dark blobs, which sailed across the darkness and stuck to *Coral Beach*'s hull. Since then, the crew has been tracking them mostly from the sound, which is a *clunk, clunk, clunk* like someone's walking around out there.

To your left, a woman stiff-legs it toward the exit. It's tempting to join her. But Maladanto, Esperanza, Bock, and White are there with the breach door open and you're struck by how they didn't have to do this. At any point, they could have decided to pull out and leave this to someone else. Even now, they could have closed the exterior door and pulled *Coral Beach* away, and maybe it wouldn't have made a difference—maybe by this point, their fate was sealed—but even so, they stood together and faced it. So you're staying, too.

"Okay," de Veers says in your ear. "Seems like they noticed. All five unknown objects converging on the breach chamber."

You see their hands tighten, the skin crease around their eyes. Esperanza takes a little step to the left, which gets him out from behind Maladanto, and you think, *Yes!* as if there's still a chance. Then he steps right back where he was. You hear someone moan quietly. There's an urge to blame here, to say, *There*, that's what went wrong. That's why it happened. Esperanza's positioning. Bock drifting away from the door. There must be something, a mistake without which it would have turned out differently. Surely it didn't have to be like this.

A vibration. Low impacts coming through the hull.

De Veers's disembodied voice: "Ten seconds, boss."

Maladanto says, "We don't know what we're going to see. Neither do they. Let's nobody turn this into something it doesn't have to be."

White's lips move fractionally. You always thought he was chewing the inside of his lip, but he's actually mouthing words. When you make out a few, you realize he's praying.

A rough, blocky limb appears against the darkness. It curls inside the bulkhead like a tree root. Then another limb, and more: too many limbs. An irregular shape rises into view. There's a rough-hewn head and shoulders and a massive torso and it looks like some kind of gnarled wood. It's actually translucent resin. You can see a hint of movement beneath its surface, threads contracting and expanding, like a bowl of worms. A second shape clambers down from above, senses the gravity, and drops to the floor, landing on six thick limbs. The tremor comes up through your shoes.

"Oh, God," someone behind you mutters.

Maladanto, Esperanza, Bock, and White don't move. That's always seemed remarkable, but now it's flat-out amazing. They watched two alien nightmares climb on board and they didn't fall apart and run.

The creatures move tentatively, taking stilted steps. Their heads bob. You know what they are. They have several names, nowadays, but most commonly, people call them salamanders. You know a lot about them that Maladanto and his people don't.

The salamanders seem to notice them. There are moments of stillness: one, two, three, four. Maladanto raises a hand in greeting.

The salamanders don't respond right away. It's not clear whether they understand. Then the first begins to bow. It was standing on four hind legs; now it goes down onto all six. Its head dips.

Maladanto isn't an expressive guy and even here his face is half-shadowed by his helmet, but you can see what's blazing in his mind. He didn't dare hope it would be life, and he didn't dare hope it would be intelligent, and he didn't dare hope it could communicate. He begins to lower his own head, mirroring a gesture he's read all wrong.

The salamander's face splits open. What you're seeing is its protective resin breaking apart to reveal its true face for the first time. But to Maladanto, it must appear as if the creature's head disintegrates. Its jaws crack open. It makes a movement in its throat, which has since been named for the noise it accompanies: *huk.*

Maladanto's body jerks. Fluid hits the wall behind him.

You know that salamanders are capable of spitting little quark-gluon slugs, which are essentially tiny black holes. They leave behind a trail of mangled matter, because what happens when that much gravity passes an inch from your heart and five feet from your toes is that different parts of your body experience monumentally different forces. The crew of *Coral Beach* doesn't know this. They only see Maladanto's body implode.

A chunk of what's left hits Esperanza. He's the one with the cattle prod, which is actually an emergency ignitor for *Coral Beach*'s fuel collider and has never been used in practice. It's capable of putting out a heart-stopping charge, but Esperanza falls and loses his grip on it, because he was standing too close to Maladanto.

White runs. This is the part where Bock should take two steps back and drop the door. But the cattle prod rolls toward her and she hesitates, then runs forward and scoops it up. The salamander advances and she raises the cattle prod above her head. White reaches the door and yells for Bock to come. This is how it happens: Bock won't leave Esperanza and White won't leave Bock.

The salamander pauses. Bock could strike at it, but doesn't. She's holding a cattle prod in front of an alien and no one would blame her for freezing up in fright, but that's not what's happening. Bock is a biologist, and there's a line of concentration between her eyebrows, and you see her hearing Maladanto's words: *Don't fuck it up.* Before she stabs the first intelligent life ever found beyond Earth's warm blue bubble, she's making sure in her own mind that it's the right thing to do. Maybe she could have killed one. Hurt it, at least. Who knows. She's still deciding when the two salamanders *huk* and turn her and White inside out.

Esperanza grunts, the sound loud in your ear. He shoves away the rearranged nightmare that is Maladanto. The door is twenty feet away and he crawls toward it. The salamanders watch him. There's nothing to read in their faces. They're both split open now, loose strings of resin dangling obscenely, but what's underneath—the wide, lipless mouths, the black, orblike eyes—is incapable of expression. Esperanza is a fifty-eight-year-old botanist who made his name in flowering gene strains. The salamanders let him get almost to the door before they turn him into meat.

People around you are crying. Alert lamps are cycling. Those *huk*s passed all the way through *Coral Beach*, leaving ten-inch-diameter tunnels behind, so air is venting. The salamanders don't seem bothered. Resin is already threading across their faces, forming a fresh layer. Behind them, more salamanders climb into the breach chamber. They explore slowly, thoroughly. They go through the door that nobody closed. There's another behind that, which stymies them briefly, but when they can't force it open, they *huk* at it until they can. *Coral Beach* isn't large. It's not long until they find de Veers. He's working the engines, trying to bring the craft around on the alien ball. He has no weapons, so he's decided to ram it.

The salamanders don't speak. They don't try to communicate. They just kill him. You don't know why. There are a lot of theories. Some people say it wasn't their fault. We wandered into their territory and they defended it. They're mindless animals, unaware of what they're doing. Something Maladanto did registered to them as a threat. There are a lot of opinions. All you know is that when the video finally, mercifully stops, you want to kill salamanders, as many as you can.

SEVEN YEARS
AFTER CONTACT

1

[Gilly]

THE LAUNCH

Before he could go before a global audience of two billion, they wanted to fix his eyebrows. He sat before a light-ringed mirror, on a chair that went up and down at the whim of a woman with silver lips, and tried to keep still.

"The left is fine," she said. "The right concerns me."

He'd been in the chair for two hours. There had been a makeup person, a hairdresser, a stylist, and now this second makeup person. His face felt like a plaster model, ready to crack and fall to pieces if he smiled.

"Smile," she said. It did not crack. "Can I get some three-base paste for Gilligan?"

"Gilly," he said reflexively. He didn't like Gilligan.

"I'm so nervous, I could barf," said the person to his left. "That blueberry yogurt is definitely starting to feel like a mistake."

Three others were in chairs alongside him; the speaker was Talia Beanfield, the Life Officer. Gilly glanced at her but she was recording herself on her phone. He was supposed to be recording clips, too.

Service wanted to stitch them together into a behind-the-scenes feed of the launch ceremony.

She caught his eye and smiled. For most of the last half hour, Beanfield had been immersed in towels and clips. She looked good now, though. Her hair was artful and honey brown and glimmered as she moved. "Did you try the yogurt, Gilly?"

"No."

"Smart," she said to her phone. "This is why Gilly's Intel and I'm Life."

"I'm sorry," said the makeup woman. "I need to get in there." She stood between them and resumed her attack on Gilly's face.

"Stop giving the makeup people a hard time, Gilly," Beanfield said. "You and your unruly eyebrows."

"Eyebrow," said the woman. "It's only the right."

"A deviant," said Beanfield.

"Len's here," called a woman by the door. "Last looks, please!"

Gilly took the opportunity to check out the others. Jackson, the captain, was reclining with a white bib tucked around her neck, eyes closed, possibly asleep. She hadn't recorded any clips, either, as far as Gilly had noticed. Between her and Beanfield was Anders, the Weapons Officer. He had a shock of dark hair and light stubble and was probably the most handsome man Gilly had ever met. On the occasions Gilly hadn't been able to avoid seeing his own press, he was always struck by how out of place he looked, like a fan who'd won a contest to meet celebrities. Jackson, the war hero; Anders, the tortured dreamboat; Beanfield, the effortlessly charming social butterfly . . . and Gilly, a permanently startled-looking AI guy who couldn't find a good place to put his hands.

The door opened. A man in fatigues entered and clapped his hands. This was Len, their handler from Service: thirtyish and upbeat, carrying a little extra weight. "It's time. How's everybody feeling?"

"Like a painted whore," said Anders.

"That's perfect," said Len. "We're good to move, then, yes?"

"Yes," said Jackson, awake after all. She peeled off her bib and was at the door before the rest of them had managed to extract themselves from their makeup thrones. The silver-lipped woman stepped back and, for the first time in a while, looked into Gilly's eyes instead of around them.

"Good luck out there," she said.

The van's windows were heavily tinted. But as they crossed the tarmac, Gilly caught sight of the shuttle gantry: a towering metal lattice that would launch them into the upper atmosphere. From there, they would rendezvous with the ship, which had recently finished its two-year construction in high orbit. They would then perform a monthlong burn, followed by a hard skip to join four other Providence-class battleships that were fighting an alien race farther away than anyone could imagine. Before any of that, though, was the part he was anxious about.

"Here's the rundown," said Len. "Your families will be seated to the right of the stage, all together. Feel free to give them a wave, blow them a kiss, whatever you like. You can do that at any point. But especially at the end, as you're leaving for the shuttle."

"I did my good-byes this morning," Gilly said.

There was a half second while Len tried to figure out whether he was joking. "Well, this is the one people see. So, you know, give them a wave."

"Yep, okay," he said.

"Like you mean it," said Len. "Like you're about to embark on a harrowing four-year mission to save the world and you might not see them again. You know what I mean?"

"Yes," Gilly said.

Len eyed him another moment, then turned to Anders. "Paul, there will be two empty seats beside your uncle."

Those would be for Anders's brothers, who had been lost in an earlier engagement of the war. There was a third brother who'd taken his own life, Gilly knew, as well as a father who had drunk himself to death. The only member of Anders's family to attend the launch was an uncle, who, when they'd been allowed to mingle this morning, had repeatedly squeezed Gilly's shoulder and entreated him to invest in his mattress store.

"The governor will deliver the opening address," said Len. "Six minutes. For this part, you just need to stand still and look attentive. We then have a two-minute spiritual but strictly nondenominational blessing, during which you may look down or skyward. Alternate between the two as your heart tells you. But please do not, repeat, not, make eye contact with families, wave at anyone, or give off the impression of being bored or distracted." He eyed Gilly. "Understood?"

"Got it."

"There are times when your bumbling obliviousness to protocol is seen as endearing," Len said. "I just want to make it clear: This would not be one of those times."

"I've got it," he said.

"I believe in you," Len said, and looked at Gilly a moment longer, which, Gilly felt, undermined the message. "After this, we get into the politicians and corporates." He rattled off a few names, only some of which Gilly recognized. He'd spent the last year being trained by Service but was still technically a civilian: an employee of Surplex, the company that had built the ship. Of the crew of four, he was the only one who didn't have a military background. He was also the youngest, at twenty-six, beating out Beanfield by six months.

"At one point, the admiral will refer to your husband," Len said to Jackson, who was gazing out the window at the gantry. She'd put on dark sunglasses, which made Gilly wonder how much she could see. The van's weak interior light carved lines into her face. Jackson had a decade over any of them, coming up on forty. "He may ask him to stand up, or may just call attention to him. Neither of you need to do anything. I just want you to know there will be this moment of acknowledgment."

"That's fine," said Jackson.

"Then the admiral will face you and say something like 'So are you up to the job?' And you'll say . . ." He pointed at Gilly.

"Well, our job is pretty simple," Gilly said. "When the ship detects salamanders, we attend station. Beanfield goes to Life, Anders to Weapons, Jackson to Command. I attend Intel, back where you can feel the engines. Then we pound everything in a thousand-mile radius into bite-size pieces."

"Rousing," Len said. "If, however, we want to sound a more upbeat note . . ."

Beanfield said, "We're going to spend every day working to repay the faith that nine billion people across two hundred countries have placed in us. If we're not up to it, we're sure going to try."

"Better. Maybe lose the part about two hundred countries."

"I always say that. Shouldn't I be inclusive?"

"As a rule, yes," said Len. "However, some of our international allies are yet to fully discharge their funding commitments for Providence Five, or, just between us, to begin discharging them at all, and the negotiations are ongoing. I'd like to steer clear of that whole area."

"Also there aren't two hundred countries," Gilly said. "I think it's one ninety-six."

Beanfield looked at him.

"I guess you were approximating," Gilly said.

"Also a fair point," said Len. "Let's not accidentally grant statehood to any unrecognized nations. Every flag on that stage has been carefully positioned so we can get an angle of the four of you with the Stars and Stripes behind and the ship visible above."

"Visible?" Gilly said. It was a popular idea that you could see the ships being built from Earth. But they were the tiniest of dots, little pinpricks distinguishable only at night.

"Sure," said Len, "after a few filters and adjustments."

"Oh," he said.

"And that's it," said Len. "Then it's a direct walk to the shuttle gantry and you don't have to worry about any of this bullshit anymore."

"There's always more bullshit," Anders said.

"That's true," Len said, "but this is the worst of it. Any questions?"

The van slowed and turned down a path marked by glowing orange cones. There was a rising white noise, which Gilly hoped was from the shuttle's engines but probably wasn't. Earlier today, during the family meet-and-greet, when tiny frilly nieces and nephews in dark suits were running around the legs of politicians and generals, one of his cousins had asked, *Do you know how many people they say will be there?* and Gilly had a rough idea, because the send-off crowds had been huge for every Providence launch, but before he could insist that he didn't want to know, the cousin had said, *SEVENTY-FIVE THOUSAND.* Gilly couldn't stop thinking about that. He might be able to pretend the broadcast audience didn't exist, but he was going to have trouble ignoring that many faces.

"Hey," Beanfield said, kicking his shin. "You'll be fine." She was smiling, and it did make him feel better, not just the smile, but the reminder that Beanfield made crew because she had preternatural people skills, to the point where she occasionally seemed to read his mind. They were all here because they were among the best in their fields. They'd been chosen by a sophisticated and demanding software-guided selection process. His presence wasn't an accident. He was where he was supposed to be.

The van stopped. The doors were pulled open. He stepped out into a light wind and a high sky and hundreds of people scurrying about in black caps and headsets. Between huge trucks were stacked crates and heavy equipment. A short distance away rose the back of the stage, fifty feet high and twice as long in either direction. Even so, he could see the crowd spilling around its edges, an indistinct mass like a single creature. The noise was like the rolling of an ocean.

"Flight crew have arrived at stage rear," said a woman in a black cap.

"How many people?" asked Beanfield.

"Latest estimate is eighty-five thousand," said Len. "We've had to open up the overflow areas."

"Oh, God," Gilly said.

"Don't sweat it. There'll be so many lights in your face, you won't be able to see a thing."

A drone buzzed over Len's shoulder and hung there, watching. Beanfield gave it a thumbs-up. Gilly turned away and peered skyward, trying to approximate the ship's location.

"Can you see it?" Beanfield said.

He shook his head. "Too bright."

"But it's there." She smiled.

The crowd gave a roar. Something must be happening onstage. A moment later, he heard a booming voice, echoing weirdly because all the speakers were facing the other way.

"All right," said Len. "This is where I leave you." He eyed them.

"Don't make it sappy," Anders said.

"I want you to know, you're the best troop of performing monkeys I've ever had," Len said. "In all seriousness, I've been nothing but impressed with the way you've carried yourselves through pre-launch. I know you didn't sign up for the media circus. It makes me very happy that we've reached the point where you can finally start doing your real jobs. I know you'll make every one of us you're leaving behind very proud."

"Don't make me cry," said Beanfield. "This makeup took hours."

"Jackson," said the woman in the cap, pointing where she wanted her to stand. "Then Beanfield. Anders. Gilligan."

"Gilly," he said. The announcer said something at the same time and the crowd roared and he didn't know if she heard him.

Len straightened into a salute. They returned it, even Gilly, who had never quite gotten the hang of it. The woman began to lead them toward the stage steps. When Gilly glanced back, Len was still holding the salute.

"There's one more step than you expect at the top," Len said. "Don't trip."

When it was over and he was strapped into a force-absorbing harness, his knees pointed skyward, blood draining toward the back of his head, he watched a wedge of blue sky turn black through thick polymer glass. The shuttle shook like an old carnival ride and roared like a waterfall but all of that was normal. It was actually comforting. He knew what to expect here.

"Look at Gilly," said Beanfield, her voice crackling through his earpiece. "He's more relaxed than he was onstage."

Anders laughed.

Jackson said, "Clearing the Kármán line. We're officially in space."

"This is the closest you'll be to home for four years," Gilly said. "And now this is. Now this is."

"This'll be a boring mission if you do that the whole time," said Anders. "How much longer to the ship?"

Gilly knew, but Jackson answered. "Three minutes until we reach synchronous orbit. Ten until we can pull alongside."

"Look," Beanfield said. "Stars."

"There have been stars for a while," Gilly said.

"But so many." She was right: The glass was full of them. It wasn't like home, where you gazed up at a sky scattered with a few bright pinpricks. Here was a city of endless lights. "And they don't twinkle."

"No atmosphere."

"Deceleration burn," Jackson said. "Brace yourselves."

The shuttle clunked and whined. An invisible hand curled around Gilly's body and pulled him forward. The harness creaked.

"Shit," said Anders suddenly.

"What?" said Jackson.

"I think I left my phone back there," he said. They laughed.

They established synchronous orbit ahead of the ship, so it was coming up behind them, drawing closer in a way they couldn't see. The shuttle had no artificial gravity; they would have to remain strapped in until they docked. Jackson called out distances until at last something white began to slide across the polymer glass, which Gilly recognized as a section of the ship dedicated to Materials Fabrication. Then came more, section after section, some stenciled with flags, some with designations. He knew the ship's design intimately but hadn't seen it firsthand since early in its construction, and felt surprise at its size. It was one thing to know it was three miles long and a touch over one million tons, another to see it.

"It's like a city," Beanfield said. "Or an island."

"Mass projector," Anders said, pointing as a cubelike protrusion slid by. It was in a retracted state, but he was right: It was one of the guns. "That's the good stuff."

"Anders, we'll pass your station in a minute," Gilly said.

"Where?"

"You won't be able to see it. It's a couple layers beneath the hull."

"Oh," Anders said. "Thanks, Mr. Tour Guide."

Gilly shrugged. "You won't get to see it from the outside again."

"I can't see it from the outside now."

"Well," Gilly said.

The ship continued to pass by: laser batteries, flat sensor arrays, and housings that would generate their electrostatic armor. "All right," said Anders. "I don't know about you, but I'm ready to get out of this harness."

"Almost there," said Jackson. The ship was appearing to slow, which meant they were matching its speed, preparing to dock. Until recently, a hundred people had worked out here with tens of thousands of drones. For the last two weeks, though, the ship had sat practically empty, waiting. The last remaining skeleton crew would ride this shuttle back home.

The ship revolved and disappeared from Gilly's view. The shuttle bumbled around for a minute, adjusting position. There was a solid *clunk*.

"Welcome home," Jackson said. "Let's go to work."

The ship was silent. It had a faint smell that put Gilly in mind of orange peel. The breach room was large enough for only one person at a time, and on the other side was a low-ceilinged corridor, sprouting protrusions and bundles of cable, which threw shadows in the glow-lights. They would have to get used to clambering around, ducking beneath or squeezing past all the stuff that apparently mattered more than space for the crew.

Jackson and Beanfield milled ahead of him. Behind, Anders cleared the breach door and Gilly shuffled up to make room. "Fuck, this is small," Anders said.

"You didn't know?" They had undergone hundreds of simulations. Service had hangars dedicated to mocked-up Providence sectional layouts, inside of which they role-played scenarios.

"I thought they were exaggerating." Anders rotated his shoulders reflexively. "The thing's three miles long; we can't get an extra ten inches here?"

"I'm sure there's a good reason," Gilly said. "I could ask the Surplex hardware guys."

"It's for appearances," Beanfield said. "We don't want people back home seeing our feeds and thinking their sacrifices have funded some kind of luxury cruise ship."

"I feel like there's a middle ground that got missed," Anders said, "by about a thousand fucking miles."

"There will be an engineering reason," Gilly said. "I'll find out."

"Everyone oriented?" Jackson said. "Then let's proceed to quarters. Collect your film and survival core and begin preflight checks."

Film was a clear plastic band that fitted around the upper part of their faces and provided information display, local comms, and a variety of ways to interact with the ship. Survival cores were bulky black boxes they had to wear strapped to their backs whenever they left their cabin, and which would, during a catastrophic depressure or thermal event, throw a thin suit and helmet around their bodies and attempt to keep them alive. The cores were awkward and uncomfortable and almost certainly pointless, it seemed to Gilly, since anything that managed to get through the ship's hull would definitely kill them all outright. But it was protocol, so he would wear it.

They moved deeper into the ship. At the first ladder port, Jackson spun a hatch to reveal a lit ladder shaft and gestured for Gilly to step inside. When he did, motorized rungs hummed beneath his feet, bearing him upward. Their quarters all lay in the same section of C Deck, with just enough separation to keep them from tripping over each other. He maneuvered through the corridor until he found a door marked QTR-4: GILLIGAN. There was a tactile panel and he pushed it to reveal the only private space he would possess for the next four years.

He stepped inside. The door jumped closed behind him. It was small but efficient. Retractable bunk, retractable desk, retractable sink. Sunken handles that would reveal drawers and a closet. The lighting was pleasantly soft. He moved to the bunk, removed his shirt, and fitted his survival core. When he slid the film over his face, the word HELLO materialized on his closet, as well as above the sink and on the door: places that could serve as virtual screens.

"Cute," he said. He fiddled with the film until he figured out how to dismiss the welcome message.

He moved toward the door. Then he glanced back. It was hard to imagine how much time he was going to spend here. It was really too much to comprehend. But he supposed he didn't have to. He would just take it one day at a time. He hit the tactile button and went out.

The ship burned for thirty-three days. During this time, Gilly acclimatized to his routine and the various weirdnesses of being on board a ship, such as having plastic over half his face and not being able to stretch out without hitting something. Most of each day was spent alone, but they all ate together at least once in Con-1, two of them headed on duty and two coming off, hunched around a retractable table with metal plates and bowls and some nutritionally dense soup, maybe a loaf.

"Ugh," said Beanfield to Anders. "Is there any chance of you eating like a decent human being?"

"What?" Anders said. There was loaf all over. From clips and pics, Gilly had gotten the impression that Anders was calm and self-assured, but in reality he was kind of manic. He just went still for cameras.

"I don't want to sit opposite you anymore," Beanfield said. "It pains me."

Jackson said, "We've reached S-min velocity."

They looked at her. "When?" Gilly said. "Just now?" He checked the numbers on his film. She was right: The ship was now traveling fast enough to perform a hard skip, which would take them into the fighting zone.

"Yep," said Jackson.

"When do we skip?" asked Beanfield. "Next twenty-four hours, right?"

"*Where* is the question," said Anders. "*Sword of Iowa*'s bogged down in Orange Zone. They might want a hand."

Gilly shook his head. "Two Providences in one zone is a waste. We'll go somewhere new."

This was speculation. The ship would decide when and where to skip after processing more information than any of them could imagine. That was how the AI worked: It sucked in unimaginable quantities of raw data and produced decisions that were better optimized and more nuanced than any human could manage. They would be notified once it had made up its mind, and have just enough time to scramble to station and strap in.

"If everyone could file clips first, that'd be super," said Beanfield. "There are a lot of people back home following our feeds, and leaving the solar system is a big moment."

"Clips," Anders said. "How long do we have to keep that up?"

"Forever," Beanfield said. "You know this. Gilly, that means you, too."

He nodded. He'd been lax with his clips. He'd never enjoyed them in the first place and had instead sunk time into tinkering with the ship, which so far had turned out to require a slightly shocking amount of maintenance. In theory, the ship was self-sufficient, able to diagnose and repair faults via a fleet of small crablike welder robots. But in practice, everything it fixed seemed to break again three days later. There hadn't been a problem with anything that really mattered, but Gilly had spent a lot of time shooing crabs away from leaking pipes so he could figure out the root cause.

There was a short silence. This time tomorrow, they might be engaging with salamanders. They had spent years imagining it and twelve months intensively training for it and now it was here.

"About time we did something useful," said Jackson.

"Amen," said Anders, his mouth full of loaf.

They skipped but there was only empty space. This was to be expected: It would probably take a few skips to locate the enemy at first. After their first engagement, the ship could use the data it had gathered to search more effectively.

A week passed and Gilly began to wonder if the war would be over before they did anything.

"Look at this," Anders told him over comms. He sent a clip to Gilly's film: *Sword of Iowa* deploying a million tiny drones to unpick a salamander hive. Everywhere was debris. "We should have gone there."

"Don't question the ship," Gilly said. "It's smarter than you are."

"Then why can't it find anyone to shoot at?"

Gilly opened his mouth.

"I don't want a real answer," Anders said. "I'm venting."

"Oh," Gilly said. "Well, I'm sure it will be soon."

Anders sighed dramatically. "If I don't get to grill some salamanders, I want a refund."

The next day, Gilly was on F Deck, clad in a coverall, heavy gloves, and a helmet, wrestling with a pipe that kept wanting to spray the corridor full of steam, when the walls turned orange. A klaxon began to sound. His film displayed:

ALERT ALERT ALERT
ENEMY IN PROXIMITY
PROCEED TO STATION

It was all he'd been thinking about, but still his breath caught. A feather of fear tickled the back of his throat. He pulled off the gloves, ditched the helmet, and began to squeeze through the corridor.

Jackson popped into his ear. "Crew to station. We have hostiles."

"I see it. On my way."

Anders and Beanfield chimed in, confirming their locations. They sounded calm and focused, as he hoped he had. The floor was painted with animated arrows, or so it appeared through his film, and he followed them to a transport rail and let it shoot him back through the ship. He then proceeded through two thick doors to Intel station, which was a cramped room with a harness of heavy, flexible straps, a board, and a wraparound wall of screens—real screens, not projections, with cables wired into physical systems. Everything in here was insulated and redundant several times over. He strapped in and felt the harness grip his body. The screens lit up with data.

"Intel checking in," he said.

Jackson: "Acknowledge. Life?"

Beanfield: "En route. Thirty seconds."

"Weapons?"

Anders: "Almost there."

Jackson: "I have eyes on the enemy. We have a single hive, eighty-yard diameter. Contact three minutes."

Gilly swept his board, just like in the simulations. "Wall-to-wall green here."

"Thank you, Intel."

Beanfield: "Life, checking in. All green. There's a little desat in Engine Two but nothing out of band."

"Thank you, Life."

"Weapons, checking in," said Anders.

"Thank you, Weapons. Hive is expelling hostiles. Counting ten . . . twenty . . . fifty . . ." Gilly could see none of this. His screens were all charts and numbers. When the engagement was over, though, he would be able to play it back with visuals if he wanted. "Intel, you're green?"

"Confirm green."

"How's Armor?"

"Everything's up."

"Thank you. We have two hundred hostiles and the hive appears about empty. Weapons, status?"

"Green as grass."

"I'll take a full status, please."

"Pulse is warming up. Mass projectors standing by. Laser batteries two, three, and four relocating fore." This meant they were crawling along the skin of the ship to reach optimal firing position. The ship itself wasn't maneuverable at all: It took an hour to turn around, in the sense of arriving at the same location with the opposite bearing. So the guns had to move.

"Thank you. Hostiles are spreading. Contact in thirty seconds, assuming a turn." Recent engagement data from other ships showed that when first encountered, salamanders would peel off their hive in every direction, as if they were fleeing, then all turn inward together, like a school of fish. "How long until we're pulse-ready?"

"A few seconds."

"And there's the turn. Contact imminent."

Anders: "Pulsing."

Jackson: "I see it. Intel?"

"Cores rebalancing."

"Pulse was ineffective. No targets destroyed."

"None?" said Beanfield.

"Confirmed. No enemies down. I'm reviewing. Ah. They turned again. Anticipated the pulse. They were outside its maximum effective range at the blip point."

"Ah," Gilly said. "That's . . ."

Beanfield: "Are they supposed to do that?"

"It's a new tactic." Gilly had studied every engagement of the war: None had involved a double turn.

Jackson: "Turned again. They're coming again. Weapons, advise pulse status."

Anders: "Pulsing now."

"I see it. Pulse effective. Eighty hostiles down. A hundred or so remaining."

Gilly said, "Three turns! They've figured out our pulse range."

"Noted. We'll discuss in debrief. Weapons, full status, please."

"Laser batteries one, eight, nine in position. Two, three, four in transit. Pulse ready in five seconds, three, two. Pulsing."

"Confirmed. A good one. Got just about all of them. Life, update?"

"All green here."

"Your desat is normal?"

"Yes. We get dips in Engineering after each pulse, but it balances out right after."

"All right. We're coming up on the hive."

"Firing. Laser batteries one and eight, thirty percent."

"Thank you, Weapons. Hive is destroyed. Ten to fifteen hostiles remaining. We've got a lot of debris now. Intel?"

"Engines scaling down. We're forty points off peak. Those laser batteries are decommissioning, too—correct, Anders?"

"Yep. They're heading home." This could happen before the end of an engagement if the ship believed they wouldn't be needed. "Guess we've got this one in the bag."

"Weapons, please continue to call in activity. We just pulsed, yes?"

"Ah, we did, yeah."

"Then report it. There's some kind of bubble hanging around the hive. Three or four workers, maybe. Confirmed. I can see them." Workers were small, fat, pale salamanders who didn't fight. Every hive had at least a few. They were harmless, but it was Service policy to destroy them.

"And pow," said Anders. "Pulsed."

"All hostiles down. Scanning debris. Please stand by." They waited. "Confirmed no target. There's nothing out there bigger than a golf ball."

"That's it?" Beanfield said.

"That's it."

Anders whooped. "We're on the board."

"*Fire of Montana* has 604,322 kills," Gilly said. *Montana* was the first Providence. It had been roaming around space for two years, cleaning out target-rich environments. "We've got a ways to go to catch that."

"But we've started," Beanfield said.

"A journey of a thousand miles begins with a single step," Gilly said.

"What's that? Poetry?"

"Just a quote."

"So that's why they selected Gilly," Anders said. "Bring a touch of class to the place."

"Why'd they select you? Because that was some shoddy-ass work on Weapons."

"Oh-ho-ho," Anders said.

"Shut it down," said Jackson. "This is a combat channel. Intel, close engagement, please. We'll meet for debrief in thirty minutes."

"Engagement closed," Gilly said, smiling.

They fell into patterns. Each day, Gilly rose, ate in the mess with whomever he was sharing a duty rotation that day, and performed ship maintenance. Sometimes he wrote reports for Service. He recorded clips. When the klaxon sounded, he attended station. The engagements changed in the details, but the underlying dynamic was always the same, always salamanders dying in the hundreds before they could get anywhere near enough to spit a *huk*. It became routine, and occasionally he felt his mind drifting, as if he were watching a movie he'd seen before and knew by heart. This was something Service had warned them about, and which Gilly had initially found hard to believe: that the mission would get boring. They were pushing into unexplored space inside the mightiest piece of military technology ever created, fighting an alien species; it was hard to think of anything more interesting he could be doing. But the reality was that the ship's AI controlled almost everything that mattered and was so good at its job that there wasn't much for him to do. So he felt restless.

"What about the valve problem?" Beanfield said, in one of their check-in sessions. "You fix that?"

"Not yet," he admitted. Even now, he was plagued by intermittent pipeline failures. He had developed a dozen painstakingly researched theories that had all turned out to be wrong.

"Because that would be good. To not have pipes bursting all over."

"I'll fix it. I've been spending time on swarm analysis." Beanfield's eyebrows rose. "Figuring out why salamanders move the way they do. Trying to predict their tactics."

"Did Service ask you to do that?"

"No." He felt slightly embarrassed. It was unlikely he could figure out anything Service didn't already know, or that the ship couldn't deduce in a fraction of the time. Gilly, who had developed sequencing algorithms for Surplex's AI division in his life as a civilian, knew this better than anyone. Still, it was the part of his day he looked forward to more than anything else. "It's just kind of fun."

She smiled. "You're a puzzler. I bet you do crosswords, the really impossible ones."

"I do," he said. "Those are the best."

"Good," Beanfield said. "Keep that up."

They reached a hundred thousand salamander kills in six months, and doubled that only a few months later, when the ship discovered a particularly richly infested part of Firebrick Zone. Gilly kept up his clips, but found himself increasingly disengaged by news from back home, which felt less relevant with each passing day, like a show he used to enjoy but had lost track of.

Two years in, Anders pinged him from L Deck and said he had something to show him.

Gilly was in his cabin, checking his messages. By now they were so far out that they could only communicate with Earth when they came within range of a relay, which had just occurred for the first time in five days. But he headed down to L Deck. It was mostly storage down there, rows of tightly racked crates rotating on a belt system. Inside the crates were raw materials the ship could craft into whatever it needed, including parts of itself. Gilly could toss a boot into a recycler and a day later it would be part of a pipe.

Anders stood by one of the belts, holding something flat and shiny. "Check this out." In his hand was a *shuriken*, a throwing disc with vicious points. "Ninja stars."

"You had the ship make ninja stars?" To keep themselves amused, he and Anders had invented a variety of games to play in their downtime, like stalking each other around the ship, armed with rubber balls. Whoever hit the other person first won. The last time they'd played, Anders had said, *You know what this game needs? Ninja stars.* Gilly hadn't thought anything of it.

"They're super-sharp." Anders touched the point of a star to his palm and blood welled at the spot. "Yikes. Look at that." He sucked at it.

"You're not suggesting we throw these at each other."

Anders nodded. "I am suggesting that."

"Uh," Gilly said.

"You do not want to get hit by one of these bad boys."

"No, I get that," he said. "It's just, it looks genuinely dangerous."

Anders nodded. "It is. It is genuinely dangerous." He peered at his hand. "Look at that. Still bleeding."

"I mean, it's one thing to get injured." Medical could fix almost anything. "But I'm thinking, what if somebody takes one in the neck?"

"There are first-aid stations. Apply a patch, take a quick trip to Medical, you'd be fine."

"Or the eye?"

"Bah," Anders said. He had let his hair grow longer and his stubble had become a beard. "That's not going to happen. But I tell you what. No head shots. That can be a rule. What about that?"

"I think you're assuming a level of control neither of us possesses. What's wrong with the rubber balls?"

Anders sighed. The crate behind him was full of ninja stars, Gilly saw. There were hundreds. "The balls are boring, Gilly. They're played out."

"I don't think they're boring."

"That's because you're low-sensate." This was a reference to a psych metric of sensation-seeking behavior. Gilly's score was so low that the evaluator had wanted him to re-sit the test. But the officer who had been assigned to steer Gilly through a year of Service assured her that that wasn't necessary; from his observation, Isiah Gilligan was indeed perfectly content to sit motionless in a darkened environment for four hours with nothing but his thoughts. Gilly hadn't seen Anders's scores, but he presumed they were high. Very high. "We're two years into a four-year tour, Gilly. We can't use those little pussy balls forever."

"Isn't the fun part the stealth? Not the hurting."

"It can be both," Anders said.

Gilly's film said:

☐ [01800 HRS / -00020 HRS] ALL-HANDS BRIEFING (REC-1)

"You get that?" Anders said.

Gilly nodded. "I'll think about the stars."

Anders grinned and clapped him on the shoulder. "You're a good man, Gilligan."

"I said I'll think about it." But Anders was right; he would probably do it. He usually did what Anders wanted. They were different people, but Service had good reasons for putting them together. They were complements, making each other better.

"I'll see you at briefing," Anders said, clutching his wrist. His hand dripped. "I need to go to Medical."

Gilly arrived early and took a seat. The ship had five rooms like this, which could be used for meeting or briefing purposes, or as temporary bunkers in the event of an emergency while the ship vented air or suppressed fires or whatever. All were spacious, with room for four people to sit comfortably around a small table. One had a three-person sofa where Gilly could lean right back and stick out his legs. It was luxurious.

Beanfield appeared in the doorway, nursing a steaming coffee. She had spent a lot of time working out over the last two years, becoming long and lean. She smiled at him. "Hey, G. You see we had a sync window?"

"I did."

"I have a bunch of new interviews." She levered herself into a seat and set down her coffee. Her elbows splayed. "You did one with *Good Morning America* last sync, right? How did that go?"

"Fine, although we were interrupted by an engagement. I don't know if they want to redo it."

She shook her head. "That's a great finish for them. That's like gold."

He hadn't considered that, but she was right. Beanfield was much more aware of public relations than he cared to be.

"I haven't opened my personal messages yet. Every sync, I tell myself I'm going to save them. I'll open, you know, ten a day, so I won't run out before next sync. But then I start thinking, what if we sync again tomorrow? So I open everything and have nothing left. Sorry, did you want coffee?"

"No, I'm good."

She smiled. Beanfield wore her Service jacket unzipped most of the way down the front, a standard white tee beneath. "You need to get yourself a vice, Gilligan. You're too perfect. It makes me suspicious."

Jackson entered and took her usual seat, the one farthest from the door. If Gilly or Anders tried to sit in the same place more than three times, Beanfield would camp out in it before they arrived. Anything that looked like a rut, Beanfield was all over. But there was a captain's exemption, apparently.

"Captain," said Beanfield, which Gilly echoed. Jackson nodded. Sometimes Gilly thought Jackson was reading something on her film when she wasn't. She was still inscrutable to him, even after two years. "We synced."

"We did," Jackson said. "And there's news."

"Oh?"

"I'll fill you in when Anders gets here. Where is he?"

"Medical," Gilly said. "He might be a few minutes."

Jackson looked at Beanfield. Gilly wasn't totally across everyone's roles and duties, but he had figured out that whenever Anders did something bad, Beanfield was in trouble. "I'll ping him," Beanfield said.

"While we're here," Gilly said, "can we pull up the last engagement? There was an interesting attack pattern variation." Jackson shrugged, so he spun up a projection of their last battle. Points of light and stats coalesced on their films, appearing to play across the table. "You see the ripple here?" The salamanders closed in an arc, as usual, but their line wobbled, with sections moving in and out. "I'd love to know whether any other crews have seen that."

"We're in a sync window," said Jackson. "Find out."

"It wasn't very effective," Beanfield pointed out. "They didn't get any closer than usual."

"The battle did actually take eight seconds longer," Gilly said. "That's almost a whole standard deviation."

"Only because some of them stayed out of pulse range."

"That's still longer."

"So?" Beanfield said.

"They're learning."

"They're always varying their tactics," Jackson said. "That's not new."

"But it isn't random. Almost everything they try is more effective than before. It's steady improvement. And that shouldn't be possible, because we leave no survivors. They have no feedback on each tactic they try."

"This feels like a question for back home," Jackson said. "Or the ship."

"Yes," he admitted. "It's just curious."

"You're curious," Beanfield said.

"All right," said Jackson. The salamander cloud vanished. "Anders can catch up in his own time. We have an all-hands from Len, but let me give you the spoilers. We're going into VZ."

VZ was Violet Zone, an area devoid of beacons and relays. Ships that went into VZ couldn't sync at all.

There was a moment of silence. Beanfield said, "How long?"

"It's situational," Jackson said. "Depends on what we find. You know that."

"There must be an estimate."

"Listen to Len," said Jackson, and keyed a video.

Len's upper half appeared above the table, looking more somber than usual. "Evening, monkeys. Hope you're well. There's no easy way to say this, so I'll just say it: Strategic Command is sending you on a trip to VZ. All expenses paid, but it's going to be a long one. Preliminary estimate is six months."

He thought he'd misheard. Beanfield said, "Six months? Six months with no sync?"

It was funny: They'd talked about VZ before and the joke was that Gilly would love it, since there would be no interviews, no one badgering him to record clips for his feed, just them and the ship. But six months was a long time to go dark. Even for him. No messages. No new books or movies. He said, "We must be going deep."

"We're winning the war," Jackson said. "It's where you go to find the enemy now."

"Boy," said Beanfield. On the table, Len continued to burble. "Anders will be a challenge."

"Well," Jackson said, "that's what you're here for."

"Mmm," said Beanfield. Gilly liked Beanfield a lot, but sometimes she seemed to be under the impression that her job was the most important thing anyone did. In reality, it was the other three of them who ran the ship. Beanfield was only monitoring them. "If we win the war, can we go home early?"

"Yes, we can," Jackson said.

"We missed what Len was saying," said Beanfield. "Can you rewind?"

"No," said Jackson. "Rewatch on your own time."

"In other news," said Len, "from what I hear, we're signing with Freco to produce the next generation of warship. So you'll all be obsolete in about eight years."

"Ugh," Beanfield said. "Freco."

"What's wrong with Freco?" Gilly said.

She glanced at the Surplex logo on his jacket. "Aren't they your competitor?"

"Yes. But Freco is fine. I'm not married to Surplex."

"Don't let the ship hear you say that," said Beanfield.

"What do you have against Freco?"

"It opposed the war. Don't you remember those ads?"

"Only at first. It changed its mind with new data." Freco had a lot of political opinions and spent big to share them. But that wasn't unusual; many companies lobbied for or against various things, for reasons Gilly didn't care too much about.

"Well," she said, "that's shifty."

"You're anthropomorphizing," Gilly said. "Mental flexibility is desirable in an AI." Like Surplex, Freco's executive decision-making was largely controlled by software. That was practically the most valuable thing about each company now: its machine intelligence code. It was used everywhere and guided everything.

"Shouldn't have computers in charge anyway," Jackson said. This was an outdated opinion, and Gilly let it go.

Anders entered. "What'd I miss?"

"Sit down," said Beanfield.

"Len!" Anders said. "You've lost weight, you handsome devil." He squeezed into a seat. His hand was wrapped in clear plastic.

"No sync window for six months," Gilly said.

"That's preliminary," Beanfield said. "That's only an estimate."

"Bullshit," Anders said, and looked to Gilly, who shrugged.

"You know what," Beanfield said. "There are actually some pretty cool mental stimulation programs we can run in VZ that we're not normally allowed."

"Like what?"

"I don't know. I have to check."

"Fuck me," Anders said.

"Anders," Jackson said.

"Six months?" Anders said, and stood, for no apparent reason.

"We always knew this was a possibility," Gilly said.

"Sit your ass down," Beanfield said.

"I'm sorry," Anders said. "I'm feeling the need to externalize my feelings. Don't you say I should do that?"

"There's a time and place."

Len began to talk about election news. Anders said, "Shut up, Len."

"You should appreciate Len while you can," Gilly said. "You won't see him for a while."

"Len can bite me," Anders said. He began to unbuckle.

"Anders!" said Beanfield. "Stop that. Anders. No one wants to see that."

Anders shucked his pants. He had a long penis. They had all seen it a few times. "Let's go, Len. Right here."

"This is a briefing," Jackson said. "Put on your goddamn pants."

"It's a debriefing now," Anders said.

"Get out of here," Beanfield said. "You're disgracing yourself."

"Goddamn," Anders said, losing all his fight. He collected his pants and shuffled out of the room. There was an awkward silence.

"I want to apologize for that," Beanfield said.

"Mmm," said Jackson.

"He went to Medical," Gilly said. "Maybe he was, uh, affected by medication just now."

"I'll look into it," said Beanfield. She closed her eyes and rubbed her forehead. "VZ is not going to be easy."

"It's not supposed to be easy," Jackson said.

———

Beanfield caught him on the way out. "Gilly. Wait up?"

He waited. Jackson ducked through the doorway and disappeared into the corridor.

"Are you going to see Anders now?"

"Do you think I should?"

She nodded. "You're good for him. You help him blow off steam."

"I was going to check on the downstream distributors."

"Could you do this first?"

"Uh," he said. "I guess so."

"Thanks." She smiled brilliantly and squeezed his shoulder. Beanfield was very touchy-feely. It was best practice for a Life Officer, Gilly presumed. She was providing human contact. Personally, he found it distracting. They were trillions of miles from anyone he could have a relationship with and he preferred not to be reminded about it. He could do without the touching. "You're a good dude."

"Thanks," he said.

Anders didn't respond to ping so Gilly went and knocked on his door. After a minute, Anders pulled it open and stared at him. "You're *knocking*," Anders said. "I thought there was something wrong with the door."

"You were dark on ping." He glanced around Anders's cabin, which he hadn't seen in a while. There was crap everywhere: empty bowls on the floor, a boot on the bed. Gilly could not have lived like this. He wondered if Anders was cropping the mess out of his clips or just leaving it to Service to edit out. "Are you all right?"

Anders nodded. His breath was not great. "Is Jackson pissed at me?"

"Probably. Beanfield's concerned."

"I bet."

"You want to play something?"

Anders scratched his face. "Nah. I'm going to lie down. The ship gave me hydrexalin and now my head feels huge."

That explained a lot. "Okay." Then he hesitated. "Beanfield told me to visit you."

"Heh," Anders said. "She ordered you to play with me?"

"Yeah. Instead of doing my job. Do you feel like Beanfield gets in the way sometimes?"

"Like how?"

"Like I'm trying to keep the ship in one piece," Gilly said, "and she's interrupting with stuff like this." Anders was silent. "I mean, it's annoying, right?"

"That's Beanfield's job," Anders said. "To be annoying. Like everyone's mom. That's a Life Officer."

"I work for Surplex," Gilly said. "I'm not some Service cadet she can boss around."

Anders yawned enormously. "Are you sure?"

"Yes." His role had been the subject of careful negotiation between Service and Surplex. He was expected to act within the Service chain of command, but he was also an independent civilian, exempt from military punishment.

"Well, then tell Beanfield that your job is more important than hers."

"That's not what I think." It was. It was exactly what he thought.

"Then I don't know what to tell you, Gilly," Anders said. "I'm going to sleep now."

"Okay," he said, and Anders closed the door. Gilly stood in the corridor for another few moments. It still bothered him. He felt he hadn't explained himself very well. It wasn't that Beanfield was annoy-ing; it was that when she prevented him from doing his work, she was potentially endangering them. Maybe he should confront her directly.

Before he could take a step, his film changed:

☐ LOSS OF PRESSURE / HYDRATE FILTERS (SPT-2)

"Oh, goddamn it," he said. He headed to his cabin to collect his tools.

2

[Beanfield]

THE DISTANCE

She was the most famous, according to the numbers: 311 million people back home following the clips, pics, and quips of Life Officer Talia Beanfield as transmitted from her Providence-class battleship in an undisclosed but, trust me, incredibly dangerous part of space. Frankly, she could see why. She sometimes browsed her own feed to admire the Talia it presented. Here: Talia taking you through her workout routine, bright and bubbly, glowing with health. Here: Hilariously trying to unravel the mystery of where the robot crabs went when they were finished doing something (how long *was* that chute??). Here: Waking with puffy eyes and matted hair (so vulnerable!), missing you all so much. This Talia was amazing. This Talia was an inspiration. It was no surprise to her that this Talia had three hundred million followers, because she would love to be this Talia, too.

She took snaps and clips every day and sent them back in sync windows. The sync after that, she would see what Service had done with them: clean them up, cut out anything that could be misinterpreted or taken the wrong way or show Service in a bad light, add a little fancy editing, a few filters, and publish them at regular intervals. Because her followers didn't want six days of silence followed by a giant info dump. They wanted continuous contact. They wanted to feel like they were with her. So that was simulated. She liked the cleaned-up clips, even though—or because—they didn't exactly resemble what she remembered recording, or resemble it at all, in some cases, like how on the feed she moved smoothly down corridors, rarely banging a wrist or catching a shoulder on a doorway, which in real life happened all the time. In fact, she was covered in bruises, because the ship was unbelievably cramped. It was the smallest enormous spacecraft you could imagine. Only her most endearing awkwardness made it to the feed. But that was fine. She knew very well that what the four of them were doing out here with the salamanders was only half the war, and the other half was back home, convincing a war-weary public that, yes, we really did need to build new Providences, even though they were unbelievably expensive, and—let's admit—each new warship was less exciting than the previous one, and the intelligentsia was growing increasingly cynical about the war because it had been a long time since anyone had been in actual jeopardy from salamander attack, years, in fact, and what was our end goal, exactly—total genocide of another species? Really? The feeds were part of that war. Her personal story, or at least the edited version thereof, was part of it. This had always been clear, even though Service would never come right out and say so, since the perception of caring about public relations was itself bad for public relations. Back at Camp Zero, so named because it was zero degrees on a good day, when she was just one candidate among many hoping to make Life, she had undergone media training, learning how to smile and reassure and look like a competent, dependable officer. There were roleplays, which she loved. They roleplayed almost everything, including scenarios they might

encounter on mission. Sometimes she was dropped into a group scenario and assigned a personality to play, e.g.:

*You are intolerant of authority and become angry when you feel your
opinion isn't being listened to.*

*You are jealous of the captain and will act counterproductively in any
situation where she receives more attention than you.*

*You are deeply lonely and trapped with an introvert, a narcissist, and
a veteran with posttraumatic stress disorder, all of whom you sometimes
imagine flushing into space.*

She made up that last one. That wasn't real. But sometimes the in-
structions were *No character,* which meant you had to be yourself, and
also that you were being scored by the examiner based on how effectively you resolved the scenario. Those were nerve-racking. But fun: the
playing pretend, the ordering people around, the trying to figure out
what was going on in someone else's head. She adored that. And she was
great at it. In one of her first group scenarios, she diagnosed four personality disorders and corralled her group into scenario completion with
twenty-two minutes left on the clock, and the examiner, a famous hard-
ass, had said, "I think we need to start making these more difficult."
From that moment she had known she was going to make crew.

"You were amazing," said a boy in the corridor afterward. He had
been one of her personality disorders. He was tall and light-haired and
refreshingly friendly in a class where everyone was competing for the
same crew slots. She couldn't ask for a pencil in there sometimes without the girl looking at her like, *What are you trying to pull.* "All that
touching you did, putting your hands on people's arms and shoulders,
was that dependent personality disorder?"

"I didn't have a character," she said.

"Oh," he said.

But screw him. She was incredible at this. She cried genuine tears for

You experience an intense fear reaction if the exterior door is opened. When she played *Your commanding officer is severely depressed and will order a suicide mission if not stopped,* people leaned forward in their seats. Everyone died in that scenario because they wouldn't listen. "I don't even know what you're doing here," a girl told her. "You should be, like, famous."

That was maybe overselling it. That might have been the girl thinking, *I wish stupid Talia Beanfield would go be an actor so I can make crew.* But she was happy to be the big fish in the small pond of Camp Zero Life candidate roleplays. She had played piano as a kid and meant to make a career of it right up until she attended a state conference with approximately two hundred kids who had more talent and discipline and a fascination for music she found slightly frightening and which made her own interest seem, on reflection, more like a fondness for public approval and applause. So this was fine.

Especially fun were fraternization scenarios. These began in her second year, once they'd weeded out the candidates better suited to Intel or Weapons or, let's be brutally honest, something far, far away from a Providence. They were kind of silly, because policy was clear enough: Don't have sex on the ship. That seemed hard to get wrong. Of course, six months or so in, thirty trillion miles from home, it started to feel less clear. She had begun to have thoughts like, *Fraternization, is it really so bad?* and *Would anyone even know?* But she had a handle on it. It helped that her choices were limited to Anders and Gilly, who were, respectively, offensive and oblivious. Or maybe it really was the roleplays.

Hey, Oscar. I really enjoyed last night.

Me too, babe.

I was thinking, maybe you and me could hang out. Just talk, you know. Open up. Really get to know each other.

Uh, yeah, I don't know, babe, I've got a long tasklist today . . . all these hydrate filters needing changing . . .

But Oscar, I already checked your tasklist. I can track your movements, you know. I can see every room you go into. I know you have nothing to do right now except spend time with me.

To be honest, I just want some space, Talia.

Space? There's plenty of that outside, Oscar. Why don't you take a little walk from the airlock, then? Get all the fucking space you want!

Can we stop? I'm not comfortable with this roleplay.

And . . . scene.

Good times. She actually enjoyed fraternization roleplays more than the real version. All she had in reality was a long-distance boyfriend who broke up with her approximately eight months before informing her about it, and a series of stilted relationships with other Life candidates. Two in a row had had erectile dysfunction. One, okay, but two, she couldn't help feeling like that was on her. "Just don't look at me," he said, and she protested, because what were they doing here, and he confessed, "I feel like you're always analyzing me."

She got better at hiding that.

Being on the ship was performing all the time. It was roleplays around the clock. There was no conversation where she wasn't noting tone and word choice and body language. *That joke from Anders, how much of that was serious? Gilly's gaze is drifting, does he need more mental stimulation?* And as much as she enjoyed the work, it was exhausting. She would like, just for a minute, to hang out with someone she wasn't responsible for. She would like to relax. Talk like a normal human being. That was the part she hadn't thought through: She had gone into Life because she loved other people, yet gotten herself sent into space with only three of them.

Not a big deal. This was what she'd signed up for. Duty to protect humanity, etc.

But VZ was going to be hard.

———

"You fucked up," Anders told her.

It was the day after Jackson dropped the news about VZ and Anders's pants had followed. She was seeing Anders on a regular basis already and plainly that would have to continue. Right now he was draped across the sofa in Rec-2 because apparently he'd taken a nap in the middle of a day shift. He'd wanted to meet in his cabin but with Anders it was wise to maintain barriers.

"How?" she said. There was no table and she had to keep her arms folded, not something she normally did. She was usually open for business, physiologically speaking, like a good Life Officer.

"You told Gilly to hang with me instead of doing his duties. Now he's wondering why you think his work doesn't matter."

"Oh," she said. "Damn." In the interests of crew health and morale, a certain key fact had been concealed from Intel Officer Gilly. For two years, she had been so good at keeping it.

"Just tell him the truth," Anders said. "He's a big boy. He can handle it."

She shook her head. "No. It would be bad for him." She eyed him. "Don't you tell him, either."

"You underestimate him. He's smart."

"I know he's smart. But he needs the lie. Don't take that away."

Anders shrugged. She didn't honestly expect him to understand. To the outside world, Anders was a self-assured, devilishly handsome man with unlikely bone structure and a delightfully roguish twist. In reality, he was mostly twist. About 70 percent of her job was dealing with him, which he lacked the self-awareness to realize. They'd told her back at Camp Zero: *You will be the most important person on the ship and no one will know.* It was so true. It was *so* true.

"Don't do it," she warned. "You'll only drag him down to where you are."

"Then I'll have company."

"You have company." She tried to spread her arms. "I'm right here."

"I'm kidding around, Beanfield," Anders said. "I won't tell him."

"Don't," she said.

She had duties: interviews, messages, reports, and everything else that needed to get sent while they were still in range of a relay. Which was approximately thirty hours, according to Jackson, although that was only an estimate. If the ship detected hostiles nearby, they might spend a week floating around lighting up hives. If it sniffed something in the tilt of a frequency from a far-flung star, they could be inside VZ within an hour. As Gilly loved to explain, the ship was so much smarter than any of them, it was impossible to predict its decisions or even understand why it made them. Humans might not reach the same conclusions even if they studied the same data, because they had tiny wet meat brains instead of house-sized tanks of software writing more software. So who knew.

She felt like she had time, though. She felt like the ship was not quite as aloof as Gilly made out. The day they'd boarded, after all the ceremonies, the salutes, the tearful hugs with family, once everyone had shuttled off and the engines were warming, the ship had greeted them. Every screen, both tactile and virtual, had displayed:

HELLO

"Hello?" she'd replied. She was trained in the subsystems, but hadn't known the ship did greetings. "This is Life Officer Talia Beanfield."

The ship didn't answer. She tracked down Gilly, who was doing something with a torque wrench in a corridor, a bunch of testing equipment scattered around. Talia was confident that nothing on this ship needed the application of a torque wrench ten hours before launch. That would imply a fairly colossal fuckup in the preflight checks. But if it kept Gilly happy, fine. She pointed at the nearest HELLO. "Are you seeing this?"

"It's a default message," Gilly said. "It doesn't mean anything."

"It's nice," she said. "It's pleased to meet us."

He tilted his head to one side. She would come to know this gesture well over the next two years: Gilly mentally ratcheting his intelligence down until he found a level he could share with her. "The ship isn't alive. It can't communicate with us."

"But it is communicating," she said.

He shook his head. "This is software that wrote itself. It has a completely alien way of thinking, which can't be translated into any human language. It doesn't even really know we're here. It would be like you trying to communicate to your white blood cells that you want them to fight an infection: Even if you could somehow physically talk, there's no overlap in how you convey meaning or understand motivations. You frame concepts in totally different ways."

"Then where did the 'hello' come from?"

He shrugged. "Someone programmed it, maybe. Or else it really is similar to how you communicate with your white blood cells: via a process that's so far beneath conscious thought, you're not even aware of it."

She smiled, because she did enjoy Gilly's dorky explanations, and it was important that he feel understood. If she seemed confused, he would become anxious and throw words at her brain until she faked it. "Well, I like it." She reached out and touched a HELLO. It was nice, she thought, even if Gilly was right and the ship wasn't really talking. She didn't know her white blood cells, not as individuals, but she was grateful for whatever work they did. She wished them well and cared that they remained unharmed. If that was similar to how the ship felt about its crew, she was happy. She liked that just fine. "Hello, ship," she said.

Gilly looked at her like she was crazy. "It's just a message."

"Yes, I know," she said. Obviously it was just a message. Obviously messages were for exchanging bare, dry facts. There had never in history been a message that conveyed more than its most literal interpretation. "I get it."

Speaking of messages, she had a few from her sister and her parents, but she dutifully deprioritized these in case she lost the relay. It was more important to file clips for her feed. She combined the latter with a workout, pedaling at 120 revolutions per minute, a white towel draped across her shoulders, narrating to camera about the burn in her calves, which she related only slightly tortuously to the fight for galactic supremacy. "I think there's a fight in each of us," she said, pedaling. "If you're back home, pushing your bike, or lugging groceries, or sweating your job, you're fighting. And that fight connects us. I know I keep saying it, but I don't feel alone out here because I know you're with me. I'm carrying your fight, our fight, out there." Then she said good-bye for six months, or however long it turned out to be. And it was honestly emotional, because she would miss them, her followers, who sent her messages like *I love you!* and *Keep kicking salamander ass!* and *How do you do your eyes, they're so beautiful.* Oh, how she would miss Feed Talia.

The process left her drained and she granted herself a brief nap before resuming her tasks. But when she woke, she could feel something was different. She applied her film and pinged the relay and it came back with NO CONNECTION. It had happened. They were in VZ.

Three days later, they had an engagement. The walls flushed orange; the klaxon sounded; she scrambled to station. Her place was on A Deck, up at the top of the ship, which she liked as a concept. There was no view; it was a hardened room with a harness and a bunch of screens, the same as any station. But it was fun to imagine herself up top, a puppet master, strings dangling to the three below. Because that was what she was doing: monitoring Jackson, Anders, and Gilly. All the garbage she called in about thermals and desats during an engagement, that didn't matter at all. Nothing could go wrong with any of that. The crew were a different story.

The harness curled around her, holding her tight. She quite enjoyed that, too. It was like getting a hug from the ship. "Life, checking in."

Jackson: "Welcome, Life."

Gilly: "Intel, checking in. All green."

"Anders?"

"Yeah."

"Where are you?"

"C Deck. Give me a minute. I'm coming."

"Can you go live on ping, please?"

"Sure. Sorry. We were playing ninja stars." On Talia's film, Anders's name brightened. He was near Medical, she noticed. He and Gilly had found some new game that caused them to require trips there. She filed that away for further attention: *Anders: Deliberately seeking self-harm?* He had an addictive personality; he could get hooked on almost anything.

Jackson: "Getting our first look at VZ hostiles. One ring, six hives. Lot of traffic. Maybe five hundred soldiers in flight."

Gilly: "Any fliers?"

Jackson: "Negative."

Over comms: Anders breathing. *Huh, huh, huh.*

She said, "You all right, Anders?"

"Yeah. Head hurts. Almost at station."

Concussion? Hangover? Tumor? She would review his medicals.

"Hurry," said Jackson. "Contact in sixty seconds. It would be nice to have weapons. Intel, what am I seeing in Armor? It looks low."

"We're undercharging. Not a problem. Lots of spare capacitance."

"We'll have full armor in sixty?"

"Before that. In thirty."

"Thank you. Life? How are we looking?"

"We're looking beautiful," she said.

"Hives discharging," Jackson said. "Eight hundred in flight. A thousand. Twelve hundred."

"How big are these hives?" Gilly asked.

"Standard. Eighty yards across. But take your point. It's more than we usually see from this kind of cluster."

"It's a lot more."

"Topping out at sixteen hundred. Yes. It's a lot more."

"Intel," Talia said. "You've been running swarm analysis. Anything unusual in their behavior?"

"It's too early to tell. We'll find out if they turn." He sounded pleased to be asked, so, mission accomplished.

Jackson: "Contact in twenty seconds. Anders?"

"Weapons, checking in."

"Thank you. How does it look?"

"Pulse ready. Laser batteries . . . have not deployed."

"We're going in with just the pulse?"

"Yep."

"You want to figure out why?"

"Roger." The ship deployed weapons based on its situational assessment, which was often too complex and fast-moving to follow. But Anders was supposed to be across it.

"Hostiles converging," Jackson said. "There's the turn. Contact in five."

"*First* turn," Gilly said.

"We're in range. Weapons, why aren't we pulsing?"

Anders: "Uh . . ."

"Hostiles turned again. Same as last time. They're spreading out again."

Gilly: "Same tactic."

"And here they come again. Third turn."

"Pulsing," Anders said.

"Thank you, Weapons. That was a good one. Caught them on the bubble. Four hundred down."

Gilly: "Oh, that's good. We anticipated their turn this time. Outsmarted them."

Anders: "Pulse ready in ten."

"Clever ship," Gilly said. "Very clever ship."

Jackson: "Hives are breaking formation. Leaving the ring."

"We hit them?"

"No. Think they're leaving."

Anders: "Pulsing."

"Acknowledge. That got a lot of them. Five hundred remaining. Four hundred. Debris is cascading. Three hundred."

Gilly: "Still all soldiers?"

"So far. There may be some we haven't picked up. Hives outputting a whole mess of spores. Doesn't matter. Tracking is stable. Weapons, we're still going pulse-only here?"

"Affirmative. Next pulse in eight seconds."

"Incoming fire," Jackson said. "Two hundred in *huk* range."

"Again, just soldiers?" Gilly said.

"Correct."

"Pulsing."

"*Huk*s destroyed. Soldiers destroyed. No hostiles in flight. Looks like we got them all."

Talia said, "That puts us over half a million mission kills, yes?"

"Oh, yes, just," said Gilly. "That's a milestone."

Jackson: "Contact with hives in ten seconds."

"How many do we need to overtake *Fire of Montana*?"

"Another four hundred thousand, at least," Gilly said. "We need a lot more hives."

"Maybe we'll get lucky." Personally, she didn't much care how many confirmed kills anyone had. It was mainly a goal to keep them on task.

"That was more salamanders than normal, though. Target density seems to improve as we get deeper."

"Speaking of which," Jackson said. "We just crisped the hives, correct, Weapons?"

"Yep."

"Please continue to call in until the end of the engagement."

"Roger that."

"Zero hostiles. Zero structures. Debris is scan-clear. Engagement complete."

"Logging it," Gilly said.

"Congratulations," said Jackson. "You have now survived combat in VZ."

"Is there a medal for that?" Talia said.

"Yes," Jackson said. "They mail it out to you."

"Huh," Gilly said. "So this is what VZ feels like."

"What does it feel like?" Talia said.

"Different. I dunno. I guess it's not, logically. But it feels different. Don't you think?"

"Yes," she said, validating his feelings. "There's something about it."

"Feels like the same old shit to me," Anders said. "We sit around holding our dicks while the ship takes care of business."

"Don't be gross, Anders," she said, reaffirming boundaries.

"That's enough," Jackson said. "Engagement closed."

She caught Anders before he could make it back to his cabin. "What's wrong with you?"

He squinted at her. It had been a long time since Anders had had a haircut, and she wasn't a fan of his beardy look, which had progressed from rugged survivalist to grizzled homeless. Even though they couldn't send clips home, they were supposed to still be recording them, so this wasn't ideal. "What?" he said.

"We just talked about this."

"Gilly?"

"Yes, Gilly."

He rubbed his face. "Beanfield, I feel like dirt. It slipped out. Can you give me a break?"

"You are not to tell Gilly. I'm very serious about this. Why do you feel like dirt?"

"Gilly hit me in the head with a ninja star."

She stared.

"It's fine. It won't happen again. I just want to get some sleep."

"I'm pulling your medical records, FYI."

"Aw," he said. "Don't do that."

"Why not?"

He rolled his tongue around his gums. "You're going to see some hydrexalin usage."

"Shit, Paul," she said.

"We get serious wounds. The ship suggests it."

"I'm banning that game."

"Beanfield. It's all I have. We're in VZ, what do you want me to do?"

He had her there. The reality was, Anders needed something. He couldn't be left to his own devices. All his devices had built-in self-destructs.

"No more hydrexalin, though," she said. "I'm cutting that off. You need anything serious, you ask me or Jackson for authorization."

"What am I supposed to do when I get hit? Grin and bear it?"

"Figure it out," she said. "You need a challenge."

Anders *was* getting hydrexalin, a lot of it. After reviewing the records, she became sure he'd constructed this new game for the primary purpose of going to Medical and getting drugged up. She went back through the timestamps of his visits and found they lined up neatly with other Anders behavioral incidents, including the time he'd dropped his pants in briefing. It was good that she'd caught this.

She tweaked her VZ plan. "Stop me if this is crazy," she told Jackson in Con-1, a tiny conference room on A Deck, during a briefing. Captain and Life Officer only; these were for discussing crew behavior. "I'm thinking of instituting a hug program."

Jackson said nothing for long seconds. Jackson was not completely convinced of the need for a Life Officer in the first place, Talia had picked up. She gave off an unmistakable *everything-about-you-is-useless* vibe. But, you know, Service disagreed, so.

"We could do it a few different ways," Talia said. "A special event, if we wanted to make a thing of it, or a new informal routine to end regular social meetings. I'm leaning toward the latter, even though it means blurring the lines of authority. To, you know, slip it under the radar. So it's not so artificial."

"A hug program," Jackson said.

"Yes." She tried to wait Jackson out and failed. "I think we need it."

"Why?"

Because I'm a little worried that we're losing Anders, Jolene. That we're going to have an engagement and only three people will call in. Some things about the crew, like Anders's hydrexalin usage, Jackson couldn't be told, because it would only undermine her relationship with them. Jackson was intelligent and determined and an inspiring role model for girls around the world, but honestly, there were holes in that woman's brain. Pieces that had been left behind six years before in Fornina Sirius, where thousands of people had died and the survivors took three months to crawl home and then never talked about it except in Service-polished platitudes. Jackson was incapable of sympathy, for example. If Talia said, *I think we need to work around Anders's psychological fragility,* Jackson would nod and ask her to explain, but inside she would be clutching at the table and dry-heaving, because they were soldiers on a warship and if you didn't like it, you could step out the fucking door and wait for them to swing by on the way back.

A roleplay that might have been useful to Talia, back at Camp Zero:

Good morning, Captain Jackson! I've been thinking that rather than follow the exact same routine for every day of our four-year tour, perhaps we could mix things up by—

Stop right there, Life. Do you think this is a game?

No, Captain.

Does this look like a vacation to you?

No, Captain.

Do you think the salamanders swap around their attack formations for fun every once in a while? Do you think they like to "mix things up"?

I just mean that repeating the same actions over and over can become psychologically numbing for—

Hold up, Life. Do you think I'm about to reverse my position based on something you just said?

Well—

Do you think I got where I am by admitting fault? Let me educate you, Life Officer Beanfield: I did it by sticking to my opinions in the face of prevailing counterevidence. I stopped evolving as a human being six years ago, Lieutenant. I found that I quite liked it when people called me a war hero and decided it meant I didn't need to change a goddamn thing thereafter. Allow me to ask you a question, Life: Have you seen close combat? Because I was in the general vicinity when some other people did and to my way of thinking that makes me an authority. Do you see this sidearm I'm wearing?

Yes, I was wondering why you needed—

Do you think I understand it's purely ceremonial? Because I don't. I sleep with it underneath my pillow. All I am is symbols and talismans and empty heroism, Life, and let me ask you: Do you really believe I'm capable of hearing other people's ideas as anything other than a personal attack?

Noooooo.

Talia shrugged and said, "Call it a Beanfield thing. I like to touch. I'm a hugger."

Jackson's eyebrows rose. "Do you want a hug?"

"Nah," Talia said. "Get out of here."

Jackson smirked. They moved on to other business.

When they concluded, with nothing actually concluded, Talia climbed down to her deck, sat on her bed, and turned off ping. Then she sobbed for a while. That was a good thing, by the way. No one should get the wrong idea. When you were this far from home, you had to cry every now and again. She hid it, of course, because, not a good look, your Life Officer in tears. The others might fail to realize it was an outlet, not a breakdown. That she was simply acknowledging the reality that what she was doing out here was incredibly lonely and left you vulnerable to the most surprising things, like Jackson offering a hug. Because goddamn. She would actually love that.

She cried and then was done. She wiped her face and checked herself in the mirror. Not ideal. The truth was written plainly on her face; it would be apparent to a close observer. But there weren't any of those on the ship. Once Gilly had surprised her when they crossed paths on the way to an engagement, her face literally red, wet, her eyes bloodshot, and Gilly's eyebrows had shot up, and she had panted and said, "I just smashed the elliptical," and he relaxed and nodded like: *Oh, right, of course.*

She set down the cloth. Enough. A planet relied on her. She was here to do a job. She hit the tactile panel and went to do it.

3

[Gilly]

THE PUZZLE

The same valve in the SPT-1 hydrate filters blew twice more in the next five days. After Gilly patched it and traced the fault back to a pressure imbalance at a junction, a different pipe two decks down that had nothing to do with any of that exploded, sending water cascading down a corridor, sloshing into chutes and falling like rain in the ladder shaft.

"I thought you fixed that," Anders said. They had met to play ninja stars, but now this had happened.

"So did I." He shook his head in frustration.

"Anyway," Anders said. "We playing?"

"This invalidates my whole theory of the problem. I have to figure it out all over again."

"It's just water."

"The symptom is water," he said. "The cause is unknown."

Anders just stared at him. "So we playing?"

He squinted at Anders. "This doesn't bother you?"

"What?"

"Mysterious water. Shit going wrong for no reason."

"You're describing my life," Anders said.

He had to fetch his tools. "We'll play later."

"Come on, Gilly. The crabs can fix it."

"If they could fix it, it wouldn't keep happening."

"Unnh," Anders said.

Gilly didn't answer.

"So, later?" Anders said.

"Later," he said.

But later he went to his cabin to study the latest attack pattern. He pulled up old footage of an early encounter at Moniris Outer, where *Silver Bark*, a destroyer, had come upon a salamander hive and begun hitting it with fusion missiles, which were what they used back then, before Providences. He watched the hive break apart and spill salamanders. At first, their movements were chaotic and random, all anger and no direction, like ants boiling from a disturbed nest. Some moved toward *Silver Bark* but most didn't, and the destroyer picked them off leisurely with drones. That was their mistake: taking too long. Because one of the salamanders came close enough to *huk* a quark-gluon slug at the ship, and the instant that slug punctured the hull, the entire swarm turned and plunged toward it.

This was swarm behavior, Gilly knew: a bunch of relatively dumb creatures acting in ways that could appear coordinated. But there was no battlefield commander steering seven hundred salamanders into *Silver Bark*'s heart, just many individuals responding to the same environmental cues.

He paused the playback on *Silver Bark* taking fire. He'd seen the rest: the desperate retreat and escape. Their survival had been celebrated at the time, but the next encounter after this was Fornina

Sirius, the greatest defeat of the war, where salamanders displayed none of this milling around but rather attacked with coordination and precision from the beginning. Ever since, it had been clear that they learned quickly and couldn't be taken for an unintelligent enemy. It was just a different kind of intelligence. Service had a hard policy of total extermination in order to prevent the dissemination of any tactical feedback to the rest of the species.

He pulled up *Fire of Montana*'s combat log and paged through engagements. *Montana* had been out a long time, and Gilly had the idea that maybe they weren't sticking strictly to policy. This was a silly idea—it was two silly ideas, actually: that *Montana* would be so careless, and that if they were, Gilly could detect it first. Service liked to promote the idea that the war was being won by human pluck and determination, but the truth was that every part of it was guided or directly driven by AI systems so effective that Gilly sometimes wondered if he needed to be here. Random pipe failures notwithstanding, the ship had performed well above his expectations, to the point where it seemed capable of going ahead and hunting down salamander hives without any human input.

But he liked a challenge. Beanfield was right about that: He was a puzzler. He had come out here partly because it was the most challenging thing you could do and partly because of the allure of discovery: of exploring places no one had ever been and answering questions about what they found there. Maybe that required a kind of creativity the AI didn't possess. Maybe he could beat it to an answer just once. Maybe not. But it was fun to test himself.

They had no engagements for five days, then three in a row. Each time, the salamanders performed a new variation of turns and the ship's pulse fried them slightly later. Nine days after that, they were called to station and there were no enemies, only a wide field of debris, which seemed to be composed of dead salamanders.

"Battlefield," Gilly said. "Maybe *Montana* went through here."

"There's nothing to kill," Anders said.

"No, doesn't look like it."

"Then why call us to station?"

"I'm sorry," Jackson said, "do you have somewhere to be?"

"It's annoying," Anders said. "Getting here and finding there's nothing to do."

"We're over half a million kills," Beanfield said. "Not enough for you?"

"Not even close." He sounded irritable. "This is bullshit."

"Hive debris at one fifty-niner," Gilly said.

"I see it," said Jackson. "Weapons, this battleship was not designed for your convenience. It was designed to blow the ever-loving crap out of an alien species."

"So call me if you see any."

"Command, I'm getting something in that hive debris," Gilly said, before Jackson could start tearing strips off Anders.

"Like what?"

"I don't know. Maybe nothing."

"I'm not seeing any movement larger than our minimums."

"Yeah. But there's something that's not spin." He brought up a visual and filtered out the wrecked hive. Some part of a salamander was in there, encased in resin. Beneath the resin, something twitched.

"I see it," Jackson said.

"What is that?" said Beanfield.

"Wriggler," Gilly said.

"What's a wriggler?"

"I don't know. Something that's wriggling. Can we hold here?"

"Requesting," Jackson said. The ship would either comply or not, depending on its threat assessment. After a moment, the engines began to rotate on his board. "Green-lit. Prepping for deceleration burn."

"Thanks." He queued up probes. "I'm seeing more of them."

"More wrigglers?" Beanfield said.

"Yeah."

"Where?" Jackson said. "I'm not seeing that."

"They're not moving, but they match composition. All over."

"You're referring to the body parts?"

"Yeah."

"What?" said Beanfield.

"After an engagement, we leave a lot of salamander pieces behind," Gilly said. "Tens of thousands. Hundreds of thousands."

"And one of them is wriggling?"

"Yes," he said.

"Ship wants to move," Jackson said.

"That's an advisory?"

"Yes."

If the ship really wanted to move, it would go ahead and move. "I want to wait a minute and run a few more scans, if that's okay."

"What are you thinking?"

"Well," he said.

"Say it."

"Pregnant salamander," he said.

"Excuse me?" Beanfield said. No one answered. "They can be pregnant?"

"No," Gilly said. "Not that we know. Soldiers and workers are sexless. We've never encountered a breeder type."

"So what's this?"

"It's a dead salamander body part that's wriggling. If you have any more ideas for what that could be, go ahead."

"Well, heck," Beanfield said, after a moment.

"Ship has upgraded advisory to recommendation," Jackson said. "It wants to move."

"It always wants to move," Gilly said. "It's probably calculating how many more salamanders it could kill if we weren't sitting here."

"I'm doing a similar calculation myself."

"I don't understand how they are at all," Beanfield said suddenly. "How they come from nowhere and throw themselves at us like they don't care if they live or die."

"That part is simple enough," Gilly said. "Salamanders are clones. Genetically identical."

"So?"

"So life is really about gene propagation. It's common for animals to act in ways that protect their wider gene pool, even when that risks their own lives."

"Which animals?" Beanfield said. "Because that definitely doesn't describe me."

"You're literally on a warship," Gilly said. "It's what we're doing right now."

"Hold on," she said. "I didn't go to war to protect a gene pool. I did it for the health plan."

"Well, it's cute that you think that," Gilly said. "But you don't have as much free will as you think. Every time we think we're choosing to be selfless, or noble, or doing our patriotic duty, or sacrificing ourselves for our kids, we're really obeying a hardwired genetic instinct. We wrap it up in a nice story, but it's just biology. The closer any two people are genetically, the more likely one is to make sacrifices for the other. The same goes for animals. And salamanders." Results from the scans began to fill his board. "I mean, fundamentally, the war isn't even between people and salamanders. It's between human genes and salamander genes. They're just using us to fight it, as their throwaway survival machines."

"Let's put a pin in this fascinating philosophical discussion," Jackson said. "We're mid-engagement."

"Body part appears to be part of the hind quarters of a standard soldier class," Gilly said. He couldn't keep the disappointment out of his voice. "Doesn't appear to be anything new."

"Then what's moving?"

"There's a puncture in the surrounding resin. The material inside is escaping chaotically under pressure."

"All right," Jackson said. "So it's a leaking body part. Let's get this bus moving."

"Not pregnant?" said Beanfield. "No baby salamanders?"

"No." He hesitated. "Although . . . this could be how they do it."

"Do what?"

"Learn. They could create a store and recover it later."

"A store of what?"

"Knowledge. Memories. Other species use pheromones for communication. Hive species, like ants. They excrete a chemical composition that encodes information about what they've experienced, which others can read later. It could be like that."

"Explain that better," Beanfield said, "for those of us in the Humanities."

"It's possible that salamanders generate pheromones during their attack to record their actions. Where they went. How long they survived. If other salamanders can recover those, they could reconstruct a pretty good battle record."

"So they learn to anticipate the pulse?"

"Exactly. Salamanders that turned at the right time would record a longer survival time."

"Huh," Beanfield said. "You're a real nerd, Gilly."

"It's just a theory," he said modestly. He was sure he was right.

"Ship is getting anxious," Jackson said.

"One minute. I want to confirm this." He began sifting through the data, looking for chemical signatures. Then zeroes flooded his readouts. The ship had pulsed, reducing everything to ash.

"We're moving," Jackson said. "Sorry, Intel. Ship got impatient. Weapons, status? Anders?"

There was a pause. It had been a while since Anders had chimed in, Gilly realized.

"Anders is off-comms and dark on ping," Beanfield said.

"Pardon me?" Jackson said.

"I think he left station. A while ago."

"Hive reduced to sub-gram particles," Gilly said, to fill the silence. "Nothing left out there now."

"End engagement," Jackson said, and signed off.

"Engagement closed," Gilly said.

An hour later, Beanfield called in over comms to ask if he'd seen Anders. Gilly was in his cabin, working his board. "No," he said. He'd assumed Anders was being torn a new butthole by Jackson. "Want me to locate him?" In an emergency, he could force a ping from any film, even if Anders was trying to stay dark.

"Could you maybe just take a wander around the places you guys usually hang, see if he's there? I don't want to make it into a big deal."

"I'm kind of busy."

"With what?"

"I'm writing up my pheromone theory."

"Can that wait?"

"Well," he said, trying to think how to say, *No, Beanfield, it's a groundbreaking discovery.*

"I wouldn't ask if I didn't think it was important."

He took a breath. "I'll try to look up Anders."

"He's been taking VZ hard," Beanfield said. "Harder than the rest of us."

"I hear you." He was sure Anders was going to be fine. At this moment, Gilly was far more interested in getting his theory into a document before anyone else came up with it. He could practically feel the AI churning away, crunching data.

"Thanks, Gilly," she said. "You're a champ."

He wrote for three hours straight and then began to pull their past engagements and rework them, looking for chemical traces to bolster his theory. They hadn't been scanning at a micro level at the time, so it was hard to extract the data he wanted, but there was enough to make his case, he thought: that salamanders had been able to communicate even after death via chemical secretion. He bundled up the data into tables, wrapped up his text, and submitted it to the ship.

His shoulders and neck ached. He crawled into his bunk and fell into a half-dozing state. He dreamed about the ship, except it was bloodthirsty. It was hunting down salamanders not because of programming but because it wanted to. He woke in confusion and for a few moments wasn't sure which part had been the dream. Then he rolled over and thought of other things and fell back to sleep.

Anders was back on ping the next day, so Gilly made contact and scheduled a game of ninja stars. Then he read over his document. He found plenty of areas to tidy or clarify and when his playdate reminder popped, he snoozed it, and again half an hour later, then dismissed a message from Anders that asked if he was coming. When he finally made his way down to F Deck, he rounded a corner and found Anders urinating against a wall. He stopped.

Anders turned toward him, putting out a steady stream. His eyebrows rose. "Gilly!"

"What are you doing?"

Anders looked at the pool of urine. "Don't worry. The ship cleans it up."

"But you don't have to piss on the floor."

Anders said nothing.

"Are you okay?" Gilly said.

Anders began to tuck himself into his pants, being very careful. "I didn't think you were coming."

He was beginning to regret it. "Well, I'm here." He shifted his weight. "Where have you been going, anyway? You keep dropping off ping."

Anders zipped. "Want me to show you?"

"Sure."

"During the next engagement."

Gilly squinted. "What?"

"I found something. But it only works during an engagement."

"Are you asking me to leave station during an engagement?"

"Forget it," Anders said.

"I can't do that and neither can you."

"Forget I asked. Can you open small-arms lockers?"

The arms lockers were located on every second deck, in case they were flung four years backward in time to when salamanders got close enough to see with the naked eye. "No. Jackson has to authorize that."

"I mean in practice. You're Intel. You can cycle the locks, right?"

"Where are you going with this?"

"Guns, Gilly," Anders said. "We get a couple of guns. Then it's the same as ninja stars."

"We're not doing that."

"Not big guns. Just the pistols."

"Accessing arms lockers without approval? This is court-martial stuff."

Anders's jaw came out. Gilly could see that in Anders's head, pistols were just the beginning. After pistols, there would be rifles, junior burger guns, or lightning guns. Now he was offended because Gilly wouldn't even do pistols. "Fuck me," Anders said. "You're such a pussy."

"I'm leaving," Gilly said.

Anders came after him. The corridor was too small for Anders to overtake him, but Gilly could sense him following. "Wait. Gilly. We can play ninja stars."

"I don't want to play anymore."

"Something else, then."

His film flared. There was another burst valve, this time on K Deck. It was amazing to Gilly that he could deduce an alien species' chemical-based learning pattern but not diagnose a few exploding pipes. "I have shit to do, Anders." He reached the ladder hatch and hauled it open. When he began to descend, Anders stared at him balefully.

"You don't know anything," Anders said.

He ignored this and kept climbing. With luck, Anders wouldn't follow. Anders was weirdly reluctant to use ladders. When they played ninja stars, nine times out of ten, Anders would stay on the same deck. Gilly reached K Deck and was confronted with billowing steam.

Crabs crawled across the floor, heading into the fog. He unsnapped the gloves from his belt. Behind him, Anders's boots crashed onto the floor, as if he'd slid down the entire length of the ladder like a fireman's pole.

"I have to fix this valve," Gilly said.

"No you don't."

"Anders? I know you don't take this seriously, but I do. Let me do my job." He flipped his film into diagnostics to bring up a visual overlay of water flow.

"Take off your fucking film."

Gilly ignored him, watching fluid dynamics.

"Take off your film," Anders said, and was suddenly on top of him, his fingers gouging Gilly's face. They struggled. Anders ripped the film from him.

"You're crazy!" Gilly shouted, backing away. "You've gone insane!"

"Turn around."

He didn't want to do that, because what would happen next was Anders would jump him, or clock him with something. But as he stood there panting, fists bunched, he became aware of the silence. He turned. The corridor was empty. No steam. No leak.

"You don't need to worry about the valve," Anders said.

Gilly stared at the pipes running down the corridor. The crabs could repair things like that quickly. But the metal patching they left behind was an unmistakable dull yellow. What he was looking at were pipes that hadn't been touched in months.

"See? We can hang out," Anders said. "But don't tell Beanfield, okay? Our secret."

"Scheduler?" Gilly said. But of course that was no good; he wasn't wearing his film. He couldn't schedule a meeting. He couldn't do anything. "Beanfield?" he called.

"Shh," Anders said. "Be cool, Gilly."

"Give me my film," he said. "Give me my film!"

Beanfield sat across the table from him. Behind her stood Jackson, arms folded. Where Anders was, Gilly didn't know. In trouble, he guessed. As for himself, he was lost. He was floating in space, with nothing to hold on to.

"It's a four-year mission," Beanfield said. "It's really important that all of us receive adequate mental stimulation over that period. For our own sanity."

He looked at Jackson for her reaction to this piece of ridiculousness. Her expression remained the same.

"Think of it like a treadmill. Are you actually getting anywhere? No, but it's exercise. It's keeping you healthy, improving your strength, your conditioning. Keeping you sharp."

There had been a lot of hazing at Camp Zero. Gilly had always felt vulnerable to it, because he tended to take things literally. Pranks had to be explained to him. Even then, he couldn't understand their motivation. He kept still in case this was one of those times.

"Speak," Jackson said.

"There's no valve problem?"

"No," Beanfield said. "The ship painted that on your film. As a puzzle."

"A puzzle?" he said. "Like a crossword?"

"You're high-testing for intelligence. We have to keep your mind engaged."

He gave a short laugh. He was high-testing for intelligence. He had spent two years on a ship diagnosing engineering problems that didn't exist. He was a real genius.

"It's dangerous to send people into space for four years with nothing to do," Beanfield said. "Especially a civilian, like yourself, with relatively little mental training. So Service developed these exercises."

He felt detached from this conversation. Like he was standing back, watching it. "Who else got puzzles? You?"

"Well, no," she said.

He looked at Jackson.

"No," said Beanfield.

"Anders?" he said hopefully.

"He used to," Beanfield said.

"What happened?"

"He figured it out."

"For fuck's sake," Gilly said.

"Don't interpret this as a failure. Anders is low-testing for compliance. He interacts experimentally with his environment. That's not better. It's just different."

He put his elbows on the table. His head felt heavy.

"I know this feels like a betrayal, Gilly. I know it will take time to process."

"What about the engagements?"

"What about them?"

"Are they real?"

She looked shocked. "Gilly, this was a mental dexterity exercise. That's all. And, you might have noticed, Anders is walking proof of why they're useful."

"Engagements are real," Jackson said. "They're the most real thing we do."

"But we don't do anything. We don't even have to be at station, do we? All we do is monitor what the ship is doing. It decides where to go. It can fight without us. It doesn't even . . ." He trailed off, because the words he was about to speak, he had actually said once before, to Beanfield, without realizing their implication. "It doesn't even know we're here."

"Let's not get carried away," Jackson said. "Shit can break. When it does, you're here to fix it."

He looked at her. Nothing was going to break. The ship could diagnose and repair itself.

"It's possible your swarm analysis is useful, too," Beanfield said. "I mean, it's all data for the ship. It may help it decide one way or the other."

He closed his eyes. He couldn't take much more of this.

"Gilly, there's another really important reason we're out here," Beanfield said. "We're a humanizing media presence."

He stared. Then he looked at Jackson, because if that meant what he thought it did, he couldn't believe she would tolerate it.

"Service needs human faces out here to sell the war effort. Not drones. Providences are expensive, Gilly. They don't get built unless people pay for them. We help convince them that their sacrifice is worthwhile, via our feeds and interviews."

"What?" he said.

"War is a lot of moving parts. This is one of them."

He wanted this meeting to end. He wanted to lock himself in his cabin and not come out again. He'd thought he was someone, doing something.

"I'll give you some time to think this out," she said. "You want to hear something crazy, though? This could be a good thing. We can be really honest with each other now." The corner of her lip curled. "And didn't you always suspect? Even a little?"

"No," he said.

———

But maybe he had. It seemed impossible that he'd missed it. He'd understood the capabilities of the AI. He'd known it could do everything he could, only better. How could he have avoided the logical conclusion—that everything he did was pointless—unless he'd wanted to?

He hadn't beaten the ship to the pheromone theory, he saw now. He'd requested that it wait while he investigated. But it had wanted to move on immediately. Because it already knew what was happening, and what needed to be done.

Maybe they were right not to tell him, because now he was angry. The only thing that had kept him going at Camp Zero had been the idea that eventually he would get out and start to do things that mattered. So what now?

He stared at the wall of his cabin. He had two more years on this ship. He couldn't think of how to fill the next fifteen minutes. "Shit," he said, quietly. Maybe he really would turn out like Anders.

4

[Beanfield]

THE SHIP

Well," she said, once Gilly had left. "That was unfortunate."
Jackson shrugged fractionally. "He was always going to figure it out."

Jackson, of course, had never seen the point of concealing the truth from Gilly. Jackson held the idea that you could tell someone what to do and they would go do it and that was that. This wasn't even true with soldiers. "You're probably right."

"Service wastes too much time on that garbage," Jackson said. "Feeds and mind games."

"Mmm," said Talia. *And Life Officers*, was the next part of that sentence.

"Gilly's risking his life out here like the rest of us. He deserves the truth."

"I suppose."

"You don't agree?"

The thing is, Jolene, not everyone on this ship is trying to flee survivor's guilt. For normal people, being trillions of miles from home is kind of difficult. It's kind of debilitating. Jackson was married. This was part of her sacrifice: She had waved good-bye to her husband for four years. Talia wasn't going to say anything, but to be honest she wasn't a hundred percent sold on how much of a sacrifice that really was. If you pressed her, Talia might guess that Jolene Jackson's husband was one more person she'd run into space to escape.

"I see the argument," she said. "But it's situational. Some people struggle with this more than others."

Jackson squinted at her. "You're talking about Anders?"

Of course she was. "His boredom is creating operational problems. Gilly's now an issue because Anders was too bored to keep his mouth shut." Jackson leaned back in her seat. Her stupid sidearm gleamed. Sometimes Talia caught herself fantasizing about snatching that thing out of its holster and throwing it down a corridor, just to see Jackson's expression. She had researched it, because she had nothing better to do, and discovered it fired compressed air. It made a loud noise and disturbed hairstyles, essentially. Jackson never put it down. "I don't care what he told Gilly. I care about him skipping station. It's dereliction of duty. And he doesn't have many duties."

She honestly wondered what Jackson did in her downtime. It must be something. How else could she believe that having few duties was a good thing?

"You say he was getting hydrexalin? How?"

"Medical. He deliberately engages in games with a high injury risk."

"That stops."

"The games?"

"All of it," Jackson said. "I don't care what you have to do. He's absent from station again, I'm having him confined."

She felt that would be bad. Locking Anders in his cabin: She did not have a good feeling about that. She would like to try some tactics that didn't involve massively escalating the situation. "I'll get him to station."

"Make sure you do," Jackson said.

Anders had a history. Her first day at Camp Zero, after the Service brass with stony eyes and whip-crack voices finished telling them what a glorious honor it was to be standing where they were right now, representing humanity in its hour of greatest need, fighting to defend our brilliant blue bubble against an evil alien aggressor, et cetera, and so forth, she had looked around to check out her competition and Paul Anders had breezed by. She stared after him and a girl beside her said, "Who was *that*?" and another girl said, "I don't know, but I think I'm going to like it here," and they had laughed and bonded while Talia tried to decide whether it would be weird to start laughing, too, and decided yes.

He was beautiful. There was the jaw, the eyes, the way that when he looked at you, he seemed to be asking, *Who are you?* and the answer could be anything you wanted. You somehow became a better, more relevant person in the spotlight of his gaze. It felt that primal. And when the stories began, they only increased his allure. Here was a Paul Anders story: One day, a nice girl, usually a Life candidate, was minding her own business, waiting for a shuttle, alone, not betraying any hint of the monumental pressure she was under every single waking minute, and Paul Anders happened to sit nearby. They got to talking, and the girl discovered to her surprise that behind Paul Anders's soul-piercing eyes and unlikely bone structure was a careful thinker, not at all the shallow, narcissistic maniac you might have heard, so she allowed herself to continue to talk to him, and then they met up later—not a date, you understand, it actually didn't really fit a label—and they had the most amazing conversation, where he revealed his incredible vulnerability, like the things he'd gone through, you couldn't imagine, and she realized something: She didn't allow herself to have fun anymore, or else she was only here because her mother had such impossible expectations, or else she was stronger than she'd thought, whatever it was, one of those, and then, not to make a big deal out of this because it wasn't really the point, but they had sex. It was, let's say, how to put this, because she didn't want to sound conceited, but it did redefine her whole reality. Like it made it really clear that most people were completely out of touch with what really mattered in life. Not you specifically. She wasn't criticizing you for staying in to study interpersonal stress dynamics while she was out with Paul Anders, experiencing life. She was just saying, people should just, like, not assume things about other people. They shouldn't think they knew what was real just because of what they saw on the surface.

Then Paul Anders never spoke to the girl again and she sat on her bunk and cried into the arms of her girlfriends, who said she would be okay, he was such an asshole, how could she have known, and glance at each other, and roll their eyes, and secretly wonder if/when they might be in a Paul Anders story.

Talia didn't want to be too judgey, since this was exactly what everyone said before they fell into a Paul Anders story, but really: How stupid were these women? They were supposed to be Life candidates.

To be fair, that was part of the problem: You went into Life because you were open to people. You wanted to believe there was more to a person than anyone thought, and tease it out, and then, possibly, turn to an audience and take a bow. The thing about being Life was you were always asking other people to suckerpunch you.

One other thing about Paul Anders stories. Sometimes the girls were quiet. Twice, when she had hugged them after their Paul Anders story, they had seemed to wince. Once, a girl was absent from class for two days, and when she came back, there was a fading bruise beneath her eye. You could believe, if you wanted, that this was part of that reality-defining sex. But she didn't. Talia didn't believe that.

She assumed he'd never make crew. Even when it emerged that the selection process favored what you might charitably call media presence and less charitably call attractiveness, she couldn't imagine he would be deployed on a Providence. The process was guided by AI, but not even software could be that perverse. "Can you imagine," a girl had said, "being Life on a ship with him?" The girl wrinkled her nose but also inhaled through parted lips in a way that told Talia she was definitely imagining it, wielding nominal authority over crazy, sexy Paul Anders in a confined space for four years.

But it would never happen. Surely.

He ate like a slob. When they dined together (social! bonding!), he threw food in the general direction of his face. If something spilled, he left it, like a child. Sometimes he would pretend he hadn't heard her. She would ask him a question and he would sit there chewing and staring at nothing until she repeated herself twice, three times, then he would turn and grin at her. It was so stupid she wanted to claw out her eyes.

She had found him choking to death in his cabin in the eleventh month, writhing on the floor, his lips blue, his eyes rolled back. She'd been coming to see him to check on a deterioration in his vitals and halfway there his numbers plummeted and she broke into a run. She used her override to access his cabin and rolled him onto his side and stuck her fingers down his throat and dragged out a thick, goopy protein cookie. He gasped and retched and lay in her lap, panting. When his color returned, he smiled at her like a moron. His breath stunk of hydrexalin, a smell like rusty roadkill. He said, "I like the way your face is arranged."

"You idiot," she had said. "You could have died."

She thought about that comment later: *I like the way your face is arranged.* At first, she'd thought he was saying she was pretty. But on reflection, she changed her mind. He meant: *I like the way you're looking at me.* When he was on the floor. When she was worried he was about to die.

Next engagement, there was Anders, but no hostiles. They checked in and ran through their basic checks as the ship approached two small hives. "Movement," Gilly said. "Lots of workers. But no soldiers." There was curiosity in his voice, which she liked. Gilly needed a good mystery.

"You want I should park us here?" Jackson said.

He hesitated. "No, let the ship do its thing."

"There are *no* soldiers?" Anders said.

"Maybe we're reading it wrong," Jackson said. "Wouldn't be the first time that's happened."

"When was that?" Gilly said, and at station, Talia smacked her forehead, because how could he not recognize the Fornina Sirius reference?

"What are the workers doing?" she said, before Jackson could begin having flashbacks.

"Just shuttling between the hives. Building, I guess."

"Building what?"

"The hives. Making them bigger. They basically vomit up material and spread it around."

"So hives are barf balls," Anders said. "Floating balls of barf."

"Yes."

"I don't like it," Jackson said. "Where are the soldiers?"

"These have been encountered before," said Gilly. "The theory is they're constructed by workers first, then populated by soldiers later."

"I know the theory," Jackson said.

"Poor little workers," Talia said, to change the subject. Jackson was testy today, for some reason.

"Pardon me?"

"I just mean they're noncombatants."

She listened to Jackson choking on her own tongue for a few moments. "No salamander is a noncombatant. They're all the enemy."

"What's your opinion, Intel?" Talia said. She suspected she could put him and Jackson on the same side here. "Shooting workers: yes or no?"

"Of course. It's not even a question."

"Even the civilian gets it," Jackson said. "Every salamander deserves to die."

"Wel-l-l-l," said Gilly. "I wouldn't frame it quite that way. We're in a war and one species is going to win. We have to make sure it's us. It doesn't really matter whether they deserve it."

"Trust me, they deserve it," Jackson said.

"I'm just saying, that's not relevant to the question of whether we should be killing them."

"If you want, I can point you to a whole bunch of file footage on what they did to us at Fornina Sirius," Jackson said. "Or Moniris Outer. Or *Coral Beach*. If you need some help figuring out who the bad guys are."

"Right . . ." Gilly said, and Talia could hear him struggling against his desire to force his point through Jackson's skull. "But—"

"Desats are dipping," Talia said. They were not. "Do you see that, Intel?"

"Uh . . . not really."

"Pulse in five," Anders said. "Four, three, two. Pulsing."

"Scanning," Jackson said. "Confirmed, all hostiles down. Hives destroyed."

"Thrilling," Anders said. "Can we go?"

"It's not over," Gilly warned. "We'll get closer and pulse again to destroy any chemical residue that could be functioning as a memory store."

"Well, excuse me if I don't stick around for that part."

"Stay put, Weapons," said Jackson. "Engagement is ongoing."

"But there are no hostiles."

"Do I need to repeat myself?" There was silence. "Weapons?" They could all see that Anders had gone dark on ping. "Okey-dokey," Jackson said, after a long pause. Talia felt the weight of her disappointment as a physical force.

"Anyway, to return to what we were talking about," said Gilly, "it doesn't matter whether they're workers. It wouldn't matter if they were children. They're essentially all component parts of a single life-form that wants to destroy us."

"Now you're speaking my language," Jackson said. "Life, if you want to close out, that's fine by me. I don't know how long this part will take."

This meant: *Go find Anders.* "Roger that," she said.

She didn't find him that day, or the next, and the engagement after that Anders didn't turn up at all. She sent him a message, LAST CHANCE, to which he didn't respond. She was literally on her way to find Gilly to have him force Anders out of dark when Anders started gasping in her ear. It was just her and Anders, a private channel.

"Beanfield," he said. "I fucked up."

He was two decks down, almost directly below. She came off a ladder and found him curled in a ball in a corridor. "What's happening?" There was blood everywhere: on his hands, his shirt, the floor. A short distance away, a crab shifted back and forth like it wanted them to move so it could clean all this up. Anders's hands were pressed to his thigh. "What did you do?" Then she noticed the star, the stupid fucking ninja star, lying on the deck, bright and slick with blood. "You stabbed yourself?"

"It bounced."

Yes, she could see that: Anders practicing, hurling stars at the walls. Walking to collect them. Maybe one came back at him and he ducked and thought for a minute and then kept doing it. "Goddamn it." The walls turned orange and the klaxon howled. Her film began painting helpful arrows on the floor to show the direction to her station. "God-*damn* it."

"Don't tell Jackson."

She stared. She had to get him to Medical. "Can you stand?"

He tried and failed. She put out her arms to help, but he jerked away, his teeth pulling back like a wounded dog.

"What the hell?" she said.

"I'm good."

"Do you want my help or not?"

"Life, Weapons," said Jackson over comms. "Will you be joining us?"

"One moment," she replied, and went mute again. "Tell me where you go when you're dark on ping."

"I need Medical."

"I'll get you to Medical if you're straight with me. Deal?" He said nothing, which she decided to take as assent. She opened the public channel. "Anders is sick. I'm taking him to medical."

There was a second of silence. Then, Jackson: "Acknowledge."

It was nice that Jackson chose not to be a dick about this. Talia appreciated that. Every now and then there were these delightful instances, like rays of sunshine breaking through the clouds, that Jackson trusted her to perform her job to a standard of basic competence. She offered her arm to Anders and he levered himself up. They began to hobble along the corridor. Their movement had a weird cadence, and it wasn't just the close quarters: He was trying to keep a distance between them. Like he couldn't stand to touch her. It was amazing to her that after all this time, Anders could still have so many mysteries. What would she have done without him? He was her puzzle.

Behind them, the crab began scraping at the floor, sucking up blood. "Left," she said, when Anders appeared to have forgotten where Medical was. She helped him onto a steel table and pulled down the scanning arm. In her ear, Jackson and Gilly began to step through the engagement. There was contact in ninety seconds, apparently. Four hives. One big.

"Anders," she said. "Share diagnostics with me." Once he'd looped her in, she scrolled down her film. Subdermal puncture. He'd nicked an artery. Nothing the ship couldn't fix. She grabbed a flatpack, tore it open, and stuck it over the wound. From the outside, it was a bluish patch; on the inside, a miracle cocktail that would repair anything torn and tidy away whatever had leaked where it shouldn't have.

"Hydrexalin," Anders said.

She shook her head. In no universe was she was giving him that. If she did, the next time she found him in a corridor, his injury would be worse.

"Beanfield, I'm in pain."

"Tell me what you do when you're dark on ping."

"Then will you give it to me?"

She shrugged, like *Who knows?*

"I can't tell you," he said. "I have to show you. It only works during an engagement."

In her ear, Jackson said, "Contact," and began running through weapons, which Talia presumed she was managing via her command board. Talia was actually interested in how Jackson and Gilly would deal with this situation, just the two of them. It was a new dynamic. She would review it later.

"Okay, fine," he said. He gingerly swung his legs off the table and hobbled from the room. She followed him through the corridor and every step was against the flow of a line of glowing arrows pointing back toward her station. He reached a hatch and slid down the ladder, landing like a sack of coconuts. They descended this way to R Deck, where it wasn't even lit, because it wasn't somewhere the crew normally needed to go. In the gloom, Anders's face glowed beneath his film. He stopped before a hard door marked:

LASER BATTERY 4
HOT ROOM
DO NOT ENTER

"What?" she said. "No."

Anders pressed the tactile panel. The door emitted two short blares.

"Anders. It's a hot room. They're dangerous during engagements."

"They just say that, Beanfield." He probed around the door with his fingers.

She thought they said it with good reason. But before she could argue, a panel beside the door popped out. Anders retracted it all the way. Another warning tone sounded. Anders yanked a newly revealed lever and the door split down the middle. Heat and light spilled out in such quantity that Talia's film clamped down, plunging her into darkness. When it equalized to restore her vision, Anders was shouldering open the door and stepping inside.

"Follow me!" he said.

She breathed. Then she followed. Because she was committed to Anders; he was her job. She moved into the chamber and heat closed on her like a fist. She couldn't get a sense of the room's scale; it was too densely packed with thick cable bundles and treelike pipes. It might have been huge, a techno-jungle that went on forever. The air roared and shimmered and there was a rhythm to it, a tightening every few seconds. It felt biological, like being inside someone's bowels.

"Don't touch the pipes!" Anders shouted. "They're hot as fuck!"

He clambered over a snarl of cable toward a beige tube taller than he was. As she drew closer, she made out the identifying markings of a burn feeder, part of the system that fed the long-range laser batteries. Anders touched it experimentally. Then he pressed his body against it like a hug, his arms spread, one up, one down.

"What are you doing?" she shouted. Sweat trickled down her back. "Did you not just say not to touch them!"

"The small ones! Touch this one!"

"Why?"

"Just do it!"

Jackson and Gilly burbled in her ear. Outside the ship, where she couldn't see, salamanders were dying. She looked at Anders.

Fuck it. She pressed herself to the pipe. There was a tingling sensation, maybe? She didn't know.

"If they get close, the ship deploys laser batteries!" Anders shouted. "You know how big those are?"

Pretty fucking big, she thought. Maybe she could feel something.

That tingling sensation was building. The rhythmic tightening of the air, each time it lessened, it didn't go back all the way. Anders had his face against the pipe. She didn't want to do that.

Anders shouted, "What they put out, it comes through here!"

Jackson in her ear: "Contact in five."

Talia began to pull away, because it sounded like Anders wanted her to hug a laser feed housing at the exact moment it gushed enough fire to erase an enemy at distance, and was that not the worst possible time? Was that not precisely why the door read DO NOT ENTER? But he was staring at her and this would decide something, she saw. It might be the moment she won or lost him.

She put her cheek to the housing. She felt it coming. There was an uncoiling, like a dragon waking from sleep, its tail rising, wings unfurling, its head coming up, and she hadn't known it was so big. The air in the room thickened until she couldn't speak. It pressed against her body and she couldn't expand her lungs. She thought, *Oh no, this was wrong, I'm dying.* Then a colossal release of energy passed through her, a rush of starfire that dissolved her body.

Her legs didn't work. She sprawled in a mess of cable, her head full of stars. Her legs were numb. Anders was on the floor beside her, laughing. In her ear, Jackson said, "Hostiles down. Area clear."

"You with me?" Anders said.

She nodded. She breathed. The air was cooling. The chamber was shedding heat, transforming from a furnace to a room. She was with him.

He laughed again. They were close enough to touch. He was looking at her like he was thinking about doing something but then decided not to. "Glad you came?"

"That was . . ." she said. "Yes."

He grinned, looking abruptly like the old Anders, the one who'd departed Earth. She'd actually forgotten there was a difference. "Thanks, Beanfield."

"Sure," she said. "Anytime."

Anders attended the next engagement without prompting, and afterward performed a robust, thoughtful debrief. Jackson did her best to remain impassive, but Talia detected amazement in the lift of her eyebrows. As they were leaving, Jackson gave her a brief, barely perceptible nod, which Talia read as: *You know what, Life Officer Talia Beanfield, you're all right.*

This would be temporary. Anders had been bated, not solved.

But it meant she could relax for five minutes. She found herself thinking about the hot room. They were dotted all over the ship. She hadn't paid them attention before; they were just rooms she didn't go into. But now she couldn't pass one by without a lingering glance. She'd known the ship was powerful, of course, but she hadn't physically felt it. It reminded her of a picture book she'd read a long time ago about a little girl who lived on the back of a whale and didn't know it; the girl thought she was on an island. She battled monkeys and pirates and only at the end did she realize the whale had been protecting her the whole time.

"Hey, Gilly, I have a bone to pick with you," she said a few days later, when she was finishing on the treadmill and he turned up for a run. "You said the ship isn't alive, right?"

"Right," he said cautiously.

"Even though it said hello when we boarded."

He nodded. "That was probably a default message from a subsystem."

The treadmill beeped and she dropped to a walk. "And you said *we* are throwaway survival machines for genes. We think we have free will, but really we're doing whatever's best for our DNA. Right?"

He looked slightly impressed that she remembered. "Right."

"So the *ship* is *our* throwaway survival machine." She looked at him triumphantly.

He blinked.

"We built it," she said, "to get around in, and keep us safe, and fight to protect us. Just like genes did with us."

"That's . . . I mean, that's true. If you want to think of the ship as a body, then we're like its genes. Yes. That's a pretty good analogy."

She was thrilled, because she'd been thinking about this for a while, and had felt sure Gilly would find a way to poke holes in it. "That means the ship *is* alive, doesn't it? Because it's the same as us. I mean, genes might not consider us to be alive, because we're so different to them, but we are. We're just a different kind of life. Isn't that the same for the ship? It's life, but at a higher level?"

"I have to think about that," he said after a minute.

She felt happier than she had for a long time. She began to talk to the ship. Not when anyone could see. And, obviously, with no expectation of a reply. It was just somewhere to direct the kinds of thoughts she might otherwise have put into a feed, or a message home. "I feel bad about not replying to Maddie before we went dark," she told the ship. Maddie was her sister, pregnant, according to her last message before they entered VZ, which was really amazing. "I'm worried she might think I'm not happy for her." The ship listened. That was the thing. It was physically there. Wherever she went, it was with her. Like a friend. Her best friend in a million miles. Sometimes she didn't even need to say anything. She could lie in her bunk, facing the wall, and just reach out and touch it. She could honestly feel something. A connection. A presence.

5

[Gilly]

THE ATTACK

I t was not as bad as he'd thought. It was almost better. The first few days after discovering he had no real duties, he had lain in his cabin or wandered the decks, not knowing what to do. Then he realized the answer was simple: He could do whatever he wanted. He could study salamander tactics or review past engagements or figure out how crabs recycled each other—for as long as he wanted, just to satisfy his own curiosity. He began to wear his tool belt again, not because anything needed fixing, but in case he felt like taking something apart.

He also began to play more games, including *Gamma Fleet*, which they played through their films and mined resources and built ships and tried to conquer the galaxy. This had been popular even back at Camp Zero because it was what they all wished they were doing. Games took a few hours and usually ended in showdowns between Gilly and Beanfield, because Anders and Jackson were terrible. Gilly could now almost predict the winner from initial placements: whoever was close enough to pancake Anders and Jackson and absorb their resources.

"You should teach me how you do that," Anders said afterward. They were hanging out in Rec-3, which had sofas.

"Sure." He had tried before, but Anders's eyes glazed over when Gilly started talking about supply paths.

"You see, Gilly?" Anders said. "You didn't need those valve puzzles. You're okay."

He nodded. "I think I am."

"You just have to accept that nothing you do matters."

"Right," he said, although that wasn't how he would have put it.

"So, hey, next engagement, I want you to do something."

"What?"

"I'll tell you when it happens."

Gilly eyed him. "I don't think I'm going to do it."

"It's fine. Beanfield did it."

"Did what?"

"The thing."

"During an engagement?"

Anders nodded.

"Just tell me what it is," Gilly said.

Anders glanced around, as if Jackson or Beanfield might be about to teleport in from their cabins, where he could see their pings. "We go into a hot room."

Gilly blinked.

"I can't tell you why. You have to experience it for yourself."

"I'm not doing that," Gilly said.

Anders looked hurt. "Beanfield did it," he said again.

Gilly didn't believe this. "You can't skip engagements. And you need to dial all this shit down. Jackson won't take it forever."

"Is that right?" said Anders. "What's she going to do? Send me home?"

"We're supposed to be soldiers, Anders."

"But we're not," Anders said, standing. "That's the fucking problem, Gilly. We're passengers. It doesn't matter if we're at station."

"It matters to whether Jackson will yell at me."

"Jackson," Anders said derisively. "Of us four cheap PR stunts, Jackson is the cheapest."

"Can we talk about something else?"

"I need to get out of this room," Anders said, flexing. "There's no goddamn air."

Gilly didn't know what to say to that. In the silence, Anders left.

He considered reporting the conversation to Beanfield. But then he became distracted by an interesting salamander attack pattern from their last engagement, and next thing he knew the walls were orange. He hustled to station, and when he checked in, there was no sign of Anders. At first, no one mentioned it, then Jackson said, almost casually, "Any reason we're missing Weapons?" and Beanfield said, "I'm dealing with it, Command," and that was that.

It was a minor engagement, only a single hive. It expelled less than a hundred salamanders and as soon as the ship pulsed, they and the hive exploded enthusiastically. Gilly's screens washed white. "Whoa," he said.

Afterward, debriefing around the Rec-1 table, they tried to figure out what had happened. Jackson ran the footage, rolling forward and backward around the moment all the salamanders abruptly died.

"This was our regular pulse?" Gilly said. "Because that looks way more effective."

"Regular pulse," Jackson said.

He wanted to ask Anders, who was, after all, Weapons Officer. But

Anders was still missing. "It's like they ignited each other," he said, pointing. "It practically looks like a chain reaction. Starting with the hive."

"Is that a problem?" Jackson said.

He shook his head. "If they're dying faster, that's great. It might be because of our battlefield sanitization. They can't get feedback on what's working, so they have to try weirder experiments."

"Good news, then."

"Yeah," he said. "I guess."

Anders appeared in the doorway. Jackson and Beanfield didn't react at all. "What'd I miss?" Anders said.

"You're confined to quarters," Jackson said, not turning. Anders looked blank, like he didn't know what *confined* meant. "Twenty-four hours."

"What?" Anders said. "You can't lock me up." He looked at Beanfield. "We're on a fucking ship! Where do you think I'm going to go?"

"It's not a discussion," Jackson said. "Leave."

Anders didn't move.

She turned to him. "You want forty-eight?"

"Get fucked," Anders said.

"Five days."

Gilly could see Anders's jaw coming out, the look entering his eyes that meant he was about to do something especially stupid, so Gilly moved toward him, his hands out. "Be cool, Anders. Let's go." He reached for Anders's arm.

Anders jerked away. "Do not fucking touch me, Gilly."

"Anders." He thought he could force Anders to see reason, so he tried to take his arm again. Anders socked him in the cheek. It was so fast and shocking that Gilly was on the floor before he realized what was happening.

There was a loud *bang*. His ears rang. Jackson had her little captain's pistol pointed at Anders's face. She had fired it, Gilly realized. She had shot Anders in the face. Anders looked dazed and fell and hit the floor. Some kind of air gun, Gilly guessed. Until this moment, he had assumed it was decorative.

Jackson holstered the pistol. "Intel, you okay?"

"Yes," he said, embarrassed.

"I'm taking Anders to quarters. Please cancel his door access and comms."

Gilly nodded.

"Take his feet," Jackson said to Beanfield. Beanfield didn't move. She looked almost as stunned as Anders. "We're at war," Jackson said. "We're going to start acting like it."

Two days passed. The ship performed a series of hard skips, taking them deeper into VZ. Then the walls flushed orange and the klaxon howled and they had a single hive with no sign of life. "Abandoned?" Beanfield said.

"Maybe." In his harness, he was acutely aware of the absence of Anders. No one had talked about it and he didn't want to be the one to bring it up. "Hive is unusual."

"Unusual how?" Jackson said.

"Denser. More composite variation." He skimmed his numbers. "Much denser. It's small but heavy."

"But it's definitely a hive?"

"It has tunneling and an interlocking substrata. It's a hive. But a strange one."

"Are we scanning it right?"

"Hmm?"

"Is there a possibility of concealed hostiles?"

"No. It *is* a little harder to read, because of the density. But there are no salamanders."

He felt an invisible force tug at him. He recognized it immediately, but hadn't felt it for a while.

"Ship is decelerating," Jackson said. "Hard."

"Roger that. We're burning at eighty percent." He didn't know what that implied. They always entered engagements at high speed, to maximize the ship's reaction time advantage.

Beanfield said, "Ship wants to check out the weird hive?"

"Yeah, maybe."

"Do we want Anders for this?"

"No," Jackson said.

Data began to pour down Gilly's board, the results of scans. "I think you're right, Beanfield. This could be a discovery. Salamanders manipulate gravity fields in ways we can't replicate. This could be an opportunity to learn about it."

"Pulse is warming up," Jackson said. "Looks like learning time is over."

"Oh," he said, disappointed.

"Pulsing."

"Maybe it's just an old, abandoned hive. We should expect to find a few of those this deep in VZ. They could even—" Something lifted him up and threw him to the left. He lost his grip on his board. His harness grabbed him around the hips and shoulders. "Jesus," he said. His board bounced back into position but it was an empty slate. His film read:

CONNECTION LOST

"I've lost my board," he said.

He checked the connection. At station, everything was wired, so maybe a plug was loose? Although that shouldn't matter; the wired connection was a redundancy. He tapped his film to cycle through subsystems. One after another came back: NO CONNECTION.

"Hello?" he said.

Systems began to blink back on: Life, Command, Engineering, Comms. Something popped in his ears.

Jackson said: "Intel? Life?"

"I'm here."

"I temporarily lost comms. Now I've got nothing on my board."

"Yeah, me too."

"Life?"

"I'm here," Beanfield said. "But no board."

His board fizzed to life. "Systems are coming back up. I'm running diagnostics."

"Which systems?" Jackson said. "Tell me what we have."

"All of Life function. All Engineering. Half of Comms. Weapons coming up now. Armor . . ." He eyed it, in case it was about to change. "Armor is down."

"Repeat that?"

"Armor at zero percent function."

"Give me a scan. I want eyes on our surrounds."

"Roger that. Weapons starting to come online, by the way."

"What happened?" Beanfield said. "Did they attack us?"

"Hive was a bomb," Jackson said. "Detonated when we hit it. Some kind of hinky percussive wave."

He watched the sensing subsystem come online and begin to sift through surrounding space. When numbers began to return, he sucked in his breath. "We have hostiles."

"How many?"

"It's reading fourteen thousand."

There was a short silence. "Could that be a glitch?" said Beanfield.

"Could be. Yes."

"Verify it, please," Jackson said. "Because that would be a shitload of hostiles."

"Yes."

"I still can't see anything. How long are you getting until contact?"

"Six minutes. They're a long way out and we're slowed down. Verified. Hostiles are real."

"Fourteen thousand?"

"Sixteen thousand now. More have entered sensor range."

"We need Armor, Gilly."

"Understood. I'm investigating."

"Weapons are functional, though?" Beanfield said. "So we'll neutralize them before they can reach firing distance, yes?"

"Correct. Ship AI is functional and Weapons are online." He blinked. "Wait. Weapons are down."

Beanfield inhaled.

"You said we had Weapons," Jackson said.

"We did. I'm sure . . . they're coming up now." Earlier, he had seen Weapons scale up into the nineties. Now they were at half that. He kept the readout onscreen and watched its components light up green, one after another. When it reached PLASMA CANNON MAJOR, everything flipped back to red. "We have a problem. Weapons are caught in some kind of loop. They're coming up and going down again." He checked sensors. "Five minutes to contact."

"Am I going to get my board back?" Jackson asked. "If not, I'll come to you."

"Uh," he said. He was tracing the failure path of the plasma cannon back through subsystems to see where it was going wrong. The crazy thing was they didn't even need the plasma. It was a super-weapon that took an hour to charge and was wasted on anything smaller than a planet. They had never used it. But the ship performed diagnostics on each component as it came online, and when it tried this on the plasma, it was causing some kind of error cascade that killed everything. He found a similar effect in Armor and followed it back to a particular core bank: a hunk of computing power that constituted roughly one-thousandth of the ship's brain.

"Intel?"

"I think I see the problem. Core bank nine-nine-six is corrupt."

"Can you take it offline?"

That was exactly what he needed to do. The ship could work around a failed core bank. It simply had to know that it needed to. It should have detected the fault itself, but he could force it. "Not from here. I have to go to Engineering."

"Go. Life, release Anders from confinement. I'm relocating to Intel."

He unstrapped and hit the door's tactile panel. The door didn't move at first and then there was an extremely mechanical whirring of a kind he'd never heard it make before. Just when he thought he was going to have to use his bare hands, it juddered open. He ran through the corridor, leaping housings and ducking beneath bulkheads that he knew by heart, and took two ladders down to E Deck. The door to Eng-13 didn't respond to tactile at all. He felt for the manual release, popped the side panel, and cranked it. Inside, the cores sat beneath thick green translucent housings, each with a board mounted at eye level, spaced a few feet apart. All were reading green. He found 996 and it was green, too. That was the problem. It had gone bad, but the ship hadn't realized it.

"I'm at Intel station," Jackson said. "Contact in two minutes. Life, Weapons, you should have boards when you get back."

He brought up the board, but, to his dismay, it didn't offer him any options he hadn't had at station. He should have known: They were mid-engagement; it had locked down. He stared at the core itself. It was a thin silver brick, gleaming softly under the green housing, two feet away but sealed off from his reach. It looked fine but inside was corruption. He had to teach the ship that, somehow.

"Life, checking in," said Beanfield.

"Weapons, checking in," said Anders.

He unclipped his drill from his belt and clambered up the green housing. Once he was in position, he set the drill bit against the housing and squeezed the trigger. The plastic squealed. He forced the drill down, chewing through the material. His film flared with warnings.

"Intel!" said Jackson. "What's going on?"

"I'm attempting to inflict physical damage on the core to make the ship take it offline." He pushed the drill down until the head touched the housing. That was as far as it would go. He pressed his face to the plastic and peered through. The end of the drill bit hovered half an inch above the core. "Shit!"

"Problem?"

"I can't reach it." He pulled the drill free from the housing. He didn't have a longer bit. But he did have an extensible screwdriver. He dialed the drill open, jammed in the head of the screwdriver, pulled it out to its full length, and fed it back through the hole he'd made.

"Contact," Jackson said. "Hostiles are firing. *Huk*s incoming. Impact in forty seconds."

"Weapons are dark," Anders said. "We are not firing. Repeat, not firing."

Gilly pulled the trigger. The drill jumped in his hands. The tip of the screwdriver squealed across metal. He leaned over the drill, forcing it down with his body weight. The housing filled with white smoke and an acrid smell. His film began to bleed alarms.

"Seeing a lot of warnings, Intel."

"That's fine." He paused to lean out and check the board. He saw core bank 996 blink red and then gray. "That's it! Core is offline!"

"Armor is initializing," Jackson said. "Weapons are initializing. Good job, Intel. Great job."

"Gilly fixed it?" said Beanfield.

He scrambled down the board. He would know once Weapons and Armor managed to dial up beyond the point where they'd been resetting. "I think so. We won't be able to tell for a minute."

"Until Weapons and Armor are fully deployed, we're vulnerable," Jackson said.

He dropped the drill, slid off the housing, and took command of the board. "I can run Intel now."

"Thank you. *Huk*s still incoming. Impact in twenty seconds. Prepare to brace."

"Pulse is up!" Anders said. "Charging!"

"Armor impact in thirty seconds."

"Armor at thirty percent," Gilly said. "It's rising, but that's low. Too low."

"Understood. Armor may be insufficient to repel current incoming ordnance. Prepare to brace."

Anders: "Laser battery one online. Laser battery two online. Pulsing!"

Jackson: "Hostiles down. Ten . . . twelve thousand. Debris is obscuring—"

Anders: "Lasers firing. All batteries. Holy shit."

Jackson: "Debris cascade obscuring sensors. Unknown number of remaining hostiles."

Beanfield: "We got them?"

Anders: "We got them! We got them!"

Jackson: "Ordnance still incoming. Armor contact in ten seconds."

On his board, Gilly popped up the Armor display. Forty-two percent and rising. By his reckoning, that was enough to divert hundreds of simultaneous hits. That should be plenty; that was more than any human vessel had needed to repel at once in the history of the war. "How many *huks* incoming?"

"Two thousand," Jackson said. "Brace, brace."

There was a jolt. A noise rolled through the ship like thunder. He felt tremors through his legs. A succession of impacts, until everything was shaking. He lost his grip on the board and fell to the floor. His drill clattered to the ground and spun toward the wall.

"Breach," Jackson said. "We have depressure."

6

[Beanfield]

THE DARK

Something tugged at her. There was hair in her mouth. When she pulled it free, it went right back in. There was a breeze. A wind had sprung up, making things difficult. There was always something.

"We're hit," Jackson said in her ear. "Major damage across multiple decks, concentrated in decks A through C, aft. Weapons, Intel, Life, call in."

She opened her mouth to respond. Then she noticed a hole in the wall that hadn't been there before.

"I'm fine," Gilly said. "No damage in Eng-13."

"All good," Anders said. "Weapons station clear."

The hole was as big as her head. Its edges curled inward, reaching toward her like a metal flower. Its middle was dark and unknowable. She turned the other way. On the opposite wall, near the floor, a second hole. The edges of this one were smooth. She leaned forward in her harness until she could see into it and found herself staring through thirty feet of insulated armor and then a ladder shaft and then a corridor and her stomach lurched at the perspective and she turned away.

"Life," Jackson said. "Call in."

She looked at the first hole again. Her hair flapped into her face. Because that was where the air was going. Toward this hole. It slid past her ears into the dark flower and the heart of the flower wasn't shadow, she realized. It was space. What she had at first taken for glints of reflected light, those were stars.

She stared. Something inside her turned. As a kid, she had often visited her grandparents' farm outside Des Moines, and there she had lain on a short grassy hill and fell in love with the night sky. Years later, she had kissed a boy on a beach with his face ringed by stars. At Camp Zero, the sky was a relentless slab of cloud, but occasionally it cleared, allowing her to look up and see them waiting for her, her stars; they had been waiting her whole life and she only had to find a way to reach them. But now that she saw them unfiltered, she felt revolted. They weren't beautiful. They were the lights of anglerfish, deep-sea monstrosities with glowing lures, calling the small and stupid toward jaws and needle teeth. There was only death out here, only void and fire, and the true beauty in the universe was what she had left behind. She had grown up in a warm, safe bubble of air and failed to realize how miraculous it was. The ship had protected her for a while, but now it had a hole, and was leaking.

Her ears popped. She opened her mouth but her voice was gone. Sound was tinny, as if transmitted from far away, on bad equipment. The ship was groaning. She couldn't hear this, but she knew it was true. The air was leaving and the ship was groaning. *I'm passing out,* she thought. It was a bad thought but not an urgent one. She reached for her straps but her hands were tinny and far away, too. She couldn't remember what she was supposed to do. It was something. She had run drills. She had run disaster simulations for every possible scenario, even though, it was understood, especially by Life candidates, the chances of anything going wrong were effectively zero. There was, perhaps, a certain smugness you unavoidably developed in Life, after learning that a lot of the ship's safety features existed primarily for psychological reassurance. The jettison pods, for instance. They could shoot you all the way home, if you ever needed to abandon ship, but there were no conceivable circumstances in which anyone would be better off outside the ship, and the real reason the jetpods existed was to make the crew feel better. This was the kind of thing that encouraged Life to think of Weapons and Intel as deluded schmucks. She should have taken the drills more seriously. There were so many safety protocols. There was something she should be doing, right now, to save her life.

"Life," Jackson said, from far away. "Respond."

What had she said in her last feed post? She couldn't remember. Nothing too trivial, she hoped. Service would fake up something appropriate, of course, splicing together pieces of her clips and outtakes. She wished she had replied to her sister.

She felt an explosive impact across her back. Translucent sheeting slapped across her face. Air filled her lungs, bright and rich. Fabric slid along her limbs, inflating. Her survival core had deployed. Every day for two years she had worn that thing for the sole purpose of making the crew believe it meant something. And look at this.

"Life, come back."

She found her voice. "I'm here."

"What's happening?"

"I'm okay," she said, but then something moved in the hole.

She stared. The wind had eased, she sensed. It was hard to tell from inside the suit. But yes. Less wind, but more something crawling toward her from the hole.

"Life?"

Was she prepared to die? She had thought so. It was a job prerequisite, after all. Before she left, there was much talk of sacrifice. She had stood before cameras and spoken that word, often, and in great seriousness, with a slight frown, to let her viewers know it was for real. She had been asked straight-out by three different Service psychs whether she was prepared for the possibility that she might not make it home, and she had answered yes. She had made a will. But there was only twenty feet of hull between her and an ocean of anglerfish and had she known that? That she was one small hole away from an actual universe of death? That when the air left, the ship groaned? Nope. Nope. Nope.

"There's a salamander," she said. "My station is breached and a salamander's coming in."

Gilly: *"What?"*

Jackson: "Repeat that, Life." But she couldn't. She was transfixed by little glinting limbs in the hole. It wasn't big enough for a salamander to fit through. It must be pushing, squeezing, frustrated. "Life," Jackson said. "There are no hostiles anywhere near physical contact range. Restate your status."

A crab crawled from the hole. Its pincers moved over the torn metal. Strand by strand, it began to unweave the metal flower's petals.

"It's a crab," she said. "It's repairing the breach."

"There's no salamander?"

"It's . . ." she said. "There's no salamander. I was confused for a second. My survival core has deployed."

"You sure you're fine?"

"I'm fine," she said.

"Thank you, Life. Can you give me a ship overview?"

The crab had dissolved the metal flower and begun rapidly spinning up dull yellow threads. She looked behind her. In the other hole, another crab moved. As she watched, a third crawled out of the hole to join it.

"Life?"

She ran her board. "Damage everywhere, across all Life systems. But it's contained. Pressure is stable. Thermals are stable."

Gilly said, "Did we get them all?"

Jackson: "Awaiting confirmation. Lot of debris out there. We're sifting. Hold tight."

Anders: "We got them. I saw it."

Jackson: "Confirmed. All hostiles are down. Battlefield is clear. Commencing scouring. Good work, everyone."

"Fucking hell," Gilly said shakily. "Fucking hell."

The crabs were disappearing into the holes, filling them from the inside. Her station looked almost the same as before. The only difference now were two round areas where the metal was the dull yellow of bruised skin.

"Sixteen thousand two hundred eleven kills," Jackson said. "I believe we just set a record."

"Request to meet for debrief," said Anders, "and talk through what the fuck just happened."

"Granted," said Jackson.

They went through the engagement second by second, analyzing what they could have done better. This was slightly ridiculous, because one of the main things they could have done better was to not lock Anders in his cabin. Talia didn't say that. She was having trouble concentrating. She felt rattled. Her mind kept returning to the hole in station and what she'd seen beyond.

"We've lost Materials Fabrication," Gilly said, pulling up a schematic. Gilly didn't appear rattled at all. If anything, he was energized. She was jealous of his ability to see this as a fascinating development. He pointed. "Here."

"You mean there's no function?" Jackson said.

"I mean it's gone. It detached from the ship."

There was a short silence.

"Well, shit," Jackson said.

"The ship can rebuild itself," Gilly said. "But this will test it. Mat Fab was seventy thousand tons. We've also lost structures all across here"—he gestured—"and here. Plus there's a lot of incidental damage. At least five hundred *huk*s penetrated Armor and passed straight through."

Just when she had learned to love the ship. She had thought they understood each other. There had been a trust. Then her whale had floundered. She was gripping the table as if bracing for the floor to drop away. It wasn't the ship's fault, but she felt a little betrayed, to be honest.

Anders said, "So we have holes?"

"Had. All breaches are now repaired."

"I want you to inspect Life station," Jackson said. "Make sure it's up to code."

Gilly nodded, then eyed Talia. "What was it like?"

"What?" she said.

"The breach. Your core deployed. Must have been scary."

"Oh," she said. "I'm over it." She gave them a smile, her resolute one, and they nodded, and Jackson began to talk about subsystem damage. Talia was slightly tempted to raise her hand and say, *Excuse me, you know what? I'm actually not over it. I thought maybe someone would notice. But apparently I have to come right out and say it. Do you mind if we talk for a minute about how terrified I am?* But she could imagine how that would go. She could roleplay it:

Anders: I don't follow, since I, personally, seek out near-death experiences and find them to be awesome.

Jackson: This is a debrief, Life. Your feelings aren't relevant except insofar as they imply personal weakness. There's a time and place to discuss such things, and it's when we get back home, with someone else.

Gilly: [stares mutely].

What she needed was herself. She wanted Feed Talia to sit her down and hold her hand and tell her it was okay. *Go ahead. What you feel is important.* She should go to her cabin and watch some old clips. She could stare at the screen and let Feed Talia comfort her, since Feed Talia was the closest thing to a real person around here.

"What about the damaged core bank?" Jackson said. "Is that repaired?"

Gilly shook his head. "That's the one part of itself the ship can't fix. But it's not a significant loss. There are thousands of cores. No single one in particular matters much."

"One in particular took down Weapons and Armor."

"Yes," Gilly said, "but only because of a really unusual set of circumstances. The concussive wave from the hive bomb caused corruption in a core and also, separately, in the ship's ability to detect that kind of fault. So it couldn't tell what was wrong."

"So the enemy has a Providence killer," Jackson said.

"No, I don't think so. I doubt they had much of an idea what the blast would do. I think they got lucky."

"Justify that," Jackson said.

"Well, for starters," Gilly said, "there are thousands of core banks that *weren't* affected. So if it was a plan, it's not a reliable one. But more important, this is what salamanders do. They try something, and most of the time, it doesn't work. If it does, they all start doing it. Experiment, learn, adapt. That's their entire strategy."

"So we should expect more bombs?"

He scratched his face. "Yes. Some of them escaped, and we didn't scour the battlefield. But the ship learns, too. If we have another engagement before it's developed a counter, I'll be shocked."

"I don't want to be shocked. I want to be sure. Will we be prepared for the next bomb? Or whatever they try after that?"

"Uh," Gilly said. "I mean, you're asking me to hypothesize about an unknown tactic, which I can't do."

"What if we assumed manual control?"

Gilly blinked. "Of what?"

She gestured shortly. "The ship."

"The *ship*?" He looked at Talia like he wanted her to jump in. But Talia wasn't following the conversation closely enough for that. She was not available for dialogue guidance right now. "You're asking what I think about *manually controlling the ship*?"

"Yes."

"I think it's insane."

"Why?"

"Which part are you even talking about? Piloting?"

Jackson shrugged. "Say next engagement, we take direct control over Weapons, so that if a bomb strike neutralizes the AI again—"

"Can I stop you there?"

"—we retain the ability to fire on the enemy."

"That's ridiculous."

Anders said, "Can't be more ridiculous than sitting at station with no systems and a dead AI."

"This . . ." he said. "This is not a manual ship. This is an AI ship."

"I understand your stance," Jackson said. "Now talk me through why."

Gilly took a breath. "First of all, the ship is orders of magnitude faster than us at battlefield analysis. So even if we assume that we could arrive at the same decisions—which is absolutely not the case, by the way—we'd do it slower. Much slower."

"Why do we want to arrive at the same decisions?"

Gilly struggled for a response. "Because . . ."

"I'm just talking it through," Jackson said.

"Because before Providences, people used to die a lot," Gilly said. "Now they don't. Are we really going to question the effectiveness of AI decisions? That's . . . Everything we do is founded on that."

"What's second of all?"

"Second of all, some of the systems you're talking about, like Weapons Targeting, are flat-out beyond human capability. We're aiming at small, fast-moving targets thousands of miles away. Our hit rate would be near zero."

Anders said, "What's the computer's hit rate?"

"You should fucking know that," Gilly said. "It's a hundred percent."

Anders shook his head. "Wrong."

"I'm rounding. It's effectively a hundred."

"It's less than a hundred."

"I'm getting aggravated," Gilly said, "because it feels like you're saying that since it's not perfect, it might as well be near zero."

"When the AI goes down, the hit rate *is* zero," Anders said. "Not near zero. Actual zero."

Gilly took a breath. "Third of all, I don't even want to imagine what happens if the ship discovers that we've rendered its weapons systems inoperable. It's not going to sit there and rely on us to pea-shoot hostiles. It'll try to route around the problem in ways we can't predict."

"Hmm," Jackson said.

"Fourth of all, some systems can't be run manually. At all."

"For fuck's sake," Jackson said. "If it's impossible, open with that."

"Which systems?" Anders said.

"Anything that requires coordination between multiple subsystems. The laser matrix. The mass projectors. The plasma planet-killer. The engines you can only enable or disable, not maneuver."

"What about the pulse?"

He hesitated.

"That sounds like yes," Anders said.

"We could probably pulse," Gilly admitted. "But I'd have to detach it from the ship's control. Which would be idiotic, for the reasons I mentioned."

Jackson said, "Can you set it up so that if we lose the AI, we have the option of asserting manual control?"

He screwed up his face. "Not easily."

"But you could?"

"I can look into it."

"Look into it," Jackson said.

"I don't mind going down fighting," Anders said. "But I don't want to be sitting in the dark with no weapons while they're swarming the ship."

"That won't happen," Gilly said. "It was one in a million, and the ship already learned from it. I'm not just saying this because I'm Surplex. This is the way it works."

Jackson glanced at Talia. This was about as long as Talia could detach from a conversation before it became weird, she presumed. She replayed the last three sentences in her head and reached for a sunny platitude.

But something about Anders plucked at her attention. She had thought he was doing his usual Anders thing—being kind of a dick while seeking out the most potentially dangerous outcome for everyone— but his arms were folded tight, his legs crossed, and he was leaning back in his seat. All of this was such a classic fear reaction that it momentarily struck her dumb. Why was Anders scared?

"I hope that's true," Jackson said. "But I want a plan B if the shit hits the fan again."

The confinement? He had exhibited an extreme reaction to it in the first place. Now that he was out, he was behaving like an abused child. This implied that he didn't want to be sent back. He was terrified of being sent back.

Oh, God, she thought suddenly. *Anders is claustrophobic.*

It was preposterous. That was why she'd never figured it out. It was the last place in the universe she'd expect to find a claustrophobe. He had known what it would be like, yes? He had realized the corridors would be small? But it was true. She knew immediately that she was right.

You are Life Officer on a warship two years from home and one of your crew is claustrophobic. Go.

"That's reasonable," Gilly said. "Let me think on it."

"Good enough for now," Jackson said, and Gilly nodded.

She stared at Anders. *Why,* she thought. *Why.*

She couldn't talk to the ship anymore. It felt like they were having a fight. The silence between them became a palpable thing and it was so ridiculous, because the ship was an inanimate object, or, at best, a creature with which she could never communicate. But still, she felt abandoned. She was shaken and post-trauma with no one to talk to and at a complete loss as to what to do about Anders. At the end of her shift, she wound up in Rec-1, trying to print pancakes. But when they came out, she couldn't eat them, because they were too beautiful.

"You dealing?" said Jackson, materializing out of nowhere.

"Hmm, with what?" she said, wiping her nose. She adjusted the pancakes. Jackson. She did not need Jackson right now.

There was a short silence. "Let's talk."

She sensed reluctance and so could deduce what kind of talk this would be: It would be Jackson pretending she wanted to hear Talia's private thoughts and fears while judging her mercilessly for every one of them. "No, I'm good. Thank you." She turned and gave a smile, a bright one that said, *Aren't you sweet* and *This is the end of the conversation.*

Jackson didn't move. "I know what it's like to be close."

For a moment, Talia honestly didn't know what she meant. Close to what? But: death, of course. Jackson had been close to the cold and the dark. And she was regarding Talia with something that looked like genuine understanding, and Talia closed her eyes to not see it but it was too late. She turned away. A noise popped out of her that was part hiccup and part sob. "Oh, God," she said, mortified.

"Come," Jackson said.

"I'm fine," she protested, but she let Jackson lead her away from her pancakes. They went to Jackson's cabin, also a surprise; Talia had never been there and never expected to. Beside the bed was a picture of Jackson's husband in a collared shirt, smiling in dappled sunshine, a little cottage behind him.

"His collar is askew," Jackson said. "I want to reach in there and fix it."

Talia nodded. She had seen this picture in the background of Jackson's clips and always suspected it was something of a prop.

"Sit," said Jackson, gesturing at the bed and pulling out a metal chair for herself. "Talk."

She sat. She wanted to. But Jackson's back was ramrod straight and her perfect posture was a reminder that Jackson would never put herself in Talia's position, not in a million years. There were no circumstances in which Jolene Jackson would sit on a bed and blub about her feelings. "Honestly, I'm just having a moment. I'm okay."

Jackson eyed her. "So it's like that." She rose, moved to a drawer, and came back with a metal cup and a dark vial. She sat and began to pour it out. "I only have one cup, so we share."

Talia accepted the cup. The liquid smelled sharp and rich. "Are you supposed to have this?"

Jackson said nothing.

"Scandalous," Talia said. She tipped up the cup and fluid slid down her throat and lit her insides on fire. "Oh my God."

Jackson took the cup, poured a measure for herself, and threw it back.

"Well," Talia said. "Now I know what you do with your spare time."

"Oh, no. This is just for emergencies." Jackson poured another cup and offered it to Talia. "What I do in my downtime is write."

She rolled the cup between her hands. Her throat burned. "Write what?"

"Letters," Jackson said. "To my husband. Ask me how many."

"How many?"

"Seven hundred and twelve. One for each day we've been out here."

She blinked. "Jackson, that's a stupid amount of letters."

"Yup," said Jackson.

"Why don't you send him clips?"

Jackson sat back. "I don't know. In a clip, I feel watched. Like I need to perform. I doubt you'd understand."

"No, I get that."

"I wouldn't have guessed," said Jackson. "You're very natural." There was a pause, during which Talia resisted the urge to confess that her whole life was a performance, Jolene, all of it. There was no time when she didn't feel watched. "I don't send them."

"Pardon?" Talia said.

"The letters. They're just for me."

"You've written seven hundred letters to your husband but not sent them?"

Jackson nodded.

She laughed before she could stop herself. *Why?*

Jackson shrugged. "I never seem able to say it right." The corners of her mouth tugged.

Talia covered her mouth. "That's terrible."

"Is it?"

"This conversation never happened," Talia said, "because if I reported that to Operations, it would set off so many red flags, you have no idea."

"Deal," said Jackson, and they drank, one after the other. When the cup was refilled, she said, "Why did you come out here?"

"What?"

"What brought you to this ass-end of nowhere," Jackson said. "And don't give me the prepared answer."

She stared. There was a hot tingle at the back of her brain. "I don't know." Suddenly she felt sad. "I think I made a mistake."

"Drink," said Jackson.

She obeyed. "I thought it was important. I thought we'd be safe. I thought people would respect me."

"I respect you."

"No, you don't."

"Well, you're growing on me."

Talia snickered. "I always thought you hated your husband," she confessed. "I thought you wanted to get away from him."

Jackson looked shocked. "No, no. He's the best thing that ever happened to me."

"I'm sorry."

"I'm sorry for thinking you were an empty-headed waste of space."

Talia gasped. "I knew it. You're not as good at hiding your feelings as you think, you shitty simulacrum of a human being."

"Drink," said Jackson.

She obeyed. The liquid burned less, going down easier.

"I hate Service," Jackson said. "I hate all of it. And I hate the people who aren't in Service, too. I don't know which I hate more: Service or civilians."

"In month seven," Talia said, "I was so lonely, I started to fantasize about Anders."

"Well, now," Jackson said. "That's understandable."

"He's so pretty," Talia said. "But such an asshole."

"He's a toddler. I can't watch him eat."

She leaned forward. "*Me too.* That's the *worst part.*" She exhaled. Now that someone was listening, she couldn't stop talking. "I feel like I'm suffocating out here. As if I died the day we left but I didn't notice and I can't figure out why I'm not breathing."

"We were fools, letting them ship us out."

"We were," she said. "We were so dumb."

"I even knew before I left," Jackson said. "But I did it anyway."

"I just wanted to be good at something," Talia said.

Jackson patted her own leg like she wanted to make a point. "You shouldn't have tried to do this alone. We're a team."

"Yes." She knew that now. "You're right."

"I miss my husband," Jackson said, and, shockingly, began to cry. For a second, the sheer implausibility of the moment left Talia frozen. Then she moved to Jackson and put her arms around her.

"It's okay," Talia said. "We'll be okay."

They drank and talked more and when Talia couldn't stand straight, Jackson said she could sleep in her bed. This was such an exciting idea that Talia accepted, even though she probably could have made it to her own cabin. She snuggled into Jackson's sheets and inhaled her smell and it felt like she had crawled all the way into Jackson's life. She fell asleep happy.

At some point she became aware of Jackson making an extraction, zipping up her flight jacket. She looked yellow in the glowlights. Talia raised her head.

"Stay, if you want," said Jackson.

"Mmm." She did want to stay. She wanted to talk some more. There was so much to discuss now that she'd found a door into Jackson's brain. "Where are you going?"

Jackson nodded in the general direction of the rest of the ship.

Ah, Talia thought. *I see.*

Jackson left. Talia rolled over and hugged the pillow and closed her eyes. But she couldn't forget where she was, and opened them again. She wondered whether Jackson had run away or if she genuinely had something to do. She could actually check that, if she wanted.

Hey, Jolene, I really enjoyed our talk last night.

Yes, me too, Beanfield.

I thought maybe you and me could hang out, watch a movie. Or just talk. Do you have any more to drink? I feel like we have a lot more to explore.

Actually, I have a busy roster today, Beanfield. I'm on a tight schedule.

But Jolene, you have all that time to write letters. And I can see your schedule. I can track your movements. I can see where you are every moment.

She stayed in the cabin for five hours. At a certain point she realized she was being obnoxious; she was deliberately testing Jackson, and both of them would know it. But she stayed anyway until she finally saw Jackson heading back on ping. When the door slid back, it became clear that Jackson had been monitoring Talia's ping as well, because she was wearing her captain face, the one that betrayed nothing.

"Hi," Talia said.

Jackson pressed the tactile panel to close the door. There was a silence. "It's time for you to go."

So blunt. So Jackson. "Okay."

Jackson had clearly expected a fight. But it had been five hours, which was plenty of time for Talia to run roleplays in her head and prepare responses. "You're a good soldier," Jackson said.

"What?" she said, because this one she hadn't anticipated.

"You're a good soldier."

"Oh," she said. "Thank you." But this annoyed her. Talia was a bad soldier. They both knew that. Was that not the conclusion they'd reached? That they were failing, but that was okay? Wasn't that the comfort Jackson was offering? Now she was turning it into a lie.

"We still have roles," Jackson said. "I don't want to become dysfunctional."

"Why would we become dysfunctional?" she said breezily, and Jackson looked disappointed, and that was that. But almost as soon as Talia had left, she answered her own question. It had always felt a little overdone to Talia how Jackson walked around like she couldn't afford to crack a smile in case that was the moment the salamanders attacked, but she'd swallowed that because Jackson was captain, so, sure, why not go ahead and play the part? Clearly she was a piece of stunt casting designed to boost public sentiment and couldn't even coordinate her resource builders in *Gamma Fleet*, but fine, whatever. Now, though, she knew Jackson agreed with her. She shouldn't be here. None of them should.

She was alone again. "Somebody get me off this ship," she muttered. It became a thing she repeated to keep herself sane. She didn't mean it, of course. There was no *off the ship*. It was just a mantra. *Please, somebody,* she thought. *Get me off this ship.*

7

[Gilly]

THE CASUALTY

It took two days for the ship to rebuild Materials Fabrication as if it had never been damaged. It had been; it had been shredded by *huk*s and spun off into space in bite-size pieces. Gilly double-checked that, because when he ran his board and saw it reporting as online and fully functional, he wondered if the ship was failing to diagnose faults again. He climbed to B Deck and the blast doors stood open and the corridor beyond was almost entirely the burnished yellow of new metal. He explored for a few minutes and developed a strange feeling, a kind of nervousness, because everything was the same but also not. He retreated to his cabin to watch again how it had been destroyed.

How the *huk*s had affected the ship was interesting: In many cases, they'd passed through a room where everything was nailed down and left barely any trace but a couple of holes in the walls. Other times, the *huk*s had dragged every loose object into the air, shredded them, and sprayed the pieces like confetti. And if the path of a *huk* came close enough to a long section of metal, a wall or pipe or floor or whatever, it would unpeel it like a banana and trail a deadly cloudburst of globular shrapnel. This had happened in Materials Fabrication, which had been struck often and badly.

He pulled footage of the rebuild and watched somewhere in the order of ten thousand crabs crawling around, knitting hull. The ship hadn't had ten thousand crabs earlier, Gilly was sure. It must have manufactured more. And then the crabs had manufactured more ship.

He sat back. It was what was supposed to happen, but the scale and speed of it were amazing. By his reckoning, the ship had rebuilt Mat Fab faster than it had been constructed the first time.

His mind turned to the core bank he'd drilled into. Those weren't repairable, but as long as the ship was doing surprising things, he decided to check in on it. When he brought up the system, core bank 996 was green and online.

He blinked. He rewound the damage assessment to make sure he was looking at the right one. He was. The ship was reporting 100% functionality across all core banks.

This he had to see. He closed the board and headed to E Deck. Possibly the damage had caused the ship to stop recognizing it as a core bank, and therefore to stop knowing it shouldn't attempt repairs. But even so, it should have been unsuccessful, because core bank repair was beyond the ship's capability. It was concerning either way, because an AI rewriting its own core was a little like a human neurosurgeon opening up his own skull. Any errors could compound, affecting the ship's ability to recognize that they were errors.

He walked right past the door to Eng-13, lost in thought. When he backtracked, he couldn't find it. He stopped and checked his location on ping. He was where he'd thought. He took eight steps and stopped and touched the wall. On his film, Eng-13 was mapped right in front of him.

He peeled off his film. He looked both ways. He knew this corridor. He had been here during the engagement. There had been a door. Now it was gone.

———

"You're telling me it moved the room?" Jackson said. They had gathered in Rec-2 at Gilly's request. From Jackson's demeanor, she had been asleep.

"I think the room is still there," he said. "We just can't get to it."

"How do you know?" Beanfield said.

"Because it's on ping."

"But that data comes from the ship. It could be lying."

"Pardon me?" he said.

"Or outdated."

"The ship doesn't *lie*." There was so much insanity built into the assumptions of that comment, he didn't know where to start. "It has only the most basic concept of our existence. It can't imagine what we're thinking, let alone know how to fool us."

"You're sure you went to the right deck," Anders said.

"Yes."

"I'm not saying you're crazy. But you did spend months trying to fix imaginary valve leaks."

Jackson was silent a moment. "Check it."

"It's not there," Gilly said as Anders left. "I even took off my film."

"Why?" Beanfield said.

"Because I thought it might be a puzzle."

"Oh," she said. "No, this one's not us."

"Are the other Engineering areas accessible?" Jackson asked. "Eng-12, Eng-14?"

"Yes."

"So Eng-13 is still there, missing a door."

"Right."

"Or the ship deconstructed the room and is lying about it."

"The ship doesn't lie," Gilly said. "It has no reason to."

"It also doesn't hide doors, was my understanding until five minutes ago."

"Okay," he conceded.

"So the question is why."

"We can't know that."

"Explain that deeply unsatisfying answer," Jackson said.

"Because it doesn't think like we do. When we try to put ourselves in its shoes, we can't help anthropomorphizing and imagining human motivations. Which is wrong."

"Wrong?"

"Inaccurate. Misleading."

"Well," Jackson said, "I want to know where my door went."

"Isn't it obvious?" Beanfield said.

They looked at her. Gilly said, "Not to me."

"I get what you're saying about anthropomorphizing," Beanfield said. "But you attacked it. Isn't it natural for it to protect itself?"

"What?"

"You drilled into its brain. When you were taking the core offline."

He stared at her.

"I mean," she said, "isn't this what the ship does? Learn from experience, so it's better at defending itself the next time?"

He felt genuinely at a loss for words.

"Interesting," Jackson said.

"I was forcing recognition of a faulty core bank. I was *helping*."

"Sure," Beanfield said, "but you can imagine the ship might not see it that way, right?"

He could not imagine it. Or maybe he didn't want to. The idea felt grossly offensive in some way he couldn't specify. He had been fixing a machine part.

"I'm not saying it's angry or anything," Beanfield said. "Just that, logically, it might want to keep you out of there so it doesn't get drilled again."

He looked at Jackson, who said nothing.

"Hey," Anders said on comms. "Guess what? Gilly's right. There's no door."

"Thank you," Gilly said.

There was a *rap rap rap*; Anders knocking on the wall. "Weird," Anders said.

The ship cut engines and coasted for two more days. They had never done this before and everyone projected their own assumptions onto it. "We're retreating," Beanfield said. "We're getting ready to skip out of VZ." She was hanging around while Gilly tried to burn through the wall with a plasma cutter to see whether Eng-13 was still there. So far, he had produced heat and light but no answers.

He sat back on his heels and studied the wall. "I don't know about that."

"No? We encountered a new weapon, took major damage, and developed intel about salamander information transmission. You don't think it'll want to relay that back to Service?"

Gilly didn't say anything.

"Sure, okay," Beanfield said. "We can't guess what an AI is thinking. But even so."

He poked at the wall with a gloved finger.

"Anything?"

"This is dense. Similar to the exterior hull. I can't pierce it with these tools."

"Is there something else you could use?"

"In the small-arms lockers, maybe."

"Hmm," Beanfield said. "Let's not go shooting the ship, is my thinking."

"Agreed," he said.

"I mean, it's not like we absolutely have to get in there."

He nodded. It was true. Frustrating, but true. He began to pack away his tools. "Hey, have you seen my drill?"

"I don't keep track of your tools, Gilly. What, is it your only one?"

"No. But I like to know where everything is."

"I have noticed that about you." She unpeeled herself from the wall. "Still think it's unaware of our existence?"

"Hmm?"

"The ship," she said. "You said it doesn't know we're here. But then we hurt it. So maybe we got its attention. Maybe we made it mad."

He stopped. "You're talking about software. Yes, very intelligent software, but it doesn't think like us. It doesn't, you know, feel things."

"Not like we do, of course. But in its own way."

"Look," he said, "I can't tell you what's going on in the mind of a computer. But I'm really confident that it's not what you're thinking."

She considered. "You don't think the ship can feel hurt?"

"Uh," he said.

"Or scared?"

He chose his words carefully. "I think it would be a mistake to consider the ship as anything other than a collection of logical processes."

"Oh, Gilly," Beanfield said. "You say that about everything."

"No, I don't," he said. "I don't view everything as a collection of logical processes."

She smiled and shook her head. "Forget it. I'm starving. Let's head back."

"There *is* logic to everything," he said. "You look deep enough, there's always a rational process. You just need to figure out what it is."

"There it is," Beanfield said.

"I don't know how you can believe otherwise. I mean, don't you want to know there's an explanation for everything?"

"I can't think of anything worse," Beanfield said. She looked back down the corridor toward where Eng-13 had been. "I hope you find your answers, Gilly."

There was something in her face that disturbed him, so he stopped. "You can trust the ship. No matter what's going on, it will always want to protect us, because we're its DNA. That can't change."

She smiled brightly, the way she did in clips. "Thank you for saying so, Gilly."

"I promise you," he said.

The next day Beanfield called him over to say she could feel the ship burning. "What?" he said.

"Little tremors." They were outside Rec-4, which was configured as a gym. Her hair was plastered to her forehead, her white shirt sweat-soaked down the middle, a towel slung over one shoulder. "Are we accelerating?"

"I don't think so." He checked his film. "No."

"You can't feel anything?"

He knew she wanted him to lift his film, so he did, and listened. It was sometimes possible to feel whether the ship was burning, especially on aft decks.

"Maybe it's not accelerating *yet*," she said. "It feels like it's about to."

He wasn't sure how anyone would sense that. "I guess I could pull an exterior view and look for any unusual activity."

"I already did that."

"Oh," he said.

"It doesn't matter." She threw the towel over her face and began to rub with vigor. He remembered how, during the last engagement, Beanfield's station had been breached. They had never really talked about that, but he wondered how she was dealing with it. It occurred to him that when he was worked up about something, he could talk to Beanfield, but Beanfield had no one.

"I'll keep an eye on it," he said.

And, funnily enough, when he woke the next day, he could feel something. He ran his film and confirmed it. They were accelerating. But they weren't leaving VZ. They were going deeper in.

Three more days passed. They grew tense and excited. Anders didn't sleep, as far as Gilly could tell. He developed bloodshot eyes and a braying, high-pitched laugh. "Jesus, Anders," said Beanfield. "Your breath." He wanted to play ninja stars but hid in such obvious positions that Gilly felt bad throwing shurikens at him. On the fifth day, Gilly discovered him trying to herd crabs into a jetpod. He came around a corner and there was Anders, waving his arms, corralling crabs. Anders saw him and stopped and lowered his arms and the crabs began to disperse. Gilly kept walking because he didn't want to know what that was.

The ship opened fire. There was no klaxon. But they could feel the coil and release of power. They scrambled for station, thinking it was another emergency, another systems failure; now even the klaxon didn't work. Gilly was near Weapons at the time and Anders came storming up the corridor with his eyes full of crazy energy and shoved him aside. Gilly reached station and strapped in and Jackson's voice came through saying there was no enemy. The ship was launching drones and destroying them. It was practicing.

"Goddamn it," said Anders.

"Just a drill," Gilly said. "It's testing countermeasures to the bomb, like I said."

"Piece of *crap*."

"Cool it," Jackson said. There was silence. The ship ran through the same process over and over, launch and destroy, using different weapons.

"I want to *do* something," Anders said.

Of course, they were hoping the ship would develop a hard counter to the hive bomb so that everything could go back to how it had been, when they had destroyed salamanders with ease and minimal human input. But it was hard to deny that when things had gone wrong, it had been the most exciting part of the last two years. It was the kind of thing Gilly had had in mind when he got interested in making crew. That must go double for the soldiers, he thought, and double again for a guy like Anders. He could understand someone nursing a small wish for the ship to need them again.

"I think we're done here," Jackson said, after the thirtieth drone. "Nothing's happening."

He tried to avoid the issue of seizing manual control of the ship, but Jackson pinged him regularly for updates and there were only so many times he could stall. In the mess, where you weren't supposed to talk shop, or at least not too much of it, she sipped at a steel cup and asked whether he intended to have a report for her before the war was over, or afterward. He glanced at Beanfield, since the moratorium on shop talk was her policy, but she gave him nothing.

"It's a complicated area," he said.

"I didn't ask for an assessment on how complicated it is," Jackson said. "I asked you to tell me what we can do."

"Look, the answer is nothing. I know that's not what you want to hear, but it's the truth."

There was a momentary silence. "Gilly," said Beanfield, "there are times when you make it *incredibly* clear you didn't come through the military."

"What about a kill switch?" Jackson said.

He looked at her, surprised. "What?"

"Isn't there a mechanism to disable the AI in an emergency?"

He hesitated. The answer was yes. Furthermore, Jackson definitely knew that. It abruptly occurred to him that this was the endgame she'd had in mind for some time. She had never liked the idea of computers controlling everything and had seen her chance to change it. "There's something like that."

"Now we're talking," said Anders.

"But," he said, adjusting his position on what felt like an abruptly hard seat, "it should never, ever be used."

"Then why does it exist?" Jackson said.

"Everything would stop working. And I mean everything." Jackson didn't respond. "We're in VZ," he added. "There's no backup if something goes wrong."

"I appreciate your expertise with the ship," Jackson said. "And I understand you have a career interest in whether it succeeds. But here's what I see. We're a long way from home, the last time we engaged we got our butts handed to us, and the AI has started hiding rooms."

"One room."

Jackson smacked the table with her palm. The plates and cups jumped. There was a short silence.

"If we activate the kill switch," Jackson said, "we wouldn't have to rely on the AI to use systems like Weapons. They'd be available for manual operation. Correct?"

"Yes, but—"

"I know these systems weren't designed to be used that way. I know we wouldn't be as efficient as the AI."

"That's putting it mildly. Extremely, extremely mildly."

"So we understand each other," Jackson said. "This is a card we shouldn't play except as a last resort. Nevertheless, it's one I want to hold. So make it ready."

He took a breath. "Please promise me you won't use this unless we absolutely have to."

"I'll do you one better. I won't use it unless you say so."

He wasn't sure whether to believe that. It felt like something she might say now and retract later. But it did make him feel a little better.

"Yes?" Jackson said.

"All right."

She picked up her steel cup and took a sip. "Well then," she said. "Sounds like progress."

He'd almost given up when it happened. He was in the can. The klaxon sounded. The walls glowed orange. He bolted upright and took a step before realizing his pants were around his ankles. Before he reached the ladder, Anders was reporting in over comms. "Weapons checking in." He must have been camped outside.

Jackson: "Roger that. On my way to command, give me thirty seconds."

"Is it another drill?"

"You see those orange lights? That's how you know it's not a drill."

Gilly popped the hatch to D Deck. "Almost at station."

"Life, how far?"

"I'm here."

"Check in, please. Let's do this by the book."

"Life, checking in. All systems normal. We have good O_2, good pressure, good thermals."

"Thank you, Life."

Gilly strapped into his harness and brought up his board. "Intel, checking in. All systems online and functional."

"Copy that, Intel."

Anders: "What are we up against?"

"Give me a moment. I'm reaching station. Command . . . checking in. I'm seeing green-to-green. Sensors up. Armor up. Weapons up."

"Hostiles?"

"Stand by."

"How many?"

"Weapons, I will brief you when I have information you need, you understand? We have a six-pack of hives and they're expelling. Nine hundred total so far. Contact in forty seconds."

Gilly skimmed his fingers across his board. Not touching anything, just defining his area. He had the cores on permanent overlay so he'd know immediately if any of them flickered. Somewhere in that solid green rectangle was core bank 996, which he still didn't trust.

Beanfield: "These are regular hives?"

"Looks that way to me. Verify, Intel."

"Regular hives. No bombs."

"Batteries one through twenty-eight relocating to fore," Anders said. "That's a lot of fucking lasers. There's no way to put a few of those on manual?"

"Negative," Gilly said.

"If we lose cores again—"

"Everything's green, Anders."

"Let me know the second anything gets even a little funky," Jackson said.

"Roger that."

"You have the kill switch prepared?"

"It's ready."

"Because if we need it, I don't want to suddenly discover there's an 'Are you sure?' or a sixty-second timer or any of that bullshit."

"It's ready to go," he said. "But I want to stress again, using it will kill us all."

"Just want it in the back pocket, Intel," Jackson said. She counted down to contact: twenty seconds, ten. On Gilly's board, the pulse system juddered.

Anders: "Firing. Firing."

Jackson: "Seeing that."

"No hits. Hostiles turned. They anticipated the pulse. Now again. Coming back at us. Count me down, Weapons."

"Pulse ready in ten seconds."

Gilly: "What's that I'm seeing at range?"

Jackson: "It's . . ."

"Looks like a hive bomb."

"It's . . . yes. Seventh hive, not expelling, no soldiers. Initial composition profile resembles the bomb. Contact in ninety seconds. Should be safe to pulse until then. Intel, verify, please."

"Already on it."

"Total hostile numbers at twenty-two thousand."

Beanfield: "Twenty-two thousand?"

"Pulsing," said Anders.

Twenty-two thousand, Gilly thought. That would make it the largest engagement of the war.

"Hostiles down. Nineteen thousand remain."

"Whoa," Gilly said. "Nineteen?"

"Nineteen, affirmative."

"How can there be nineteen? Were they all inside pulse range?" He left the hive composition analysis to check the attack pattern himself. An arc of salamanders sprung up before him, closing toward a small blue dot. He manipulated the field, zooming in.

"Yes."

"This formation is new. They're in layers."

Anders: "Pulsing in ten."

"They're shielding each other."

"From the pulse?" Jackson said.

"Yes. The inner ring takes the brunt of the force. The ones behind are protected."

"Pulsing," Anders said.

"What does it mean?"

"It means they're going to get closer. A lot closer."

Jackson: "Hostiles down. Minor debris cascade. Seventeen thousand remain."

"Only two thousand casualties that time? *Two*?" The destructive power of the pulse increased as the enemy grew closer. Additionally, it was impacting already damaged units. They should have been dying in greater numbers.

"We dialed it down," Anders said. "Pulsed at only seventy percent."

"Why?"

"Dunno. Ask the ship."

He opened his mouth to make a hotheaded reply. Jackson said, "Ship is worried about the bomb."

That was probably true. The hive bomb was still outside their theoretical pulse range, but a lot about it was unknown. He could understand if the ship wasn't taking chances. "They're going to reach *huk* range."

"In thirty seconds, yes."

"Pulsing in ten," Anders said. "But we're still dialing down. Fifty percent now, and dropping."

"Shit," Gilly said.

"I'm just going to say it," Anders said. "Manual control?"

"No." He stared at the shrinking ring of salamanders.

"Pulse is cold," Anders said. "Ship has disabled it. What's it doing, Gilly?"

He didn't answer. They couldn't know what the ship was doing; that was the point.

Jackson: "We have laser contact in five, yes, Weapons?"

"Yes. Three. Two. One. Firing. All batteries firing."

On Gilly's board, lines appeared in the salamander rings. Lasers, punching through their ranks. The ship didn't normally resort to lasers, since they weren't very effective when the enemy was spread out. But of course now they weren't. They were in layers.

Jackson: "Mass casualties. Rising fast. Debris cascade. Scan obscured."

Beanfield: "Power loss. Noncritical. We're sucking juice from everywhere."

Anders: "All batteries still firing."

The salamander rings broke, fuzzed.

Jackson: "What are you seeing, Intel?"

"What?"

"The cores. Everything look normal to you?"

"Uh . . . everything's green, yes."

Anders: "Batteries eighteen through twenty-nine topping out."

Jackson: "Intel, I want to be absolutely clear on this, you're seeing no systems change? Nothing at all?"

"Nothing at all."

Beanfield: "Power levels returning to normal across decks."

Anders: "Retiring batteries eighteen through twenty-nine."

"Thank you," Jackson said. "One or two thousand surviving hostiles, but they're dropping fast."

"Banks nine through eighteen retiring. Banks one through eight. All batteries have ceased firing."

"Reading zero hostiles. But with this much debris, it'll take a minute to verify. In the meantime, we're coming up on contact range with the hives."

"Ship knew what it was doing," Gilly said. "Had a plan all along." He felt embarrassed. And worse than that: exposed. He had been trumpeting the ship's infallibility since he boarded. But apparently he didn't believe in it as deeply as he'd thought. "I want to apologize for my behavior."

"No need," Jackson said. "Hard starboard burn. We're taking a wide berth of the bomb."

"Good," Beanfield said.

"Firing," Anders said. "Batteries one through four."

"First hive is down. Second hive. Third. It's . . . all six initial hives destroyed."

"Laser batteries returning to stow."

"That's it?" Beanfield said.

"Looks like it," Jackson said. "We're moving on. Ignoring the bomb."

"What happened to scouring? Don't we need to scour, Gilly?"

"It might be too dangerous," he said. "Could be the ship's decided it's not worth the risk to scour." He felt stupid and outclassed. He had no business trying to second-guess the AI. He should have known better than to try.

"All right, then. Engagement closed," Jackson said. "If my math is right, we are now on track to pass *Fire of Montana*'s record."

"Oh my God, yes," Beanfield said. "At this rate, we'll overtake their total accumulated kills by end of tour. Is that right, Intel?"

"Sure," he said. "Sounds right."

In debrief, Jackson stepped through the engagement, but there wasn't a whole lot to say. They had encountered enemies; the ship had destroyed them; they'd done this dance before. Gilly had checked and double-checked, but there had been no unusual system activity during the engagement.

"So we're back to standard ops," Jackson said. "But we're also deeper in enemy space than anyone's ever been, so let's stay sharp."

"I wonder why we're not scouring," Beanfield said. "It almost feels like the ship's in a hurry. Like it's trying to get somewhere." She looked at him, but he didn't know what she was suggesting. "Like maybe the salamander homeworld."

"Salamanders don't have a homeworld," Gilly said shortly. "They're fully adapted for vacuum."

"Some people say there's a home."

"Those people are wrong. If they came from a planet, we'd be able to deduce what it looked like from their physiology."

"Can you ratchet down the aggression a tad?" Beanfield said.

"I'm just saying." He shook his head. "I'm sorry." He was jumpy and irritable. In between the engagement and debrief, he had run a probe on core bank 996, because it would have made a lot of sense to him if the ship's room-hiding behavior could be traced back to a fault there, sustained either during the original damage or the subsequent self-repair. But as best he could tell, the core was functioning exactly as it should be. So there was no good explanation.

"They have to come from somewhere," Beanfield said.

"A mystery for the ages," Jackson said. "I think we're done. I recommend everyone grab sleep. I'll pull a solo shift." She glanced at Anders. "You still have forty-eight hours of confinement."

Anders didn't react, but Beanfield jumped as if someone had goosed her. "We can discuss that."

"It's already decided," Jackson said, and left.

"Let me talk to her," Beanfield said, after a moment. This sounded slightly mutinous to Gilly. He didn't know why she was surprised that Anders's sentence had only been delayed. That was common sense.

Anders shrugged.

"No one's going to confine you."

"Do the crime, pay the time," Gilly said.

"Shut the fuck up, Gilly," Beanfield said.

He stood. That was a pretty aggressive comment, he felt. But he let it go. Jackson was right. They had been on edge for days. Everyone would feel better after sleep.

He returned to his cabin and recorded a clip while he undressed. Normally, he tried to structure his thoughts for a particular audience, Service or his colleagues at Surplex or the general public, but he was tired and degenerated into a ramble that was mostly for his own benefit. He figured Service could figure out what to do with it. "As we've encountered new hazards and the ship has developed more sophisticated responses, it's become harder for me to guess what it's doing, or why," he said. "It actually makes me wonder if I've ever been able to."

He unstrapped his survival core and hung it by his bed. He balled his shirt and tossed it into a chute and pulled open a drawer and there was a new shirt, of course, white and pressed and never worn before, because the ship manufactured them.

"I've been concerned about the ship exhibiting aberrant behavior. But I'm starting to think it might not be aberrant at all. I'm fooling myself if I think there's a line I can distinguish between logical and illogical AI behavior. The reality is, it's all beyond my ability to assess. Maybe the ship hiding Eng-13 is the result of a fault I haven't been able to detect, but maybe it's just natural emergent behavior from an AI system that's so intelligent, it is, in a lot of ways . . ."

He trailed off. He didn't want to say the word *alive*. And not just because it seemed so silly, putting that on an official record, but also because, alone in his cabin, it suddenly felt like the ship was listening. He didn't want it to hear him.

He shook his head. "I'm tired," he said. "I'm not making a lot of sense. I'll pick this up tomorrow."

He was yanked from a depthless slumber by a low bleating. He sat up, groggy. The walls glowed purple. He pulled on his film and saw:

☐ CORE #0127 SELF-CHECK FAILED (ENG-6)

It was the kind of thing that used to appear back when he had puzzles. He fitted his survival core, grabbed his belt and tools, and headed for K Deck.

Jackson popped into his ear, asking what was happening. "I don't know," he said. "I just woke." He reached the ladder and spun the hatch.

"We've been engaging hostiles," Jackson said, "for the last three hours."

"What? While I was sleeping?" That couldn't be right. He wouldn't have slept through the klaxon. If it was met with no response, it would become progressively louder. At a certain point, the light would become bright enough to sear through his eyelids.

"There was no call to station. I'm only finding out about it now."

The ladder was mechanized but he let himself slide as well, for additional speed. A small dark object struck his foot and blurred past his face. "What—"

"You all right?"

He gripped the ladder and punched a tactile button to make it stop descending. "There's something in the ladder shaft."

Beanfield: "Is this an engagement?"

Jackson: "Unclear. Attend station until we know. Intel, what's going on?"

He peered past his boots. There was movement down there. Multiple dark shapes. "It's full of crabs."

"What are they doing?"

"I don't know." He began to descend manually, one rung at a time. He was focused on what was happening below and didn't notice that more crabs were descending from above until they scuttled past him. "God, shit!"

"Intel?"

"Nothing. Sorry. It's fine. More crabs. They're going the same way I am."

"Toward Eng-6?"

That would make sense. If there was a fault, the ship would call crabs to it. "I think so."

"Get down there, please," Jackson said. "I want eyes."

He resumed his descent. "If we've been fighting for three hours, how many hostiles was that?"

"Not many. Two or three hundred. From what I'm seeing, it wasn't one large engagement but a dozen or so small ones."

"Three hundred salamanders from twelve engagements?" That was hardly any. They had never encountered so few at once; no one had. "From how many hives?"

"One. And that was in the early stages of construction. No soldiers."

"So, what, they just roam around in space now?"

"Apparently," said Jackson. "This deep in VZ, I guess they do."

"Or they've evolved new tactics," he said, and stepped on a crab. He kicked it off the ladder and continued. "I'm almost at K Deck. There are crabs everywhere."

"At station," said Beanfield. "Life, checking in."

He wondered about Anders. He didn't know whether Anders had actually been returned to confinement. Then his boots found solid ground and there were so many crabs he couldn't move without treading on them. The air was filled with the clicking and chittering of their movement. "Lights," he said, because it was dark, and the ship didn't seem to have registered his arrival. The walls glowed yellow, then began to cycle purple, as they had above. "Holy shit."

"What is it?"

The corridor was full of crabs. They carpeted every surface, walls, ceiling, flowing like a tide toward Eng-6, swarming over each other. They bubbled from the ladder shaft and swept by, submerging his boots. "Got a buttload of crabs here."

"Can you see Eng-6?"

"Not yet." He began to wade through the crabs.

"Intel, I'm transferring control of the AI kill switch to Command."

"Ah," he said, "why?"

"Because I'm at station and you're down there."

He hated that. But it was hard to argue. She was the captain. Ultimately, it was her call. "Everything is fine at the moment."

"Except for the unexplained fault," Jackson said. "And the thousand crabs. And the secret engagements."

"Anders is dark on ping," Beanfield said. "With permission, Command, I'd like to force his location."

"What are you talking about? He's in quarters. He's confined."

"Actually, there's an issue with that that I want to discuss with you."

"Are you telling me you released him?"

"It's complicated," Beanfield said.

There was a metal squeal. Gilly peeled off his film to get a fix on its direction. It seemed to be coming from dead ahead. He pushed on, forging through crabs, trying to ignore the sensation of little spindly legs beneath his boots. When he reached Eng-6, he found crabs massed around the doorway, limbs weaving, knitting. The edges of the doorway were disappearing. The crabs were converting it to a wall.

He lunged forward and swiped at them with his gloves. "They're walling up Eng-6!" He jammed his film back on and kicked at a cluster near the floor, scattering them. "Fucking crabs everywhere!"

"Say again?" Jackson said.

The squeal came again, louder, and this time he located it as coming from Eng-6. He ducked through the doorway. Inside was Anders, kneeling atop one of the green core bank housings, pushing Gilly's drill through the thick translucent polymer.

He was frozen by the insanity of what he was seeing. "Anders!"

Anders looked up. He had gotten himself a long screwdriver to use as a drill bit, Gilly saw. Of course he had. Gilly had described the technique in debrief.

"What are you doing?"

Anders hunched over the drill and drove it downward. White smoke leaped and twisted. Lines appeared on Gilly's film:

☐ CORE #0127 SELF-CHECK FAILED (ENG-6)
☐ CORE #0126 SELF-CHECK FAILED (ENG-6)

Anders jumped down from the housing. He began to climb the adjoining one.

"What?" Gilly said. "What?"

"What's happening down there, Intel?"

"Anders is drilling the ship!" He couldn't understand what Anders was hoping to accomplish. "He's destroying cores!"

"Anders," said Jackson. "Stand the fuck down."

Anders spun the drill experimentally, positioning it over the housing. "We don't need the AI. I can run Weapons."

"No, no, don't drill it," Gilly said. "Don't drill it!"

Beanfield: "Anders, you won't be confined. Please don't damage the ship."

Anders leaned on the drill. It began to squeal.

"There are thousands of cores!" Gilly shouted. "You can't drill them all! Anders, stop!" He slapped the core housing. "Anders!"

Jackson: "Gilly, take him down."

He wasn't sure how he would do that. When he glanced around for inspiration, he saw that the doorway had shrunk. Already it was barely a quarter of its original size. The rest was dull yellow metal. Around its edges, crabs worked, knitting, walling them in. He yelped and ran to the door and swept them away. But there were too many: As he repelled some, others surged. "Anders! Help me!" He threw a glance over his shoulder, but Anders was still intent on the drill. "Anders!"

Beanfield: "I'm on my way."

"Anders, help me!" He couldn't keep the crabs away. He remembered trying to cut his way into Eng-13, unsuccessfully, because when the crabs walled up a door, they did so in a way his tools couldn't penetrate. "Anders!" Finally he abandoned the doorway, ran to the core bank, and slapped the housing. "We have to leave!"

Anders glanced at him. Gilly pointed at the doorway. Anders's gaze shifted to it and Gilly had never seen anyone look so shocked. At last, Anders got it. Gilly extended a hand but Anders came down boots first, at speed, and knocked Gilly off balance. He fell to one knee. To his astonishment, Anders left him. He fled for the door and began to wriggle through it. His hips caught and Gilly watched his legs flailing. There was a sizzling, Anders getting too close to the burning metal the crabs were weaving. Then his legs disappeared. A moment later, Anders's face appeared outside the hole. "Gilly!" He reached back through the hole, as if leaving Gilly behind hadn't just been an act of monumental assholishness.

Gilly bent and tried to climb through, but then stopped. He took a step back and shook his head. It was too small. If he tried, he would be cut in half. He would be welded to the door.

"Come on, Gilly!" The edges of the hole glowed hotly. He could see the tips of little pincers working, eating away the gap. Anders roared. "We're losing Gilly!"

The crabs froze. Gilly hadn't realized how loud they'd been until they fell silent. The burning glow from their pincers began to fade. There was a small hole in the doorway. Enough to squeeze through if he was determined, he thought. He breathed.

"Kill switch is activated," said Jackson.

He sank to his haunches. His legs were trembling. What Jackson had said was terrible. But he couldn't find it within himself to object. "Thank you."

"You're welcome," said Jackson. "Stay put. We're coming."

He heard Jackson and Beanfield coming down the corridor, kicking crabs. By this time, he'd been able to run a board and develop a sense of what was working. The kill switch had taken out the AI but left essential systems running, including comms and basically all of Life. Jackson's face appeared in the hole. Her eyes roved over him. "You okay?"

He nodded.

"You want some help getting out of there?"

"Yes, please." Anders had disappeared; Gilly didn't know where to. He was trying not to think about Anders. When he did, anger rushed through him like water slopping over a dam. He had things to do before he gave in to that.

He stowed the board and slid his arms and head through the hole. It was tight and he became stuck and had to ask for help. Jackson and Beanfield seized his wrists and pulled on him like a breech birth and then he flopped to the floor, scattering crabs.

Jackson moved to inspect the door, where crabs dangled, inert but still clinging to the metal. "How long did this take them?"

"Only a few minutes." He found his feet. "We should reactivate the AI." They had been dark for twelve minutes. Technically, the exterior scans were working, but they returned too much raw data to parse. Anything could be out there.

Jackson nodded. "Eng-5?" He nodded. They began to wade down the corridor. "Good to know the kill switch works."

"Before we bring back the ship," Beanfield said, "can we talk about how it might react?"

Gilly blinked. Jackson said, "Pardon me?"

"The first time we drilled it, it walled up a room. We might want to expect another reaction."

"I tell you what," Jackson said. "First we'll get operational, then we can psychoanalyze the ship." She resumed walking. When they reached Eng-5, Gilly glanced around the doorway, as if there might be crabs lurking in the crevices. But the room was clean. He moved to a core housing and activated its board.

"I just think—" said Beanfield.

"Life, your stock is not high right now," said Jackson.

Beanfield closed her mouth. Gilly said, "I'm ready to deactivate the kill switch."

"Do it."

He thumbed the board. For a moment, there was nothing, just time to contemplate the empty horror of a ship with a comatose AI, drifting forever. Then he detected stirrings in the core processes. "We have signal."

"AI is back?"

"Uh . . ." He was seeing something in the readings that he didn't want to.

"Gilly?"

"It's online. But it's performing a cold restart."

"We're decelerating," Beanfield said. "You feel that?"

"Yes," Jackson said. "What does a cold restart mean?"

"It means it's initializing every single process from scratch. That could take a while."

"How long?"

"Hard to estimate." He switched into diagnostics.

"Do it anyway."

"An hour."

Beanfield inhaled. Jackson said, "We have an hour with no AI?"

"Potentially. Engines are resetting. Life is resetting. Armor is on-line but unmanaged. Weapons is online but unmanaged. Environmental scanning is online but unmanaged."

"Do we have them or not?"

"They're functional but the AI isn't controlling them. Everything we want to make work, we have to do ourselves."

There was silence. "All right," Jackson said. "This is a manual alert. Crew to station. Let's see what we can do."

He felt reluctant to leave the board, but she was right: He could do more from station. They departed Eng-5 for the corridor. The mass of crabs lay still, an ankle-deep carpet. They began to wade through it. *So many crabs,* Gilly thought. Apparently the ship hadn't recycled them after it finished rebuilding Materials Fabrication. It had decided to keep them around.

Ahead, a column of crabs leaped into the air, slapped the ceiling, and fell back down.

They froze. "Uh," Beanfield said.

The crabs didn't move again.

Beanfield prodded one with a boot. "Is this how they wake up?"

"No," Gilly said. He had seen something like this before, though. When he'd watched the previous attack on playback, the time the salamanders got close enough to cause some real damage. You couldn't see the *huk*s themselves—they were too small and fast—but you could see the destruction that followed them. You could see when one passed through a room, because everything that wasn't nailed down was tossed into the air like confetti.

"Shit," Jackson said. "Move!"

Behind, he heard another small explosion. The clattering of crabs hitting the ceiling.

"Anders, attend station! This is not a drill. We're under attack!" The corridor branched and Jackson headed for Command while he and Beanfield made for the ladder shaft. In Gilly's ear, Jackson called for Anders, with no response.

"An attack?" Beanfield said. "Now?"

He had to bring up Armor. He would have to do it manually, because the AI wouldn't complete cold restart in time. If they were already taking fire, salamanders were close. They were way too close.

"Anders!" Beanfield said. "We need you!"

They reached the ladder. He threw open the hatch. Here they had to part ways: Beanfield up, him down. If the movement system was inactive, she was in for a climb. He turned to her to say this and the hatch was pulled out of his hands. The wall burst open like ripe fruit. *Huk*, he thought. *We've been hit.* There was an excruciating force, like something trying to pull him via his forehead. He reached for something to hold on to but everything was falling to pieces and there was nothing.

8

[Anders]

THE ENEMY

Anders loved guns. If Camp Zero had been nothing but close-combat training, he would have stayed there forever. But by the time he got there, Service didn't do that; instead, it did Providence-class battleships that could kill things from five hundred thousand miles away. He'd asked once, stuck up his hand and said, "Sir, when do we get to the close-combat training, sir!" and the drill sergeant came down the line and eyeballed him and said, "Candidate Paul Anders, you want to know what to do upon close contact with the enemy?" and he said, "Yes, sir! Want to know the best way to kill them, sir!" and the sergeant said, "I appreciate your enthusiasm, Candidate Anders! Now bend down and grab your ankles! Get right down there! Now, Candidate Anders," said the sergeant, once Anders had complied, "commence kissing your ass good-bye!" This turned out to not be a joke. The sergeant waited until he made smacking sounds. "Candidate Anders is demonstrating correct protocol in the face of a close encounter with the enemy," said the sergeant, "because, by God, if any of you shit-stains let them anywhere near your personal being, you deserve everything that will happen to you."

Anders hated the ship more than he could say, but he liked its guns. He'd seen an early concept video while riding the bus, and those laser batteries crawling around the hull, converging into place, locking in, swiveling, lining up, and discharging the collective wrath of the human race in one direction . . . he'd replayed that over and over until a crazy idea took hold in his brain: that he might want to make crew. It was crazy because he could barely stand the bus, with people on all sides who might press close at any moment, with its thin, stale air. But in the video, the Providence had looked big. And it had big guns. So maybe. Maybe.

Of course, Service had tricked him. Service was lies from beginning to end, and one of the lies was that a Providence Weapons Officer got to do anything more intimate with a laser battery than observe its numbers from station. It was incredibly frustrating. Eventually he asked Gilly to open a small-arms locker. He'd been thinking about that for a while, and it would have been glorious, but Gilly wouldn't play along. "I'm not doing that, Anders," Gilly had said, like he was talking to a child. Gilly had been hanging out with Beanfield around then and so become serious and not fun. When Gilly and Beanfield spent time together, it was like Gilly's testicles, small to begin with, climbed right up inside his body, so that anytime Anders wanted to do something interesting, Gilly coughed and got nervous. Anders's idea was to get a gun, sneak up behind Gilly, and *bam*, plug him. Not badly. He just wanted Gilly to yell and fall to the deck and remember how to have fun.

It would be even better if Anders could figure out how to open a small-arms locker by himself, because they were alarmed. There would be a tone, and everyone would think, *Who the fuck is opening an arms locker?* and realize: *Anders*.

They were family out here, him and Gilly and Beanfield and

Jackson. One thing Anders had figured out in life—maybe the only thing—was that family was what you could trust. Even if it was bad, you could trust it like that. The four of them were stuck with each other out here, and that meant none of the other shit mattered, like how Gilly was unlike anyone Anders had ever known, and if you asked him even something stupid and simple, like who had a better ass, Beanfield or Jackson, there would be a half-second pause, the gears in Gilly's brain turning, and then he would produce a careful, inoffensive response, like: *I haven't thought about it.* From how Gilly acted, everything they ever said was recorded by Service for permanent archive. Which he guessed was true, but that wasn't the point; the point was that Gilly shouldn't care. Anders couldn't give two shits what Service thought, but Gilly did; Gilly gave shits about everything. Sometimes Gilly was the alien to Anders. Or the ship, thinking in ways he couldn't understand. But that was fine. Anders didn't need to understand Gilly to know they were in this together, and would be until the end, and that he would give his life for Gilly in a heartbeat.

Gilly had once asked him what he was planning to do when they got home. It wasn't something Anders had thought about; he was out here to kill salamanders and didn't want to consider what came after. "Because the way our numbers are tracking," Gilly said, "I think we're going to be received pretty well back home."

This had made Anders laugh. "Gilly, no one will care about our numbers."

Gilly looked puzzled. "Of course they will. That's why we're here."

"What people think about the war has nothing to do with what happens. If Service wants us to be heroes, they'll make us heroes. If they don't, they won't."

Gilly was silent and Anders realized he'd strayed into forbidden territory. Beanfield would not be pleased. He wasn't supposed to disillusion Gilly of his fairy tales. But it was amazing to Anders how naive Gilly could be. He was crazy smart in ways Anders could barely appreciate but swallowed everything Service told him like a child.

"I don't think people can ignore our numbers," Gilly said.

He could see Gilly getting aggravated, so he let it go. The thing was, Anders wasn't even going near the other fairy tale Gilly was suggesting, which was that the ship was an impregnable fortress that could never fail. That was the biggest fairy tale of all, in his opinion. In Anders's experience, everything failed. "If you say so."

"I do say so," Gilly said.

After watching Gilly almost get trapped in Eng-5, he turned off his ping, removed his film, and jogged through the corridors to Rig-1. Rig-1 was his favorite place on the ship. It was basically the intersection of three corridors, but weirdly wide, with more room than he'd found anywhere else. He sat on the floor with his back against a wall and could see for fifty yards straight ahead, and the same when he turned his head left and right. He came here a lot, for respite from the feeling that the ship was closing on him like a vise.

He missed hydrexalin. The problem with Rig-1 was the silence, during which his brain strayed to bad places. He had to keep busy or else he would start revisiting the past, and not even the worst places, which by now were so well trodden that they'd developed something of a hard crust, becoming memories of memories, scenes that played out behind filtered glass, but instead smaller things, faces, expressions, little cruelties, none of which most people knew about, of course, because Service had taken him and buffed and polished until those parts were all gone, and the person he saw on the feeds he didn't even recognize.

He had gone a little crazy in the last months before they shipped out. He had kept expecting someone to say, *Wait, we're sending Paul Anders? That's a mistake.* But no one did. No matter how much of an asshole he was, or how clear he made it that he was unsuited to the role, they remained intent on sending him out on a spacecraft—a *spacecraft*, for fuck's sake—which was, it turned out, a hell of a lot smaller on the inside than it appeared from the exterior. The gap between who he was and who he was presented to be in public became a chasm, and he had the idea that if only he pushed enough, it would become untenable, something would have to break, and whichever way it went, for better or worse, things would make sense again. There would be no more gap. There were many girls in those months, and one of them, whose name he couldn't remember but whose face he would never forget, jumped on his back, just slammed herself on there, and they were in the dark with the curtains drawn and the old terror burst inside him and he threw her off with such force that her head had struck the bedside table. It wasn't the first time something like that had happened, but it was the worst; she was bleeding, her eye already swelling, and he tried to help her but she didn't want him anywhere near, and there was a fear in her eyes that he recognized and understood. She left with only half her clothes. He had sat in the dark and waited for consequences that never came.

The beauty of Rig-1 wasn't even the sight lines. It was the three doors. The options. A small space could be tolerable if there was a way out. That was the only reason he could bear his cabin—until it was locked.

Tough to explain this to anyone.

He had spent his entire career waiting for someone to find out. For a corporal to call him in and say, *Candidate Anders, this is going to sound crazy, but are you claustrophobic?* And then discharge him, because what else would you do with a claustrophobic flight crew candidate? Instead, he passed one psych eval after another. He was practiced at putting up a front, especially about this, so he could possibly believe that he'd managed to fool the human doctors. But the AI was supposed to be some kind of perfect. Passing that one was a surprise. Once he was selected for crew, Service monitored his physical and mental state almost constantly, and during one automated test, a series of Rorschach slides and word association tests, a wild impulse seized him and he said, "Kid in a box" to the first dark mess that appeared on screen, and "Kid in a box" for the second, and in response to *evil*, "Kid in a box," to *death*, to *never*, all these words and pictures, he came right out with it and told the truth. When he passed that test, too, he knew they didn't care.

The ship annoyed him. It did more than that, but the thing about it being supersmart, that got under his skin, too. When he tried to discuss this with anybody, they'd only say how much safer it was, and couldn't see why Anders didn't care about that. He wanted to escape the person he'd become, and to kill salamanders, and the ship didn't let him do either. Instead it was driving him around the universe and would deposit him safely back home, and he could see exactly how that would play out. How Service would do a spit and polish on their growth narratives and give the audience the closure they craved. *They killed his brothers and he went out there and killed a million of them back. Now, at last, Paul Anders is at peace.* He could feel that future closing in on him like a box.

It had felt good to drill it. Real good.

He eyed his film, which lay a foot or so away. Sooner or later he would have to put that back on and face the consequences of his actions. But not just yet. He turned to the left, then the right, then looked straight ahead. Right in this moment, he was okay. He had options.

———

A minute later he felt a kick through the floor. It was unlike anything he'd felt in the ship before, and he pressed his palms against the cool metal to see if it would repeat. There was something else now, a kind of juddering rumble. Also new.

He reached for his film.

As soon as he got it on, Jackson squawked in his ear. "Status. Status."

Gilly, his voice strangled: "Beanfield's hurt. I can't get her out."

"Can you reach station?"

"Everything's . . . we took damage. I can't see."

Anders said, "What's happening?"

Jackson: "Anders, get your ass back here. Intel, I need you at station."

"I can't reach her!"

He got up and moving. He fixed Gilly's location on ping and saw Beanfield in the same location. "I'm coming."

"Intel, you need to leave."

"I can't. I can't. She's hurt."

Shit, he thought. He had done it again. Gotten wrapped up in himself and let other people get hurt. He spun a hatch and began to ascend the ladder. The rungs didn't move. Apparently he would have to do this manually. He loathed ladder shafts so much. Couldn't see the bottom of them. Couldn't help thinking he'd never reach the end. He would climb and climb and the walls would inch closer behind his back.

Jackson: "Intel, I can't do this by myself."

"I won't leave her."

"I'm almost at you," Anders said, although that wasn't true.

"Intel, we have six hostiles and they're tearing us apart because we can't control Armor or Weapons. The survival of this ship depends on you restoring basic function."

Six? He couldn't imagine the ship being taken down by six salamanders. That was ridiculous. He said, "Gilly, I'll deal with Beanfield. Go do your job."

Gilly: "Do my job? Do *my* job?"

Jackson: "Gilly."

"She's not responding!"

"I don't care," Jackson said. "Get to station."

He broached A Deck and the relative space of a long corridor. "I'm here."

"Where?" Gilly said, and then: "You're half the deck away!"

"Gilly, we need you, buddy."

"Why don't you shut the fuck up?!"

"Hostiles have ceased firing," said Jackson.

"You left me in the core room," Gilly said. "I don't want you. I'll do this myself."

"Physical contact in three minutes," said Jackson. "Prepare to be boarded."

"Did you say boarded?" Anders said.

"They're approaching; not sure what else they'd have in mind."

Gilly said, "Wait . . . do you have Sensors?"

"Yes. Correction. I have Ring 2 Sensors. I can't make sense of anything else as it's coming through as raw data."

"Do we still have Life?"

"Yes."

"Can you shut it down?"

"Why would I want to do that?"

"Just do it."

"We need Life, Gilly."

"I realize that! I'm not an idiot!"

"Dialing down," said Jackson, after a brief pause.

The lights blinked out. Anders stopped. His film projected a faint blue light but everything beyond ten feet was darkness.

"The ship won't drop core function," Gilly said. "It'll always maintain thermals and air pressure as a priority. But disabling the rest might let it skip ahead to systems we really need, like Weapons and Armor."

"Thank you," Jackson said. "How's Beanfield?"

"She's breathing. I don't know. She needs Medical."

"Can you leave her?"

Gilly hesitated. "How close is Anders?"

"Close," he said.

"I'll leave Beanfield when Anders gets here."

"Armor is still unmanaged," Jackson said. "Weapons unmanaged. Physical contact in two minutes."

"Okay," Gilly said.

Anders saw a red glow ahead and it turned out to be a ring around a small-arms locker. He hadn't known they had emergency lighting. He tugged on the release. "Can I get a cycle on a weapons locker?"

"Where are you? I thought you were coming!"

"There's a locker on the way." He ran his hand across its surface. "If we're getting boarded . . ."

Gilly cursed. There was scuffling. "I'll take her to Medical myself."

Jackson: "Anders, you're off mission. Go to Beanfield."

He exhaled. Salamanders at the front door and guns beneath his fingertips that he couldn't reach. But he turned his back on the locker. The darkness ahead seemed thicker. It was a blanket poised to wrap around his body and squeeze tight. He'd prepared for this, though.

Sometimes he ran around the ship with his eyes closed just to see if he could do it. Drove his knee into a bulkhead once and it sounded like a bag of peanuts and felt like hot knives and he had to drag himself to Medical. The ship gave him hydrexalin, which was the start of a whole thing. Another time he'd cannoned into Jackson and she said, "*What are you doing?*" like there was no good answer, and he couldn't think of anything to say except the truth, "Running to station in the dark," and Jackson looked impressed, like, *Bravo, training for an emergency.*

"We have a gravity well situation," Jackson said.

"What?" said Gilly.

"We're getting close enough to a planet to have to care about it."

"Maybe the ship wants to use it to evade."

"Has it taken control of Engines yet?"

"I don't think so. Are we on an impact trajectory?"

"Negative."

Ahead was a faint blue glow like an itching on his eyeballs. It resolved into a mess of shit, broken beams and twisted metal and dark holes in everything. In the middle of all that was Gilly, a blue glowstick in his hand. Beanfield was slumped across his legs. Her eyes were closed. In the blue light, her skin from her chest to her chin was black. There was a first-aid patch on her left side and that was black, too.

"She got impaled," Gilly said. "A piece of the ship went through her."

Anders knelt and saw that she was alive. The patch wrapped around her side, and as terrible as it looked, it would be performing the essential function of preventing Beanfield's insides from leaking out. "Go fix the ship," he said.

"Her leg is stuck. I can't get her out."

He hadn't even noticed that. Her left foot was trapped beneath a slab of rubber and metal. "I can do that. You need to go do your thing."

Gilly hesitated, then pressed the glowstick into Anders's hand. "Okay. Take this."

He nodded. Gilly eyed him and left. He bent to inspect Beanfield. Her hair was covering her face; when he pushed it aside, her face was dark with dust and dirt. "Hell of a day, Beanfield," he said. He explored her leg until he found the place she was caught. When he tugged, she gave a low, guttural groan. He peered into the wreckage and saw immediately that there were two ways to free her: the way that required him to lift ten thousand pounds of busted ship, and the way that would snap her ankle.

He wriggled down and set himself as best he could. Her pants were torn. From the angry look of her skin, Gilly had removed some debris before he arrived. He took hold of her leg and her eyes popped open and she gave a small cry. "It's okay," he said. "Worst part is over, Beanfield." But his promises had never been worth much and she'd always known that about him and she kept protesting, making a terrible, feeble mewling. He pulled as hard as he could and there was a noise and her leg slid free and she fell silent and limp.

He carried her to the ladder shaft. He was glad she was unconscious. He didn't know if he could do this with someone clinging to him, trying to grab his shoulders. It was bad enough already.

His brothers had put him in a toolbox. He'd had a thing about small spaces even before and he made the mistake of telling Eddie, the youngest, whom he trusted, and Eddie told the others. After that they would come anytime. Hands on his shoulders. *Hey, Pauly.* He kicked and screamed but there was never any help. Sometimes they sat on the lid and didn't lock it, so he could believe that if he pushed hard enough, he could escape. Each time he saw a sliver of light before the dark slammed down again. He died a whole lot of times in that box. Screamed and cried with wet terror bursting inside his mind. It felt like they left him in there for hours, for days, or not even that, a spongy, indistinct amount of time that could grow or compress and conceivably last forever. That was his real fear, that they might not let him out. He couldn't close his hands into fists when he got out because of how he'd punched the lid. Couldn't write well, either, or manipulate a board, or do much of anything that required fine motor skill, and he tried to cover for it with horse-ass behavior, which got him appointments with the school counselor. *I want to help you,* the counselor said, but Anders had heard that before and not once had it been true. When he did get around to asking that man, in a roundabout kind of way, what would happen to a person who killed a member of their own family, he was silent awhile and then said, *Sorry, Paul, but we have to leave it there.* No school for a while after that.

One time in the toolbox he had kicked and there was a sharp noise. He pulled himself free and lay on the cool concrete floor and it was the sweetest moment of his life. He'd never found anything quite so good again, and not for lack of trying. Lying there, things had become very clear to him: one, that when his brothers found him, they would put him back, and two, he would do anything to prevent that from happening. So he took down a wrench and waited by the front porch. He knocked Eddie off his bike before any of them noticed him. The others jumped him pretty quick and beat him half to death, but Eddie was still out four teeth and never spoke right again. Anders caught all kinds of hell from his father for that. And he always felt bad for how it went down, because Eddie was the nicest, and just happened to come around the corner first. But it was the end of the box.

"I'm at station," Gilly said.

He wedged Beanfield into the ladder shaft. "You hear that? Gilly's on the case."

She didn't reply.

"I'm going to trigger the pulse manually," Gilly said. "Stand by. Three. Two. One. Pulsing."

"Was that it?"

"What do you mean?" Gilly said. "Yes. We pulsed. Why? What happened?"

"I'm not seeing any impact. But it's difficult to assess damage without the regular scans."

"I can pulse again in twenty seconds."

"Six incoming hostiles," Jackson said. "Same as before. Twenty seconds to physical contact. Confirmed, no apparent impact."

"Shit," Gilly said.

"What went wrong?"

"I don't know. It's . . . wait. They're too close. They're too close."

"For the pulse?"

"Yes. They're inside its minimum range."

"Use the drones," Anders said.

"That's . . . a good idea for three minutes ago!" Gilly said. "I can't do it that fast!"

"Breach on A Deck," Jackson said. "Breach on B. Second breach on B. Breach on D. Third breach on B. We've been boarded."

Small-arms lockers, Anders thought, but didn't say, because he was trying not to drop Beanfield down an unmotorized ladder shaft. He managed to work her down to F and then it was easier through the corridor. He reached Medical, cranked the manual door release, and lay Beanfield out on the table. He waited for something to happen but it didn't. "Ah, bitch," he said, because of course the ship wasn't working. He yanked open drawers until he found a blue medbag. He tugged down Beanfield's pants and she woke and tried to stop him and he said, "It's okay, I'm helping," and it was hard, because he had to be forceful. Once he got the medbag over her hips, she calmed some. He detached her survival core and set it aside. Not much use against crushing forces, that. Kind of completely useless. He carefully unpeeled the first-aid patch. Blood welled immediately, a lot of it. He drew the bag up tight so it could press to her skin and watched it begin to inflate, turning her into a big blue cuddly toy. The medbag would apply pressure where it was needed, and dispense medicine, anesthetic, whatever. It would also drug her out of her mind, most likely. But that was probably for the best. "Beanfield's bagged."

Jackson: "Anders, I want you out of there right now." There had been some conversation he hadn't followed while he was figuring out the medbag.

Gilly: "Is Beanfield all right?"

Jackson: "Anders, they're on your deck."

He looked at Beanfield. He wished she was awake. *Salamanders on the ship, Beanfield.* Two years of nothing, and when something finally happened, she was unconscious.

"Did you hear me?"

"I heard you. Beanfield's okay."

Gilly said, "I'm locking everything down. If you want to be on the right side of the blast doors, you need to get to a junction or hatch right now."

He wondered what to do with Beanfield's survival core and decided to leave it; it wasn't going to help with her injury, and couldn't be applied over the medbag. He hefted her. The fabric crinkled. Her eyes were closed. She looked peaceful. "Going to need you to open that small-arms locker, Gilly."

Gilly: "Ah . . . all right, let me check on that."

He stepped into the corridor. It felt colder. From above came sounds like whispers. Could be anything. Could be wind, dragging around parts of the ship. Could be Eddie, coming for him with the pipe, his mouth bloody, his teeth full of gaps. He carried Beanfield, the glowstick dripping blue light.

From ahead came a low dragging. "Is that them?"

"Yes. Move."

"Because it sounds like they're ahead of me."

"You're okay if you move."

He moved. "You sure about that?"

"Yes."

The glowstick jiggled in his hands. He was going to drop that fucking thing. It would roll across the deck and while he was on his knees, balancing Beanfield and groping in the dark, salamanders would find him. They were big. He didn't want to face one without a gun.

"Junction right ahead," Gilly said. "Get through that and I can drop a door behind you."

He saw it in front of him. But the thing about corners was that anything could be around them. He knew that better than anyone. But if they were that close, Gilly would know, and tell him. He had to trust that. He stepped out into the junction and raised the glowstick. To port was a small-arms locker, but of course his bullshit light stopped at six feet and his imagination extended farther than that. He wasn't illuminating anything except himself, standing there.

"They to my port or starboard, Gilly?"

"Closest hostile is port."

Of course it was. "How close?"

"Close enough. Keep moving."

Gilly was cautious, though. Always thinking things were worse than they were. Anders set Beanfield against the wall, on the far side of the yellow-and-black markings that outlined where a blast door might come to rest. Then he returned to the adjunct corridor. "Beanfield's clear. You can drop the door."

"What about you?"

"I'm getting the guns."

Jackson: "Don't do that, Anders."

"Anders, you're heading right at one. Don't be stupid."

"Anders, *go back*," Jackson said, her voice thick with anger. She was hellishly sexy when she was angry. He'd told her this once and her jaw had flexed and he could see he'd offended her. But he'd meant it as a compliment. He would genuinely fuck Jackson in a heartbeat if she promised to stay mad at him the whole time.

"Salamanders on the ship," he said. "Somebody needs to shoot these fuckers."

"Don't do this, Anders."

"Just open the locker, Gilly."

"I don't even know if I can!"

Jackson, resigned: "You can. Do it."

"Thank you," Anders said. He kept moving, searching for the tell-tale red ring. The glowstick was fucking with his vision, washing everything blue, coaxing glints and reflections from every surface. Finally he saw it, a solid box projecting from the wall, red light like a halo. "I'm there. Gilly?"

"Working on it."

He pulled the release but it was not generous and did not open. He'd had an argument with Beanfield about this very thing, saying, *What kind of asshat thinks it's a good idea to put the small arms behind a lock we can't open?* and Beanfield had patiently explained that, essentially, people like her and Jackson did not want people like Anders getting their hands on a gun whenever they felt like it. Which, he had to admit, had a kind of sense to it. But now look at this. Look at this shit right here.

"Picking up more incoming," Jackson said. "A lot more. A thousand or so. The ship is lost. Evacuate."

"Now, hold on," Gilly said.

He peered into the darkness. Since he'd stopped moving, he could hear a sound from ahead, something dragging. He listened until it stopped. "Gilly?"

"The ship isn't far off attaining full function," Gilly said. "Twenty minutes. Maybe less."

"We're not going to be here in twenty minutes. And the ship can't help us purge internal threats."

"We can't evacuate!"

He got the heebie-jeebies and whipped around. The light jumped crazily, throwing salamander shadows everywhere. But there was nothing. The dragging came again, ahead, louder. "Gilly!" He tested the release again. This fucking ship. It had wanted to kill him since the day he boarded, and here it was again.

"Got it," Gilly said.

The ring glowed green. Cylinders whined, retracting. The dragging became a scraping, or a scrambling, maybe, was a better way to put it, something huge and hungry moving toward him in the dark, and he pulled the release and still the fucking thing did nothing, until at last the locks fully retracted and the door popped open and inside was everything he wanted, pistols, needlers lined up as neatly as you please, and, best of all, a stock VX-10 rifle, better known in the popular press as a lightning gun. He snapped it free and thumbed for power. He slotted the butt against his shoulder. He trained the barrel into the heart of the darkness.

Three green lights glowed on in a line along the barrel, one after the other. A high whine tickled the back of his eardrums. Some people couldn't hear that sound. They didn't know what they were missing, in Anders's opinion. He held position, measuring his breathing, keeping the weapon pointed into the darkness. Just silence, now.

Hey, Pauly.

Sweat dripped into his eye. He stayed where he was. He could wait. He knew how to do that.

"Anders?"

It was only Gilly in his ear, but he squeezed the trigger and the gun barked and kicked against his shoulder and spat lightning down the corridor. The corridor bleached and splintered into brilliance. Fat licks of electricity scoured the walls and ceiling. But there was nothing there, only empty corridor. He released the trigger and darkness fell, then silence, except for the tingling whine of the gun and his own breathing. Ozone crawled up his nostrils.

"Anders, you need to get back to Beanfield so I can drop this door. They're converging on you."

He knew this deck. The corridor ran ahead for two hundred yards and had only one branch. Whatever had been making that dragging sound had to be down there. "Drop the door."

"You'd be trapped in there with one of them."

He rose and began to move down the corridor. He could move more quietly than a salamander, he was pretty sure. "That's fine."

Gilly continued to protest, so Anders put him on mute. He needed his ears. He crept forward. There was a soft *thump*. Some scraping. He couldn't see and was sorely tempted to light up the corridor again but there was no way one of those big fucks had crawled out in front of him without making more noise than that. He had a sense of it now.

He reached the junction and set his back to it. No sound at all. He leaned out and tossed the glowstick into the darkness. It looped through the air, spreading blue light along the walls and floor, and touched a hulking alien shape that filled the corridor, thick, muscular legs, resin scales, its neck contracting, its jaws cracking open. Anders dropped. There was a sound: *huk*. It all happened faster than he expected and a force seized him and tossed him against the ceiling. He rebounded and hit the floor. But he hadn't lost his sense of direction and he aimed the lightning gun along his feet and squeezed the trigger. The world flashed and danced. The gun leaped in his hands like a gleeful spirit. He hosed the corridor until the weapon stuttered and fell silent.

He crawled behind the safety of the corner and breathed there a minute. There was a crackling sound. A yellow flickering. When he peered out, he saw small fires. The shape that had filled the corridor was slumped, rivulets of fire running from burning fissures.

He approached it carefully. The walls were charred and scoured. The smell was terrible. Like poison. As he neared the shape, it coughed fire. A piece broke off and fell to the deck. Something bubbled, red and wet. Broiled salamander.

"Hey," he said to it. His film was lighting up with muted chatter from Gilly and Jackson but Anders was on a different plane right now. The salamander popped and fizzed and he crouched beside it. "Not so tough," he said. "Not so tough." It abruptly struck him as funny and he had to sit for a minute. Look at him, here, with a lightning gun and a dead salamander. Of all the bullshit Service had invented about him, this part was true: He had loved his brothers in a way he never felt about anyone else, despite the box, because of the box—whichever it was, they had been in it together against a father more monstrous than any alien creature, and he'd come out here because the only thing he could think to do after they died at Fornina Sirius was kill salamanders. And here he was. He kicked the corpse with his foot. "Hey," he said again. "You know what I call you?"

The salamander didn't answer.

"A good start," he said.

9

[Beanfield]
THE JET

Something needed to come out of her and she retched. It was a sad retch. It had no enthusiasm. It was the most perfunctory retch of her life. A thin line of drool issued from her mouth and when she went to wipe at it, she couldn't move her arms.

She couldn't see, either, actually.

Her head dropped. She wrestled it up. She didn't know when her head had gotten so heavy. Or when her body had started hurting. And it wasn't like it was just one part of her body. It was the whole thing. Actually, it was her side. And her left foot. But also everything. She felt squeezed. She tried to call out and emitted a low, wheezy croak, like a disappointed frog.

She appeared to be in a corridor. Alone. Alone in a corridor. Also she couldn't move. Something was wrapped around her body. She felt entombed. It was very dark and her eyes wouldn't focus but she was definitely entombed, alone, in a corridor.

"Ark," she said. She didn't want to be alone. Could it not be that, please? She was a people person. Whatever was happening here, she could deal, so long as there were people.

She couldn't free her arms but managed to lift her legs. She pushed with her feet and slid her body a short distance. She wasn't completely sure this was a good thing. There was a fog in her brain she couldn't penetrate. Her left foot told her it had been a bad idea to put pressure on it, a very bad idea, and she tried to remember when she had done that. A few seconds ago. That was when.

Something creaked. The ship, she assumed. She couldn't recall hearing the ship creak before, but maybe it was something you only noticed when you lay down in the dark, entombed, and listened.

There were salamanders. She remembered that. Jackson had shut down the ship and salamanders were coming.

From far away a fairy light danced toward her. It was faint and blue and she tried to resolve it into something sensible. It grew as it approached and she became fearful, because of the salamanders. Then, all at once, she saw Gilly's face. The light was a glowstick, which he was holding.

"I've got you," he said.

"Get her up," said Jackson. She didn't seem to have a fairy light. "We have to move."

I'm okay, she tried to say, and it came out as, "Hnhh," with plenty of saliva.

"Don't try to move," Gilly said. "You're in a medbag."

Really? That would explain a lot. A medbag would have sedated her. Now that there was a fairy light, she forced her chin down so she could look at her body. He was right: There was a shiny inflatable encasing her like a fat suit. At Camp Zero, they'd practiced fitting each other into these and waddling around. They weren't supposed to, since anyone in a medbag would be in no shape to do anything other than lie still and try not to die. You didn't need to practice walking in one. But it looked so hilarious.

"Pick her up," said Jackson.

She couldn't remember what had happened to put her in a medbag but she had the feeling she was pissed at Jackson for some reason. It might have been something recent or might have been the whole *You're a good soldier* thing in her cabin, which Talia still hadn't quite forgiven her for. She didn't know if Jackson was the reason she was waking up alone and entombed, but until she learned otherwise, she was going to blame Jackson anyway.

"Beanfield, there are salamanders on the ship," Gilly said. "We've picked up more incoming and I can't get the ship back. We're going to a jettison pod."

He scooped her up while she processed this insanity. She was medicated so maybe she had missed something, but it sounded like he had said there were salamanders on the ship and they were planning to use a jetpod. This was a pretty fantastic joke if so, because the jetpods weren't actually real. They were designed for psychological reassurance. Yes, they worked, but it was absurd that anyone would ever, under any circumstances, improve their situation by departing the 500,000-ton killing machine to squeeze into a thirty-foot cylinder made from plastic and tissue paper, and Service had told her this, because part of her job was convincing the crew otherwise: that, no, actually, jetpods were a realistic escape option, and therefore no one need feel like they were trapped in a flying can of death trillions of miles from home. And she had done this. She had freaking done it, in ways people would never notice, just like they didn't notice how she defused Anders or engaged Gilly or prevented Jackson from murdering everyone on board. She had done what Service asked and now there were salamanders on the ship and they were taking her to a jetpod? *They were in VZ.* She tried to articulate her concerns and made a gargling noise.

"Relax," said Gilly. "Let the medbag work."

You are unable to speak coherently and your crew are under the mistaken impression that jetpods are a real thing. Go.

"Anders," Jackson said. "Whatever you're doing, I need you to stop it."

"Gil," Talia said. "Gilly." They couldn't abandon ship. They couldn't abandon *the* ship, either. They'd had their differences, it and she, but she didn't want to leave it. Not really. Not like this. What she'd said earlier, *Please get me off this ship,* those were just words.

He peered at her. "Beanfield's trying to talk."

"She can talk once she's strapped in."

Gilly bent and put his ear close to her mouth.

She whispered, *"No jetpod."*

"It's all right," he said. "It's just a precaution. We won't detach unless we have to."

"What did she say?" said Jackson.

"'No jetpod.'"

"There are a thousand incoming hostiles," Jackson called over her shoulder. "If the ship doesn't restore function before they arrive, it's toast."

They reached a hatch, which Jackson spun open. Gilly set Talia down and climbed into the shaft. Jackson shoved her toward him. Jackson was wearing a very un-Jacksonlike expression, Talia noticed, now that she saw it up close. She searched for a label and landed on *concerned.* Yes. That was it. Jackson was exhibiting concern for her. That was alarming.

She felt herself toppling. Gilly caught her. "It's okay. I've got you. I'm not leaving you." This last part, she guessed, was because her face was registering some concern of her own. She was glad for his words but she did feel very anxious. Even if it was a precaution, they should not board the jet. Nothing good could happen there.

They began to make their way aft, Jackson periodically barking at Anders. At first, Talia assumed Anders was ignoring her, because she couldn't hear his replies, then she realized she wasn't wearing her film. From half the conversation, though, she could infer the rest: Anders was off somewhere doing his own thing. She actually didn't need to hear anything for that. That was what she would have assumed in the absence of contrary evidence. It sounded as though he'd managed to get his hands on a weapon. That was alarming, too.

They stopped. Jackson cranked a manual release. A door jerked apart, and what was behind it lit up. And there it was. The jetpod. Two harnesses up front, facing actual manual controls. Two at the rear. Lots of padding. A whole bunch of lockers, with reliable heavy-weight fonts designating which piece of impractical equipment they contained: beacons, medkits, material converters. Everywhere were handles. She could trace the inspiration of this design back to bright, plastic toys for babies, with levers and keys that made clicking sounds.

"Begin prep," said Jackson.

Gilly ducked into the jetpod and lowered Talia into a harness at the rear, looping straps over her bulging medbag. She kicked and shook her head. He bent and peered into her eyes.

"No," she said.

"Beanfield's agitated," Gilly said.

"It's the medbag," Jackson said, breaking off an argument with Anders, wherever he was. "She's under sedation. Ignore her."

He looked back at Talia. "What's wrong with the jet?"

She rolled her eyes. *Look at it, Gilly. Just look at it.*

"Gilly," Jackson barked.

"Here." He moved to the front of the jet and began dialing up systems. "Where's Anders?"

"Deck F. He's killed one."

"One what?" Gilly said, and then: "A *salamander*?"

"That's what he says."

She saw him hesitate. His eyes roved around the jet. He wasn't stupid. He was seeing the bright handles. The padding, which would prevent injury only if they encountered improbably small forces. His expertise was in software but he could surely realize what he was seeing. He was good at puzzles.

Gilly said, "Maybe . . ."

Jackson glanced at him. "What?"

He pointed to a screen. "There's a path from here to Eng-1. I could use its board to manage systems until the AI is able to take over. Then we could try to repel the boarders with small arms."

Jackson eyed him. "Now you think you can run Weapons and Armor manually?"

"Not well. But maybe well enough to buy us some time."

Jackson was silent. Then she shook her head. "No. This is wishful thinking."

"Look at this thing," Gilly said, gesturing to the novelty handles. "We can't escape a thousand hostiles in this. We'll never make it."

Jackson's eyebrows rose. She glanced about and her eyes landed on Talia. Talia did her best to nod. Jackson's face hardened. She hadn't suspected before, Talia saw. But it was making a lot of sense to Jackson in this moment. She'd dealt with Service long enough to know how they worked.

"Goddamn it," Jackson said.

"Anders isn't even here yet," Gilly said. "Let me try until then."

"All right. But when I call abort, you abort, understand? You leave that second and hightail it back here."

"Understood." He rose. He threw Talia a last glance and slipped into the darkness.

Jackson strapped into the front harness and positioned her board. Without turning, she said, "You and Service have a lot to answer for."

That was a little unfair, Talia felt. She hadn't designed the jetpods. She had only been doing her job, like Jackson did hers. But she felt elated because now they weren't going to shoot into space in a toy coffin. Gilly would run the ship and then they would repel the boarders and they would be okay.

"Anders, status." Jackson continued the one-sided conversation for a minute more. Eventually Anders appeared in the jetpod doorway. He was carrying a bulky rifle, a lightning gun, as naturally as if it were a third-born child. Anders plus a gun had been a waking nightmare for her for a while, but now she thrilled to see him with it. He looked like he'd never been complete before.

He stopped dead. "Where's Gilly?"

"En route to Eng-1. For now, we hold here."

He raised the rifle and took a step backward, into the corridor. That was an issue, too, now that Talia thought about it: Anders likely couldn't be convinced to enter the jetpod. "I'll provide escort. I just need to get a new cell. This thing's almost out of charge."

"Negative. You're not roaming around the ship looking for lockers. Stay here."

Anders stared at Jackson. Talia wished he would check behind him once in a while. He was standing with his back to a corridor that was drowned in darkness, and how fast could salamanders move? She felt like they were fast. On flat ground, under 1G, she felt like one could scramble out of the darkness and be inside the jet before anyone could react. She attempted to raise this but her body had become even less interested in responding to her wishes. The medbag was sinking chemicals into her, she realized. It would steal away her consciousness altogether before long. She managed to cough.

Anders glanced at her. "You still with us, Beanfield?"

"I'm in," said Gilly, his voice coming out of the jet's front. "I have a board."

Jackson raised a proximity view on a screen: the ship a blue dot, an orange planet radiating gravity lines, and a thin red arc of salamanders edging closer. "You have ninety seconds. If what you're doing isn't working by then, you leave."

"Understood."

Anders tossed a glance over his shoulder, which eased her concern, but only for a moment, until he turned back again. *Just step into the jet, Anders. Come inside and face the right way.* "Can you track the salamanders from here?"

"We only have thermals, so it's an approximation. But they're close."

"How close?"

"Aft port quarter. Two of them."

"On this deck?"

"Yes."

Anders ducked into the jet. He set himself inside the door and pointed the rifle into the darkness.

Thank you, she thought.

"I thought you were out of charge," Jackson said.

"Almost," Anders said. "Almost out of charge. I should get Gilly."

"There are no hostiles near Gilly. There are two near us. Stay. Intel, how are you looking?"

"Good. The AI cold restart is almost complete. It should be fully functional within three or four minutes. I haven't looked at Weapons yet, but I think I can run Armor."

On the proximity screen, the red arc continued to tighten. "We enter *huk* range in sixty seconds. You need to be back here before they start landing."

"I understand."

"I'll come get you," Anders said.

"Negative," said Jackson. "And stop asking." The onscreen readout spun lower: fifty seconds, forty, thirty, twenty. "Gilly, don't want to bother you, but I need an update."

"Almost done. I'm committing a command sequence now."

In the doorway, Anders adjusted his footing.

"Shit," Gilly said.

"What is it?" Jackson said.

"Minor problem. It's fine. Hold on."

Onscreen, the red arc began to blossom. Pinpricks of white light appeared, moving toward them. The first timer vanished and a second, measuring time until impact, assumed its place. They had forty-three seconds. "Hostiles firing. Gilly, you need to come back now."

"It didn't work. I missed something. But I can fix it."

"If we don't move, we'll still be here when the *huk*s start hitting."

"You should detach. You can separate from the ship until it's over. You'll be safe."

"Negative. Not leaving you there."

"If you . . ." Gilly trailed off. They listened to him make mysterious sounds for a moment, bumping and scuffling around, doing who knew what. "Um. You should detach."

On the screen, white pinpricks everywhere, like snow.

"Thirty seconds to impact. Come back, Gilly."

"I've messed this up," he said. "I shouldn't have tried to run systems manually. It can't be done."

"Gilly, come back."

"I should have prioritized getting the AI back. I'm clearing out some subsystem caches. That might help."

"Gilly."

"I can't reach you anyway," he said. "There's a salamander in the corridor."

Jackson thumbed her board. A floor plan appeared on screen. A section of a middle corridor was smeared red.

"Detach so you don't get hit," Gilly said. "I'll stay here and do the best I can."

For a moment, Jackson didn't move.

Then she touched her board. The jet doors slapped closed, almost catching Anders. The jet kicked. Talia felt them detach with a metal *clunk*. The loss of gravity was instantaneous, her body floating up in the harness.

"What the fuck are you doing?" Anders shouted.

Jackson wrenched the jetpod to the side, rolling them away from the ship. The universe revolved. The engines bit and inertia pressed Talia into her harness. "Gilly, you have a path to Ext-4. We'll attach there and pick you up."

"That's—"

"If you're not there when we attach, I'm dragging you out, you hear me?"

Anders stowed the rifle and pulled himself along the handles to the front harness. "We can get him?"

"Yes. But it's going to be rough."

Onscreen, the pinpricks converged on the blue dot. The timer dwindled away.

"Got it!" Gilly said. "AI is up!"

Jackson: "Brace, brace."

Over the engines rose a chorus of bleats and tones. The right screen flipped into an engagement loadout and the universe was full of salamanders. They filled the screen like stars. She was amazed at their numbers. She had followed mission stats. She had known they were grains of sand on a beach. But look at how many.

"Our twenty-five ninety," Anders said. "The ship will block some of them."

Jackson nodded. The jet kicked. They skimmed along the underside of the ship and sections flew by on the viewport. Ahead was a heavy-liquids tank, and for no apparent reason, it burst, spraying globular fluid, and then not far away came another blowhole, and then another. Her whale, breaching. She didn't know if it could survive this much damage and was suddenly afraid because it was breaking everywhere.

Anders pointed and Jackson swung the jet around. The docking brace grew on the main screen, a flat section marked with fat white lines. As she watched, it heaved and burst open, spraying debris.

Wreckage thumped the jet, knocking it about like a toy in a bathtub. The screens spun. Jackson and Anders were shouting; she couldn't hear their words. Jolts reverberated. Jetpods weren't designed to be hit with debris. They weren't designed for any of this. On the engagement screen, the salamanders were arriving, drifting down from the stars like spider eggs in the wind. The jet was screaming. Jackson was fighting it for control. But it wasn't going to help, Talia saw. They had lost. They had gone deep into VZ and failed to appreciate how the salamanders were expending vast numbers of lives trying to get close to them, or the resolve that that implied, the hunger, the hate. They had been very complacent. She hadn't really noticed she was in a war, if she was honest.

From the ship, a core of light, clean and brilliant.

A concussive force hit her. She was at the beach, six years old, her father turning away and a wave she never saw coming hitting her from behind, plunging her into a churning watery world of confusion, not knowing where she was or how to escape. Her father had caught her hand and plucked her from the sea and held her in his arms while she coughed and cried.

The screens were filled with debris. A large chunk of the ship's rear was venting fire. "Go," Jackson screamed. "Go, go, go." The jet fled but the ship hung on the screen and Talia could see fire spreading along it like fault lines, rupturing and splitting. The fire looked small compared to the mass of the ship but each tear revealed a deeper conflagration. It was insatiable and it ran in straight lines, following the materials lines, eating the ship in bites, and there went her station, and there the place she had gone with Anders to the hot room, and where she had eaten, and lived, slept, too many places to count, all becoming light and ash.

They ran through space. "Goddamn it," Anders said. "Goddamn it." He was cursing a lot. He was wrestling with his controls like a lover; which was to say, roughly. She felt the urge to go up there and tell him he should have been the one left behind, not Gilly. *I'm not leaving you,* Gilly had said, when he was carrying her down the ladder shaft. But she had left him.

"Give me thrust," Jackson said.

"I'm fixing the redline."

"You can do both."

"Like fuck I can."

"Calm down," Jackson said.

She wanted to speak to Jackson, too. This captain schtick of Jackson's wasn't cutting it anymore. To the untrained observer, sure, Jackson was a picture of professionalism, strapped up there with her shoulders bunched, her jawline jutting, that would make a really ter-rific clip, right there, but Talia knew the truth: that Jackson had been chosen for her public profile, and that was why all of them were here—not because they were good soldiers but because they made a good feed. They sold a good war. Even herself, for all she wanted to believe she was keeping this crew together in deft and clever ways; that wasn't a real skill. That wasn't what anyone really needed in a war. They were impostors, all of them, and they had gotten Gilly killed. She felt choked with failure.

The jet shuddered. Another impostor. If it was anything like its crew, they were in for a short ride. It jumped about like a skittish cat, avoiding debris, she guessed, which, according to the screens, was all around them, most of it small, some not so much, and plenty banging against them. The only reason they hadn't been torn to pieces was they were all moving along roughly the same vector, traveling away from where the ship had been. She caught a glimpse of some large part of the wreckage, a great broken chunk like a falling moon, then lost it.

The ship hadn't said good-bye, she realized. It had said hello, but never good-bye.

"Four of them now," Anders said. "Fuck!"

"We can lose them. Keep burning."

"If they don't box us in, which they fucking will!"

"Bank," Jackson said. "Bank!"

A force pressed her against the floor. She heard something detach from the jet: *clunk*. Anders yelped. The pressure increased. She could feel blood falling from her brain. She wasn't a drinker, but the times she indulged it wound up like this, her feeling the blackout coming and realizing she should have made different choices about half an hour ago. She wasn't terrific at anticipating the consequences of her own actions, if she was honest. A part of her would see disaster coming and embrace it. Why was that? Maybe she liked to have problems to fix. Maybe she was deluded. *One more drink. I'll be fine.*

She swung into the wall. That was a surprise: She was supposed to be in a harness. There was a lot of noise from she didn't know where and her hair was all up in her face. She pushed away from the wall with a free hand but it was difficult and slow, as if she were a child. She couldn't move her left arm at all and was momentarily confused before remembering the medbag. She looked at her free hand again. She wasn't supposed to have a free hand. She was supposed to be encased from head to toe in a protective blue inflatable.

Items were flying around. Containers and cables and, hello, a boot. And not only items she would expect to float if introduced to a gravity-free environment: items that shouldn't float under any circumstances, like shreds of plastic and carbon fiber and twisted-pair metal. Items that should be part of the jet. And they were moving toward her. When the jet kicked, they heaved together, left or right or up or down, then resumed drifting in her direction, like she was pulling them toward her on strings. She swung into the wall again. She was getting annoyed with that. The express purpose of her harness was to prevent her from banging into things, and it was sucking at it. She twisted to see what was going on behind her. She couldn't turn very far, but caught a glimpse of a flapping strap, the end torn, as if savaged by animals.

She looked forward again. Up front, Anders and Jackson remained safely ensconced in their harnesses, like sensible people. Jackson's black braid stood tall, pointing straight up. They were shouting: She could see the cords in their necks, although she couldn't hear their words. The screens were full of space and stars, all going around and around. One showed a jetpod spewing white gas. That jet looked pretty fucked, in Talia's estimation. Whoever was on that thing was definitely going to die.

She shook her head, trying to beat back the chemical fog. There was a noise behind her that felt familiar but she couldn't place it, couldn't see it, either, because she was trapped by the medbag, which was strapped into the harness. It was the harness itself that was moving in a way it wasn't supposed to, she figured out. She began to wriggle her shoulders. With one hand she worked the medbag down to roughly strapless gown level, creating the perfect outfit for Camp Zero tomfoolery, or, no, better, a hilarious feed clip, since she was always complaining to her followers about the uniform. They would die to see her like this. They would absolutely die. The next part was harder because the medbag gripped her torso, all the better to maintain positive pressure in the event of puncture wounds, an oft-overlooked feature of the modern medgown, and when she revealed her legs, the left was purple and swollen around the knee, coated in a thick yellow paste. She stared at it a moment, because it was pretty gross.

She blinked. Focus. She pushed the medbag free and gripped the straps. At last, she was able to twist around and see.

At the rear of the jet was a hole. Above it, vents blasted, fighting to equalize pressure, but also, she saw now, creating a cycle of air that pushed everything that was floating toward the breach. Her medbag flapped like a flag. *Here she is! You found her!* Since her station had been breached, she hadn't been able to forget the void, and how about this, it turned out the void hadn't forgotten her, either.

She grasped a handle and pulled herself away from the hole. She had been very superior about these handles before. She wanted to apologize for that. She gripped one and then the next and pulled herself toward Jackson and Anders. They didn't notice her approach. They didn't even know about the breach. They were flying the jet manually and the screens were terrifying. It abruptly occurred to her that her life was in their hands. That was an amazing concept. She would live or die because of Jackson and Anders. If she'd needed more evidence that somewhere along the way she had made some really poor life choices, here it was.

She got a hand on the back of Jackson's harness. *We're breached,* she shouted, but couldn't hear herself. She grabbed Jackson's braid and pulled.

Jackson jerked around. Her eyes roved over Talia. "What are you doing? Strap in!" Talia could barely hear her over the whirlwind of the equalization vents. She pointed to the rear of the jet but Jackson had already turned away. She shook Jackson's shoulder again. "Get off me!" Jackson said. "Anders, bank!"

"Shut up!" Anders shouted. A tone sounded, harsh and insistent. A screen flared:

GRAVITY WELL

Anders gave an anguished roar. He fought the board. The jet kicked. Talia almost lost her handhold. Jackson shouted, "Strap in! We're going down!"

Down? Talia wasn't familiar with the concept of *down.* That wasn't really a thing on board a jetpod with zero gravity. But a dull orange-purple curve passed across the left screen and was that a planet? It looked like a planet. Which would explain the *down.* But that couldn't be right. They couldn't land on a planet. She had been trained for every bullshit scenario she could imagine and some more besides, they had trained her in what to do if *the ship were overrun by mice,* but not how to survive ditching a jetpod on a planet. That was crazy.

The proximity tone rose in pitch and hysteria until it became an unbearable electric scream. "Get off me!" Jackson shouted, and began to pry Talia's fingers off her seat. Jackson wanted Talia to return to the rear harness. But that was not happening, if Talia could help it, because back there the universe's black lips were clamped to the jet and sucking the life from it. She would not go anywhere near that. She fought but Jackson was strong and Talia felt her fingers going. She seized a fistful of Jackson's hair.

There's a hole, she said.

Jackson didn't hear or didn't care. She seized Talia's wrist and applied pain to it. Talia lost her grip and tumbled backward, or downward, or rearward, whichever it was, slowly, like a daisy in the wind. Eventually she stopped herself on a buckled locker door that shouldn't even have been open and began to drag herself forward again. She was going to tell Jackson what she thought of her. This felt important. It was time to stop biting her tongue about the truth that Jackson was the worst person ever.

When she reached Jackson's harness, the screens were yammering with information. There was something else now. Orange, like the planet, and round, but small. A hive. As she watched, it began to spit little black dots. Salamanders. The jet seemed to be heading directly for them, which struck Talia as a bad move. She would definitely have gone in the other direction.

"Get in your harness!" Jackson screamed.

There were salamanders behind them, too. Now Talia saw the problem. Hostiles on all sides. She decided not to be harsh with Jackson. Jackson was dealing with a lot. She'd come up here to say something, though. Not only to speak harsh truths to Jackson. She blinked, trying to recall. Jackson's eyes went past her to the rear of the jet and widened. *Oh, yes,* Talia thought. *The breach. That was it.*

"Oh my God," Jackson said, and unbuckled. "You sit here."

That was fine. Talia climbed into the harness. With fat, numb sausage fingers, she pulled the straps around her. They felt amazing.

She closed her eyes for a moment. She was halfway into a lovely dream when a new tone rose and she opened her eyes to see what it meant. The screen read:

COLLISION AVOIDANCE DISABLED

She looked at Anders. They were still running straight at the hive. It seemed now like they were going to smash into it. *Anders,* she said. Anders got a lot of crazy ideas and she had the suspicion that this was another. She turned to check whether Jackson was seeing this but Jackson was plugging the breach with the medbag. Talia blinked. That was really clever.

"Hold on!" Anders shouted.

The hive ballooned on the screen. She remembered Anders lying in his own vomit, months before, looking up at her and saying, *I like the way your face is arranged.* So this was it. He had finally found a way to kill himself, in the most spectacularly pointless way possible. She began to unstrap but it seemed to take forever and while she struggled the hive rushed toward her, growing exponentially, eager to help Anders get what he wanted. She leaned out and grabbed his wrist. He knocked her away. By this time, the hive was filling the screen. Maybe he wouldn't hit it, she thought. He would just shoot by, close enough to lose their pursuers. Then he punched the board and the jet lurched into the hive.

Her ears filled with screaming metal. She was flung in one direction and then the other. Wind was everywhere, the growl opening into a throaty roar. They were breached in a dozen places. Her eyes streamed. But she saw white dots vanishing from the screens. They had struck the hive and it had torn them up but also created a thousand tiny pieces of deadly shrapnel to tear apart the salamanders.

He was trying to drag the jet around but there grew a terrible shaking. The planet had them, she realized. They had flown too close and the jet was doing its best but wasn't designed for this and the shaking was turbulence. Her brain rattled. A high whistling grew behind her, and she felt joy, because as terrifying as that sound was, it meant atmosphere. It meant she had escaped the void. She was falling toward an orange-and-purple planet at terrible speed, but the universe wouldn't eat her. She opened her mouth to scream or laugh or something. She didn't know. It was a good moment to do, well, anything. *Last drinks, ladies and gentlemen. Last drinks.* One more couldn't hurt. The jet's engines thundered, the wind screamed, and she fell, fell, fell.

10

[Jackson]

THE CREW

She hadn't been to Arlington since she was a cadet. In the meantime, it had doubled in size, sprouting offices and testing fields and blocky beige buildings. All thanks to war funding, she guessed. Her escort, a young CDO with soft blond hair and no facial expressions, reeled off building names as they sped by, two of which she recognized as belonging to officers from Fornina Sirius. If she'd died out there, maybe there would've been a Jolene Jackson wing. Or an annex. Maybe a squash court.

The car stopped. Her escort bounced out to be on hand as she exited. She was in full dress and a passing pair of privates stopped to salute, which she returned. The lobby was very corporate, very glass. Among an ocean of black tile rose a titanium sculpture of a Surplex mining drone. The staff sergeant on desk knew who she was before she could open her mouth. "Sir, the admiral will be with you a few moments, sir. I can take you to a room where you can wait."

She felt eyes on her as she crossed to the elevator. She felt different on base. Outside, in the real world, voyaging into the unknown and facing an unimaginable horror and surviving, that made her a hero.

Not here. On base, people knew, even if they didn't. They sensed something a little funky about a person who crawled back home, alive, leaving thousands of bodies behind. If she was feeling charitable, she would call it superstition, the belief of the military mind that when death brushed by a person, it left something behind, something contagious. More realistically, she would say they were smart enough to realize that the only way that many people died was if there had been a monumental screwup, and there was a good chance it was hers.

The Colossus room was eight floors up. She accepted a steaming coffee from the staff sergeant, who had taken over from her escort as silently and seamlessly as if one had morphed into the other, and lurked near a window that offered a view over bunkhouse roofs and wet fields. She could see cadets rolling around the track, running drills or looking for their car keys or whatever the hell they were doing.

She heard a door but didn't realize it was Admiral Nettle until he was standing beside her, gazing out at the cadets. He had a thick white mustache. That was new. "Think you could take them?" he said. "You set a track record here, as I recall."

She said, "That was a long time ago." She had once believed she could save the world by running track.

"Yes. When things were simpler. How's David?"

"Good."

"Did he come to Arlington with you?"

"No. He has work. And it's not really his thing." It wasn't really her thing anymore, either. She'd once thought places like this *were* Service: saluting in corridors, drills, meetings. That was what the military was all about. Now it all felt slightly junior high, like watching people play dress-up, worrying about things that didn't matter. Lately she had trouble believing that even a small portion of what happened here was helping.

"I visited him," Nettle said, "when it wasn't clear who had survived."

"I know you did. Thank you." There was a pause. "I know why I'm here."

Nettle's eyebrows rose.

"I know the press is important," she said. "The talks. The shows and clips. But I'm not good at it. I can't . . ." She searched for the word. "I don't know how to talk to those people. I can't give them sound bites and slogans."

"Jolene," Nettle said, "you're doing an excellent job *because* you find it difficult. People see you struggling and they empathize. You're not hiding any of that. You have an authenticity that can't be manufactured."

She was taken aback. "Then I don't know why I'm here."

"Well, it's not because we want to critique your media performance." Nettle gestured toward the door. "If you're ready?"

For what? She hadn't even known there was a *we* in his meeting. She'd assumed she was coming in for a one-on-one with Nettle. But when she entered the Colossus room, she saw no fewer than half a dozen uniforms clumped around a mahogany table, including a general, a chief of staff, and two majors. More stars in one place than since they'd awarded her the Medal of Valor on live broadcast. At one end of the room was a wall-sized screen, reading: INCIDENT REPORT / XID FS-000-013 / FORNINA SIRIUS.

She thought: *Ah, crap.*

Nettle guided her to a chair and took the seat beside her. She took a sip of water.

"That's one of my favorite pieces," Nettle said. He was gazing at a painting that occupied most of the opposite wall: a wide, featureless plain with a hint of far-off mountains. Near a corner was a dark figure with a stick or a spear. "Do you see the gazelle?"

She hadn't, until he mentioned it. In one corner was a tiny brown smudge.

"Persistence hunting," Nettle said. "Practiced by ancient tribes across Africa a million or so years ago. They were slower than their prey, but figured out that they could exploit their basic human advantage in stamina. We can endure, you see. Keep going for hours, days, until the prey ran itself to death. That's how we survived."

He was trying to put her at ease, because they were going to make her talk about Fornina Sirius, and she would be expected to do so calmly and rationally, as if reviewing a restaurant meal. One of the men with the general was a civilian in a light gray suit with a Surplex ID tag. She'd never interacted with him directly, but knew his name, Bogart, and his reports, which, when she untangled the words, said that she had killed everyone.

"Perhaps that's how we win the war," Nettle said. "By exploiting our innate advantage over the salamanders."

"Which is?"

"I don't know." He smiled. "Maybe it's still endurance."

The brass huddle across the table broke up. Officers and staff found their seats. She didn't know if they'd planned to sit on one side of the table, with her and Nettle on the other, but that was how it wound up. The general asked how her flight had been and how long she'd been in town and she did not allow her gaze to shift to the screen, where someone was dialing through Fornina Sirius layouts. "Now, why don't you take me through this?" he said finally, and turned to the screen. There it was. The deployment map, right before the end.

She took a breath. "We came out ten tees off course. We were supposed to be in empty space, but there was a high amount of debris. I had no information on how we got off course." But she knew now: The navigation software messed up. Everyone in this room knew that.

"Commodore Hrovat ordered the gunships to establish a standard defensive zone. We dispatched drones. There was a lot of rock to check through, but nothing tripped any alarms. Two hours later—"

"What did you do in the meantime?"

"Me, personally?"

"Yes."

"I communicated with Commodore Hrovat over comms. He expressed concern for the proximity of the troop carriers to the debris. There was a lot of rock floating about and it was difficult to track it all at once."

"That's all you spoke about?"

"We also spoke about our families. His kid shares a birthday with my husband. We were both hoping for a moment to send a message home."

The general nodded. "Carry on."

She would step through the Fornina Sirius engagement. She would tell them again which officer was where, who did what. But she didn't want to describe personal conversations, which forced her to remember them as people. "When Commodore Hrovat retired to rest, I assumed command. My priority was to establish where we were and how we'd ended up there. Until that was resolved, we couldn't reliably perform a hard skip. I was also called on to resolve some ship-to-ship logistics."

"What were they?"

"The *Graham* wanted to perform a personnel transfer to *Hancock*. They had a sick midcaptain."

"At what point did you review the drone report?"

"The drones were reporting continuously," she said. "There wasn't a single point in time where they finished."

"But your system automatically aggregated their data. Compiling a report for you, essentially."

"I reviewed those at regular intervals."

"How often, exactly?"

"I would say approximately every ten or fifteen minutes."

"And what did they say?"

She glanced at the screen. It was there, the same as she remembered. A lot of text, but the critical line was up top. It was even boxed.

THREAT LEVEL: UNDETERMINED

"They said that," she said.

"What was your reaction?"

"I understood it to mean that the drones hadn't finished their scans."

"I'm not asking what you thought they meant," the general said. "I'm asking what you did."

There it was. "Nothing," she said. "We were already on alert and there was no evidence of a specific threat. It wasn't uncommon for the system to take a little time before determining a threat level. So I continued with my duties. Every so often, I checked back on it to see if there had been any progress."

"By 'every so often,' you mean every ten or fifteen minutes."

"Approximately, yes. More frequently later."

"Why more frequently later?"

"Because it seemed like a long time," she said. "It shouldn't have taken that long."

"So, eventually, you realized something must be wrong."

"Yes."

"That the system should have returned a specific threat analysis, but hadn't."

"That's correct."

"What caused this realization?"

"It occurred to me that on previous occasions, when the system hadn't collected enough data to produce a threat level summary, it would leave that section blank. It would not say 'Undetermined.'" She did not describe how this felt: the crawling sensation that she'd missed something terrible.

There was silence. She took a sip of water.

"At this time, how long had you held command?"

"Two hours and eleven minutes."

"What did you do then?"

"I reopened the most recent report."

"You didn't issue any order."

"No."

"You didn't communicate your concern to anyone."

"No."

"Why not?"

"Because I didn't understand what 'Undetermined' meant. I hadn't seen a threat level coded that way before. Not even in the manual." She had looked it up afterward. It wasn't in the regular section, but rather tucked away in an appendix designed for technical use. There it said: UNDETERMINED: SYSTEM UNABLE TO PERFORM ANALYSIS DUE TO TECHNICAL FAULT. "I reviewed the drone reports in an attempt to figure this out."

"So you continued to read," the general said. "What did you see?"

"I opened the detailed drone commentary and reviewed the results of individual scans." The screen scrolled, replaying the text. "Spectrum analysis. Materials composition. Nothing looked out of the ordinary. Until . . ." The screen stopped. She didn't look at it. She didn't want to see this part ever again. "There was an object the drones had tagged as 'inert body.' It was huge. Bigger than all four carriers combined. Everything about it was wrong. Mass. Spin. Structure."

"This was the hive."

"Yes."

"Did you recognize it as such?"

"At that point, all human encounters dating back to *Coral Beach* had been with hostiles housed in relatively small structures. We didn't know they built on this scale."

"Then what did you think it was?"

"I thought it was a hive," she said.

"And what did you do?"

"I ordered a closer inspection."

"By the drones."

"Yes."

"Did you move the gunships?"

"No."

"The carriers?"

"No."

"Did you sound a general alert?"

"No," she said.

"Why not?"

"Because the system hadn't flagged it."

"It was a ten-kiloton unknown object within your safety zone."

"We'd had false alarms before, and it didn't seem possible that the computers could miss something like that."

The Surplex man, Bogart, shuffled in his seat. "If I can make a note," he said, leaning forward. "It's not correct to say the system 'missed' it. It was identified and categorized as 'undetermined' because that's actually what it was. As you said yourself just now, we'd never encountered an object like this before."

She liked his *we*. As if this man had been there. As if he would ever contemplate putting himself in the kind of personal danger that he expected of her, and everyone who had been with her, and everyone who would follow. "Not 'enemy,'" she said. "Not 'threat.' We had your AI system that was supposed to be able to detect enemies and mobilize a response before we even saw them. Except when a gigantic ball of 'undetermined' rolled up to our starboard, nothing happened."

"Which is incredibly regrettable, I'm sure everyone here would agree," Bogart said. "But I must make the point that the system was acting as designed. It wasn't asked to speculate. That's the domain of human officers. The system—"

"I saw it unfold." No one was asking her to continue, but she couldn't listen to another word from Bogart. She could keep herself in check for the media, arguably, but she couldn't hear him talk about *acting as designed* without laying it out for him what that meant. "I had visuals, so I saw everything. Salamanders peeling off it, thousands, in seconds. We were facing the wrong way. The gunships were guarding against an enemy in the distance, and it was already inside. My screen overloaded. There were too many hostiles to display. We weren't set up for an engagement at that scale. But I saw that we lost *Spirit of Phoenix* first. I know that was seven hundred and forty-nine lives. Then *Balance of Chicago*. Four hundred and seventy-one. Hrovat took command as *Retribution of Calgary* went down. Eight hundred and two." The screen was updating in response to her words, playing out the battle. "The gunships began to engage at this time. Hrovat's own ship, *Joy of New Orleans*, reported that she was breached, with hostiles on deck. We theorized that this would signal a shift in their pattern of attack, from exchanging fire at a distance to boarding and capture. But the enemy pursued both strategies at once and did not cease firing at any point. *New Orleans* was lost. Two hundred and eleven. At this stage, I became the highest-ranking surviving officer, although this was not communicated to me for several minutes, at which time I was leading a strafing run on the undetermined inert body. I observed that it continued to issue salamanders. By which I mean, it was spraying them like mist with no sign of stopping. We had lost all of the carriers and a third of the escort. I gave the order to retreat."

She forced herself to stop. The room was silent. The screen paused its replay. It was awash with red, four small white markers arrowing toward the left corner. She took a sip of water, her hand trembling.

"This kind of engagement must never happen again," Nettle said. "We can't allow them to get close. You've heard of the Providence program?"

She took a shaky breath. "It's a new class of battleship."

He nodded. "If we can get funding approval, it will win the war."

"The public was united before Fornina Sirius," said the general. "Afterward, they were burning flags. Now there's a pacifist leading the polls. We're smarter than our enemy and better resourced, but we will lose if we can't convince people they need to fight. The real war isn't out there. It's down here."

"The design is truly remarkable," Nettle said. "If they work like they're supposed to, a handful of Providences may enable us to achieve total military victory with zero casualties. What do you think?"

She said, "I think our plan was zero casualties, too."

"Indeed," said Nettle. "But, to speak bluntly, your fleet was constructed in peacetime. This is a new generation of war machine designed specifically to destroy this enemy." He turned to Bogart. "Would you like to present the software?"

Bogart cleared his throat. The main screen flipped to a diagram. "I work in Surplex Machine Intelligence, liaising with Service Strategic Command for—"

"I know who you are," she said.

He nodded. "There were, obviously, serious performance shortfalls at Fornina Sirius, not only during the encounter itself but also at various stages leading up to it. Immediately afterward, Service and Surplex launched a number of inquiries into, one, establishing how these defects were able to occur, and two, recommending strategies for avoiding a repeat in the next generation of military hardware."

"Take it out."

Bogart's eyebrows rose. "Ah . . ."

"It doesn't work," she said. "Remove it. That's my recommendation."

"With respect," Bogart said, "it's not practical to, as you say, 'take it out.' Software is integral to the military. It's in every vehicle, vessel, and practically every piece of equipment. There's no question that it will be present. The question is how much executive authority it should wield."

She turned to Nettle. "Is this why I'm here? You know my opinion. Keep software out of command. I'd rather have nothing than have a computer I can't trust."

"That's not why you're here," Nettle said.

"Now, we actually agree on this," said Bogart, shuffling forward. "Because, and perhaps this will surprise you, we at Surplex find your actions at Fornina Sirius to be fairly reasonable, under the circumstances. But we also think our software was reasonable. In our opinion, what created a catastrophic failure was not software, or human command—"

"*Not* software?"

"—but the communication between the two."

She jabbed a finger toward the screen. "Were you watching? Did you see the computers let that hive breeze up to our front door?"

"It was correctly categorized as an unknown object. The fact that no officer ordered a closer investigation—"

"Not one alarm. Not so much as a red light."

"—is attributable to inadequate shared understanding between the human and artificial components of command."

"You've got to be kidding me," she said.

"Our conclusion," said Bogart carefully, "which I believe is shared by Service, was that Providence-class battleships should be commanded by machine intelligence, free from human input."

There was silence. "Well," she said. "That's a terrible idea."

"It's not an idea," Nettle said. "It's happening."

"If you'd like to review our simulations," Bogart said, "you'll see that software outperforms human decision-making in practically all areas by orders of magnitude. It's not even close."

"Simulations," she said. "Computers grading themselves."

"Your reservations are understandable," Nettle said. "You have more reason than anyone to be cynical about AI running command of a Providence. That's why we'd like you to captain one."

A laugh popped out of her. Just a short bark, but inexcusable, given the company. She searched for composure, but the absurdity of the question was so great that she couldn't figure out how to address it directly. "If software runs the ship, what do you need a captain for?"

"The real war," Nettle said.

She felt air leaving her body in a slow, tired way. Of course. Of course.

"You've done a bang-up job speaking around the country," Nettle said. "People admire you. They trust you. The message it would send if you captained a Providence . . ."

"No," she said. "Please."

"It would be a tremendous vote of confidence. Not just in this program, but the entire direction of the war. It would tell people that the sacrifices they're making to fund the fleet are worth it."

"I'm sorry. I can't."

"The AI is sound," said Bogart. His tone was apologetic, but she couldn't look at him. "It's advanced a great deal in the three years since you shipped out to Fornina Sirius. And this isn't just a Surplex innovation. There's machine intelligence driving decision-making at all levels in most major corporations these days, with incredibly positive results. The political parties are using it to drive candidate selection and platform generation. I don't want to sound glib, but by the time you come home, it may be running the country."

She stared at him.

"It can fly your ship," Bogart said. "It can do that better than you can."

She kept her mouth shut. Nothing that would come out now would do her any good.

"You know what?" Nettle said. He seemed unperturbed by her reaction. "Let it roll around in your mind. We don't require a decision today. Take a week. A month."

A year. A lifetime. There was nothing that could put her in one of those ships.

"You may change your mind when you meet the crew," Nettle said.

It was a bundle of hangars and habitats forty miles north of Anchorage, where they could shoot birds over the pole without blowing out anyone's windows. There were nine hundred candidates, drawn from every branch of Service and corporate fast-tracks, vying for twenty-four crew slots. As the shuttle dipped toward the snowfields, the polite young flight lieutenant who was accompanying her leaned across and pointed out landmarks. There weren't many. She spotted a squad in the snow, struggling through drifts.

"Including officers and support staff, the permanent base population is about five hundred," he said. "Not counting visitors."

"Why is it named Camp Zero?" she said.

"Because this is where it starts. Where we win the war." She looked at him, but he was completely serious.

She spent a week lurking at the rear of classes and watching field training through binocs. On her second day, she was called to deliver a speech on an actual stage in a hangar. She gazed out at a sea of bright young faces and did what she'd done ever since she'd returned from Fornina Sirius: spoke of the nobility of Service, the depravity of the enemy, and the confidence she possessed that the awesomeness of the human spirit plus a Providence-class battleship would give birth to victory so splendid, it would inspire a thousand songs.

Nettle called her on the flight home. "Well?" he said.

"They're children." The flight lieutenant was sitting across from her, his expression neutral, his eyes on the wall. "Do they even know that a Providence doesn't need a crew?"

"We don't emphasize it."

"They think this is for the best. That's why they're here. Not because they want to fight. To further their careers."

"And?"

"I saw a round table on what they wanted to get out of the mission," she said. "What *they* wanted."

"It's the younger generation. They're less motivated by patriotism and duty. It doesn't make them bad soldiers."

"It doesn't make them good ones."

"I'm not letting this go, Jolene," Nettle said. "I'll ask you to visit again, in time."

She shook her head. She was more convinced than ever that the Providence program was a colossal mistake. It made her wonder whether they could win.

"But not for a while," Nettle said. "Say hello to David."

She caught a shuttle from Arlington to New York, arriving late. David was asleep, so she extracted herself from her uniform and crawled beneath the sheets and snaked her arms around him. He was the world's heaviest sleeper, but she knew he would get there. Finally his eyes cracked open. "Hey."

"Hi."

"How were they?"

"Young."

"Mmm," he said. "We were, once."

"Not like that."

He was silent awhile. "So you're not going out?"

"No," she said. "Of course not."

"Good." He kissed her hair.

David was very patient, which she hoped one day to deserve. She felt like she had tricked him. Pulled a bait-and-switch. They would be strolling together, or eating dinner, and she would drift into a universe of shredded polymer, where salamanders unpeeled from nowhere and everyone began to die, and she wouldn't even realize until she saw his face. It had been six years and she was still clawing her way through therapy and Service-approved medication toward the person she used to be, the young, happy, ambitious bride David had married, before Fornina Sirius crawled into her head and turned her into this.

Nettle sent her back to Camp Zero three months later. Then three months after that. Then six months later again. By then, the first Providence, *Fire of Montana*, was almost complete, a bright star in the early evening sky. It had a named crew. She watched their interviews and felt not the tiniest mote of regret.

"Who's picking these people?" she asked Nettle on their next call. She had been surprised by at least two of the selections, whom she knew from Camp Zero.

"AI."

She had suspected. "So now you're letting software choose the crew on your new ships that will be run by software?"

"Yes," said Nettle.

"Boy," she said.

She heard the shrug in his voice. "Welcome to the future. It works."

"But you don't know *how* it works." She didn't even want to learn about the AI; it only made her more angry. But she couldn't stop herself from picking at it like a scab. "It's made from computers writing software no one can understand."

"But it works."

"Boy," she said again.

The candidates did grow on her. She became somewhat inured to their ignorance, their self-centeredness, their wildly optimistic worldviews. There was even something charming about their irrepressibility, how they would run three miles through snow with a ninety-pound pack and no hesitation. She watched a class of Intel candidates perform a Task To Completion Under Stress, where NCOs roamed around screaming at candidates attempting math puzzles. "You ugly piece of dog shit!" one yelled at a girl in the front row. "I hope you're smart, because your face makes me want to puke!" Most candidates exhibited defensive reactions of one kind or another, revealing the extent of their distraction, but there was a young man at the back who seemed genuinely oblivious and only registered the torrent of abuse with a small jump in his eyebrows when he'd finished the task, like he'd forgotten that was going on.

"Isiah Gilligan," an NCO told her when she inquired. "Surplex civvy. He's provisionally scheduled for Providence launch five."

She told David about her experience in a New York diner, slurping noodles, thinking he'd find it amusing. Instead, he grimaced. "Ugh. That sounds horrible."

"What does?"

"The test. It's cruel."

She said nothing.

"Did I say something wrong?"

"We shouldn't hurt their feelings?" she said. "Before we send them to war? Is that what you think?"

He eyed her. "All right."

She dumped her fork and walked out. She was choked with a ridiculous seething rage and didn't even know where it was directed. What David had said—that complacency and ignorance was everywhere. Sometimes even in her: She would watch a report about *Fire of Montana* sweeping away salamanders and just for a moment it would feel like an interesting show, a series she could tune in to and then forget, that was happening far away, to other people. She walked down Third Avenue with her hands stuffed into her pockets against the cold, passing bright stores and bubbles of conversation, and salamanders were pouring down from the sky, falling like a plague of stars that no one else could see. She felt disassociated from the human race. She felt like she'd never left Fornina Sirius, a trillion miles away. Like the most important part of her was still out there, with her fallen brothers and sisters, who'd seen the enemy and learned its horror. She felt like she might never make it home.

Out of curiosity, she looked up the rest of the crew of Providence Five. The Weapons candidate, Paul Anders, she didn't know. The Life candidate, though, was Talia Beanfield, whom she'd seen struggle toward the finish of a grueling pack run, then return to help those behind. Afterward, Beanfield had sat with a cadet who'd recorded a disqualifying time, genuine grief written across her features. She would make a good Life officer, Jolene thought. For a few days, she began to feel that Nettle's suggestion might not be completely preposterous; maybe there was a set of circumstances in which she would consider going back out. The idea was curiously exhilarating. David picked up on her good mood and, on the spur of the moment, suggested they go away. They rented a cabin in western Massachusetts where they woke to bird calls and explored red gums and pulled wicker chairs together on a porch to watch the sunset and talk about small things that didn't matter. In the mornings, he made eggs. It was the closest she'd felt to him since she left. She hadn't given herself the choice, she realized. She had felt, on some level, compelled to stay and heal and become a good wife, but she couldn't do that unless it was truly voluntary. Only by walking to the edge of leaving her life with David could she discover that she didn't want to.

"You're happy," he said, on the return trip.

"Yes," she said. "I made a decision."

"A good one?"

She nodded, and he smiled and didn't press, as always. She would like to have a baby with this man, she thought. It had been one of their plans and then she had gone away and they'd not discussed it since. She would like to discuss it.

She had to leave for Camp Zero the next day, and daydreamed as the aircraft skipped over snow and ice. She'd never felt a part of this place but was now an outright fraud, returning empty salutes, mouthing meaningless ranks. She passed three days in reviews and meetings, her mind already on the shuttle home. And then in line at the mess hall there was shouting and flying trays and two men throwing punches. The shorter of the two gained ascendancy and drove the taller man to the floor, then fell on him to continue the assault before being dragged away by others.

"Who is that?" she asked a neat, clipped Life candidate in line behind her. Because that was not cool, carrying on the fight after he'd already won. That was no way for a candidate to behave.

The girl's pencil-thin eyebrows rose. "That's Paul Anders, sir." Her tone implied surprise that Jolene didn't already know. As it happened, she recognized the name: Anders was the Providence Five Weapons Officer. That night, out of curiosity, she pulled the tape from his postincident interview, the vision following her around her quarters as she brushed her teeth. An unimpressed NCO asked Anders to explain why, exactly, he'd felt the need to assault a fellow candidate, and why he shouldn't be discharged on the spot. Anders's answers were spectacularly unimpressive, and Jolene wondered again about the AI that selected these crews. How bizarre did its choices need to be before people stopped ascribing them to advanced intelligence and realized it was simply broken? she wondered.

"Your brothers gave their lives at Fornina Sirius," said the NCO, and she stopped, because she hadn't known that. "How do you think they'd feel about your conduct today?"

"I reckon they'd understand," Anders said. His demeanor was cocky, as if he didn't realize how much trouble he was in, or didn't care.

"I disagree," said the NCO.

"Well, let me tell you something about my brothers," Anders said, and leaned across the table. "They taught me that when you get hurt, the only way to make it stop is to go find whoever gave it to you and give it back."

She stared at him in dismay. His words were a knife in her heart. Just like that, she knew. She was going back out. And she was taking Paul Anders with her.

11

[Anders]

THE SURFACE

He coughed. Around him, the jetpod was battered and deformed and on fire. Someone had him by the shoulders. He jerked and twisted but it was only the harness.

Beanfield lolled beside him, half-naked and caked with soot. She looked dead. He turned away. Flames crackled. His sense of direction was wrong. He was looking into the nose of the jet, which was filling with thick curls of winding black smoke, but it felt like up, not forward. Down was behind and a metric fuckton of gravity was trying to usher him in that direction. They had ditched, then. He hoped he hadn't killed Beanfield. He looked at her. "Beanfield," he said. She didn't respond.

He wrestled free of his harness to look for Jackson. Below was a blanket of smoke and crackling fire. Beneath that was a sound: *gloop, gloop.* He didn't know what that meant. But it wasn't good. He considered moving Beanfield, but it was probably safest to stay above the smoke. That was a strange thing about the smoke: It wasn't rising. It was low smoke. He eyed it. Jackson had gone to the rear, to that exact area. He hadn't seen her since they'd sideswiped a hive and tumbled through atmosphere. That had opened up a lot of holes in the jet. There was a good chance Jackson had exited mid-descent.

He felt Beanfield's neck for a pulse. He squeezed her chin and shook her head back and forth until she groaned. Her eyelids fluttered. So she wasn't dead. That was good.

The smoke was closer. It was rising, eating away at the room he had. The back end of the jet was badly breached, he figured; possibly the whole fucking thing was gone altogether. They were holed and sinking. That was the *gloop, gloop* sound: liquid coming in.

He felt for the lightning gun but couldn't find it. He didn't know why he might need a gun, but he wanted it badly and groped around near where he'd stowed it. When his fingers closed on its grip, everything immediately felt better. He hauled it out and slung its strap over his shoulder. He began to extract Beanfield from the harness, but she weighed a ton and he struggled for leverage. Smoke blurred his eyes. The gun on his back clunked against something: his survival core. He'd long lived in fear of that fucking thing deploying with no warning, springing wet plastic around him, trapping his face, but he would need it now, if he was going to jump into that mess of flame and liquid and survive. Then he looked at Beanfield. She didn't have a survival core. He'd left hers in Medical, on the ship.

"Beanfield?" he said. "We've got a problem."

He was unstrapping his own core when the smoke below heaved and something came out of it. It was Jackson, her head bulbous, her body glistening. She was encased in a thin suit with a boxy little helmet: Her core had deployed.

She pulled herself toward him one rung at a time, fighting the gravity. "What are you doing?" she said. "Put your core back on."

"Where did you come from?"

She yanked open a locker and pulled an EV suit from it. Anders had forgotten that the jet contained stuff. Jackson had been scavenging: She already had a matter converter strapped to her back and supply belts at her waist. When she reached him, she flopped the EV suit onto a harness. "We're sinking fast. Can you take Beanfield?"

He nodded.

"I'll be right behind you. But the liquid's dense. If we get separated, find each other on ping."

He began to feed Beanfield into the EV suit, dressing her for the second time that day. By the time he'd finished, water was lapping at the harness's lower straps. Or not water: a thick black liquid that smelled like death. He fixed the EV helmet onto Beanfield's head and peered at her face. He was a little jealous of her right now. Not only did she get the good suit, the one with the bigger helmet, but she got to do this unconscious. He heaved her out of the harness. He eyed the roiling blackness below. *Dense liquid,* Jackson had said. It was going to squeeze him like a bitch.

"Go," Jackson said.

Anders had been written up twice for untidy quarters in his first month at Camp Zero, which meant that during a room inspection, a floor sergeant with nothing better to do had discovered a crease in Anders's bedsheet, which existed because another floor sergeant had called an assembly drill at four in the morning. Service, Anders had quickly figured out, was a bunch of assholes who claimed to be family but acted like they hated you. And that was okay; that was actually very true to his own family experience. But he'd joined for the opportunity to hold the whip handle for a change, not realizing how much whipping he would have to undergo himself first. He was thinking of quitting and this untidy-quarters bullshit felt like it might be the final straw. Because no one else was being written up: They'd all figured out they should sleep *beneath* their beds, leaving the sheet undisturbed, in a tight little space you could create under there by pulling out the storage tubs. Anders did not do this, because that small, dark place was far too much like a toolbox. But faced with crashing out of Service, he realized he wanted to stay. Even with the bullshit, there was nothing better for him out there, just a father he didn't visit anymore, a string of mistakes, and three gravesites, the most recent, barely a year old, being the one into which Eddie had put himself. So Anders made himself crawl under the bunk. The funny part was how there was a kind of comfort in its familiarity. It was bad, but in a way he recognized. It was the closest he'd felt to his brothers for a while.

The point of all this was that you could do anything. You could suck it up and do the worst thing you could imagine, if you had to. He nodded to Jackson. He dropped the lightning gun and the smoke swallowed it silently. He heaved Beanfield after it. This time there was a sound of wet acceptance. He jumped.

There were layers. At first he swam through muck, thrashing his legs and pulling with one arm, tugging Beanfield. Then they came to a place of clear amber light full of tiny bubbles. It was harder to swim, the liquid offering him less purchase with which to fight the gravity. His mind volunteered a terrible idea: At a certain point, he would reach a place of equilibrium, where he couldn't rise any farther, not unless he let go of Beanfield. He decided that wasn't going to happen. He swam. Eventually he broke some kind of surface and droplets began to spatter his faceplate.

He swung his head left and right. The light on his helmet illuminated only a few yards, and even that barely at all, but there were thick, undulating waves, which were furry. The water had hairs on it. He waited until he'd developed a sense of the direction of the waves and then began to swim. He could barely move his arms. But there was a current and he went with it.

At some point, his hand scraped rock. He couldn't feel his arms, but he dragged Beanfield up the shore and fell onto his back. The gravity was terrible. He was beginning to understand how unrelenting it was. It would be everywhere forever. It hurt to breathe.

"We made it, Beanfield," he said.

That might turn out not to be exactly right. But it was true for now. Before his body could surrender, he fought to his feet and pulled Beanfield from the water, dragging her until they reached a hollow, something like a cave. Then he slept.

He woke to something scrabbling on his faceplate, trying to get into his helmet. "The fuck!" he said, but it was only his own hand, his fingers digging at the plastic. For a second he was too disoriented to recall which was the bad one: removing the helmet, or leaving it on. When he remembered, he jammed his hands under his armpits to keep them still.

Beanfield's EV suit was dusted light orange, the same color as the rock. The sky was a dark soup of boiling orange-purple clouds. It looked like the most furious storm he'd ever seen, but it was silent, with no rain.

He crawled out from the shallow cave. In all directions lay cracked orange rock. No vegetation. No sand on the beach. Only thick black water, bulging and withdrawing without sound. His breathing was loud in his own ears. *How toxic is this air?* he wondered. Pretty toxic, probably. He still wanted to take off the helmet.

"Jackson," he said.

"Anders," she said in his ear. "Are you out in the open?"

"Yes."

"Hide."

He looked around. Nothing moving as far as he could see. Nothing at all but rock and black water and bruised sky.

"You still have the gun?" she asked.

"Yes."

"Good."

He hunched in the cave with Beanfield. Occasionally their suits exhaled waste like the gasps of drowning children. Whenever he moved, his suit fabric crunched and crinkled; as he sat against the rock, his survival core dug into his back. He hated it even though it was keeping him alive; even though it was sucking in whatever toxic mix of gases passed for atmosphere on this planet and making it breathable, as well as regulating his temperature and monitoring his vitals via an array of tiny pins he couldn't feel. Once he became dehydrated or malnourished, one of those pins would become significantly more feelable, opening up a line that could feed him intravenously. He'd spent thirty-six hours in one of these suits during a training exercise, and when they let'd him out and asked him how it was, he'd said, "It sucked." The supply officer said, "Better than the alternative, though."

Yeah. That was right. "Better than the alternative," he told Beanfield. Beanfield didn't respond. He checked Jackson's location on ping, which was about all his film was good for now. She was a white dot surrounded by emptiness, as if she were moving through space, with none of the usual complementary information the ship provided. He felt a pang at that, a weird twisting in his guts. The ship had been a prison for two years but he missed it, too.

Thirty minutes later, Jackson clambered into the cave, her suit and helmet dusted orange. "Stop pinging me," she said. She forced her way alongside Beanfield, who squashed against him. "It uses power."

He'd been thinking about that. "You still have a matter converter?"

She nodded and unslung the metal box from her shoulder. His understanding was that you could feed just about anything into a matter converter and it would accumulate juice, which could be used to charge their suits and the lightning gun. "How's Beanfield?"

"Hasn't woken up yet."

Jackson peered into Beanfield's faceplate. "The rock is inert. Same with the ocean. The atmosphere contains oxygen but also sulfur trioxide. The whole place is chemically depleted. Like they stripped it."

"Who? Salamanders?"

She nodded. "I've seen fliers. Not many, but we have to keep out of sight."

"They followed us down?"

"I think they got here first. This could be what a planet looks like once they're done with it."

He rubbed his thumb along the gun. "Any solar?"

"Not enough."

"Maybe the clouds will clear."

"Yeah," she said. "Maybe. How much charge on that?"

"It switches between zero and one." He shook it. The readout flipped. "Right now, one."

"If we want our cores to keep running longer than a few days, we need to find something to feed to the converter."

He nodded. There was silence. He went ahead and said it. "Any chance of a rescue?"

She said nothing. He couldn't see her face clearly.

"If there's not," he said, "just tell me."

"There's not."

He felt surprised, even though he didn't know what else she might have said. He shifted on the rock, his suit tugging against his skin. "So, what? We're going to die here?"

"Well," said Jackson. "Not today."

"Shit," he said. He couldn't think of anything else to say. "Shit."

Jackson wriggled, trying to get comfortable. "You know what I've been thinking? How they kept at us until they got us. They shouldn't have been able to take us down, but they found a way. Maybe we can do that."

He thought about this. "Yeah, but millions of them died."

Jackson was silent. Then she snickered. "True."

"I mean, we really annihilated them." His suit was sticking to his arm, and he plucked at it with plastic fingers. He thought he knew what Jackson meant, though. Even when it seemed hopeless, there could be a way out. If you kept fighting, sooner or later you could break open the lock. He said, "I'm sorry about Gilly."

"Yeah," Jackson said. "Me too."

They watched Beanfield awhile.

"Can you carry her?" Jackson asked.

"I think so."

"Then let's move," she said, "and see what we've got here."

Orange rock extended to a hazy horizon, flat and featureless but cracked with fissures, gullies through which they could pick their way to avoid detection. Anders carried Beanfield on his shoulders; she felt as if she were made of stone, so that every step in the high gravity wanted to break his ankle. He had to move slowly and stop often, and when he did, Jackson climbed the side of the gully and eased her head over the lip, slowly, as if a salamander might be crouching there. He watched this with sweat trickling down into places he couldn't reach. He wondered how much power he was burning through, working so hard physically; how many hours he was shaving off his life expectancy.

Jackson slid down the rock on her ass, using her feet to brake, exhibiting what Anders felt was a pretty impressive mastery of the conditions. "Anything?"

"Rock," she said. "Lots of rock."

They moved on. The next time Jackson climbed the rock, she stayed there for a long time. Eventually, he called, "What are you looking at?"

"Salamanders. Far off. Half a dozen."

"Do we need to move?"

"Not yet." There was silence. "They're all heading in the same direction."

"So we go the other way?"

Jackson came sliding down, boots first. "Or we head them off."

"Why would we do that?"

"There's nothing out here that's rich enough for the matter converter," she said, "except them."

"Oh, damn," he said. "Yes. Yes."

"We have one shot. If we make it count, we can feed the converter. Recharge the suits, charge the gun."

"It's more like half a shot." He pulled the gun around in front of him and peered at its display. He shook it until the gauge flipped to one.

"I'll keep my eyes open for an alternative," Jackson said, "but let's angle in their direction. Work for you?"

It did. It did work for him. It was amazing how much better he felt now that he might get to shoot something. He crouched and scooped up Beanfield and she seemed lighter than before. "I sure don't want to die with a charge left on the gun."

"Me neither," said Jackson.

They pushed on beneath a bubbling stew of purple and orange cloud. The storm still hadn't broken and he was beginning to think it never would. *What a piece of crap world,* he thought. Orange rock and ugly cloud and water that had hairs.

They spied a small hill that was utterly featureless but still the most interesting thing he'd seen that day. Jackson studied it with intensity. Reaching it would have meant crossing a lot of open ground, so they decided to move on. They couldn't keep pace with the salamanders Jackson had spotted, they discovered, so they began to angle farther inland, hoping to cross paths with others coming from the same direction. When the light began to die, they found a flat space beneath a rocky outcrop. He set Beanfield down and her eyes opened.

"Hey," he said. He gestured to Jackson. They helped Beanfield into a sitting position, because upright was better. When Anders had lain down earlier, he had felt like his brain was trying to drain out through his eye sockets. "Can you talk?"

"I feel sick," Beanfield said.

"You were banged up pretty bad. I don't know how much the med-bag was able to do."

"Try not to vomit inside your suit," Jackson said.

Beanfield looked at her.

He bent Beanfield forward and checked her suit over. When he levered her back, she said, "What happened?"

"We lost Gilly," Jackson said. "And the ship." Beanfield didn't react, so Anders suspected she had been conscious for a while and reached this conclusion on her own. "We're stuck with no resources and no chance of rescue."

Beanfield nodded and looked away.

"But we're not dead yet," Jackson said.

Beanfield didn't turn. "Yes, we are," she said softly.

He glanced at Jackson. But Jackson shook her head. Things were pretty grim if Jackson was allowing that kind of bullshit to stand, he figured. He exhaled. "Well, I'm turning in," he said. "Wake me if anything interesting happens."

Beanfield cried out in the night and he woke in confusion. The gun was in his arms and there was a yellow flicker ahead and dark movement like the curve of a salamander's head. He swung the lightning gun up and Jackson heaved herself on top of him. "It's a storm," she said. "It's nothing." He realized she was right. The cloud was boiling, silent lightning flicking around its edges. He had been about to waste the only hope they had.

"Okay," he said. "I'm okay." Jackson released him. He hunkered back down. He put the gun on the rock beside him and then shifted it a little farther away. Then he brought it closer again. He closed his eyes but didn't sleep.

They rose at first light. During the night, Anders's survival core had apparently opened up a line to feed him, and every step he felt something rubbing against the back of his ribs. He wondered how much it would feed him. He was pretty hungry.

Beanfield moved slowly, needing assistance and unable to put weight on her ankle. Despite this, they made good progress, and the fissures were numerous enough to allow them to choose their direction more often than not. After half a day of this, Jackson slid down from a wall and announced that they were within range of two salamanders.

"All right," said Anders, hefting the gun.

Jackson shook her head. "We can't take two. We need one by itself."

He supposed this was true. Beanfield said, "What if we can't find one by itself?"

"Then things will get exciting," Jackson said. They moved on.

On the third day, a smudge appeared on the horizon. It was indistinct but put Anders in mind of a volcano: a single sharp mountain, surrounded by flatlands. He lay against the rocky lip of the wall alongside Jackson and squinted at it.

"Most of them are moving away from it," Jackson said. "Just about all the salamanders we've seen are headed the other way."

"Maybe we should keep our distance, too."

"Mmm," said Jackson. "But it may contain something we can feed to the converter."

He nodded. They moved on. The fissures became larger, which made travel easier, and Beanfield was able to hobble along by his side. When they needed to rest, Jackson would scout ahead a short distance while Anders and Beanfield waited. During one of these periods, Beanfield said, "Did it say anything?"

"What?" he said.

"The ship. Before it died."

"Did it say anything?" She nodded. "What would it say, Beanfield?"

"I don't know."

He was silent.

"It said hello when we boarded," she said. "I thought it might say good-bye."

"No," he said.

Beanfield was silent, then: "Why are we walking?"

"To find something to feed the matter converter. So we can charge the suits." He was sure she knew this.

"Then what?"

"Then we do it again," he said, "for as long as we can." She didn't respond. "Hey," he said. "It's better than the alternative." Jackson reappeared at the far end of the fissure. He waved and wearily rose to his feet. Beanfield did not. "Come on, Beanfield."

She stood, took a hitching step, and began to cry. He offered her his hand, not knowing what else to say. She took it. "Talk to me," she said.

"About what?"

"I don't care. I just need to hear your voice."

He tried to think. Most of his thoughts were about food.

"Tell me why you enlisted."

"Aw," he said. "Who knows."

"You would have been about nineteen for *Coral Beach*. That's when a lot of people signed up."

He shook his head. "Not me. I didn't give a shit."

He remembered the moment, though. He'd been downtown, lounging with a friend, the sun on his face, doing nothing but watching human traffic pass by. And then it slowed. A few people at first, like they'd remembered something they had to do, then more, until the sidewalks stood still and mute. He saw a man reach out to a woman threading her way between them and touch her arm, and she stopped, too. *Paul,* said his friend. She was looking at her phone; there was a video.

"Your brothers?" Beanfield asked.

He clambered over rock. "Yeah. Two of them, anyway. Eddie tried, but didn't pass the physical." Eddie was already pretty far gone into drugs and alcohol. It was hard for him; he got frustrated in social settings, when he couldn't keep up with the conversation. He had trouble making himself understood. Each year since Anders had hit him with the wrench, Eddie had disappeared a little further into himself.

"Tell me about that, then," Beanfield said. "What it was like when they were in Service and you weren't."

"It wasn't like anything. I was just a kid, partying. Wasting my life." The world had gone insane, all at once. All anyone wanted to talk about were the aliens. And everyone had a different opinion, even then: The aliens were coming to kill us, or were harmless animals, or God's final plague. There were vigils for *Coral Beach* as well as rallies and protests about the military response, the hasty convening of several branches of the armed forces as well as a host of government agencies into a single, all-powerful Service, and you couldn't escape it. Anders was tending bar at the time, and every night the place heaved with hope and fear. People were having sex in the bathroom stalls, getting married, quitting their jobs. It was crazy, because the aliens were so far away, and no one knew anything.

Service sent out drones, a lot of them. Over the next eighteen months, they found aliens in five places, including two that had been mapped before. Which meant they were expanding. By then the term *salamander* had stuck, even though it became a political thing, with people saying the term was demeaning, or derogatory, or something. He dropped it once to a girl he'd brought back to his crappy apartment and she got steamed and told him they weren't animals, they were an intelligent species. *We're being taught to want to kill them,* she said. *Like a cult.* This was a thing, this theory that everyone was being manipulated by Service, or by the companies that supplied them, the military contractors like Surplex and Freco, into sucking the government dry in order to finance war spending. Anders even marched in an antiwar rally—not because he believed in it; he was trying to sleep with a girl. She was a pacifist and when she talked, her cheeks flushed and her jaw stood out. He carried one of her placards, which read, THE UNIVERSE IS BIG ENOUGH TO SHARE, and walked beside her, chanting *No war* and *Sonata Six, what do they know,* which was a reference to a conspiracy theory that some people had discovered evidence of Service doctoring videos before getting themselves arrested. When Anders arrived at the monument, he listened to a bunch of coat-wearing college students shout about corruption and convenient enemies and how in the age of media manipulation, democracy had become a sham.

His brothers returned home for Thanksgiving, just before shipping out. It meant Anders had to go home, too, which he'd sworn he would never do. But it was either that or miss them, and everyone put on their best face and the game was a good distraction. Toward the end, their father put a hand on his brothers' shoulders and said, "These are good boys. The bravest boys," and Anders had found that impressive, how they didn't flinch at all when their father touched them. They had gotten out, he realized. They'd found an exit. He shook their hands but they didn't hug, of course, and he watched them drive away with a mix of emotions he couldn't untangle. He wasn't sure if he was glad they were going or wanted to join them.

They died two years later, in the worst defeat of the war, when salamanders appeared out of nowhere and tore apart a military convoy outside of Fornina Sirius. They were in sleep. Almost everyone on board was. He was told what had happened by two uniformed Service personnel who knocked on his door early one morning, but he didn't feel anything until he saw the video: the hives spewing salamanders, the ships turning to gouting flame and debris and death. Only then did his feelings resolve into a hot flare of loss. He'd both loved and hated his brothers and their absence hollowed him out.

"After Fornina Sirius, then," Beanfield said. "That's what changed your mind?"

He exhaled. "Pretty much. Do you remember what it was like about a month after that?"

"What was it like?"

"Like everyone got used to it. They still talked about it. But not like it was a tragedy. It was . . ." He couldn't find the word. "It was something people used when they wanted to make a point."

He especially couldn't stand the pacifists anymore. What they rallied against, what he'd marched against, once—the profiteering, the secrecy, the hints and whispers of war under false pretenses—even if they were right, it didn't matter. It was irrelevant against the fact that there were salamanders out there killing people. He sat drinking beer at a party while a guy told them how much money Surplex made from every ship, how they had a secret plan to put their own AI inside them, how they were so deep inside Service that you couldn't tell the difference anymore, and Anders imagined him on a transport, the alarms going off, the salamander *huk*s falling. His eyes going wide. No longer so idealistic as the hull peeled open and sucked him into nothingness. But Anders didn't have the words to explain this, or anything that was happening inside him. He put down his beer and left the party and the next day he enlisted.

"Yeah," he said. "I didn't like that."

Every time Jackson spotted salamanders, there were at least two. Eventually Anders wriggled up the side of a fissure and lay beside her on a sloping slab of rock to check for himself. The fractured orange landscape ran flat and barren and across its dinner-plate surface crawled two fuzzy black dots. After a minute, one disappeared. "There you go," he said.

"They go into the fissures," Jackson said. "Just wait." The dot reappeared. Then two more.

"Shit," he said.

"Yeah. We need to be careful."

"They're heading away from the volcano." The mountain, or whatever it was, still hung in the distance, hazy and inscrutable, refusing to draw closer no matter how much ground they covered. "Maybe they know something about it that we don't."

Jackson was silent for so long, he began to get the feeling she knew something about it that he didn't, too. Then she shrugged. "We're not going to find power anywhere else."

He guessed that was true. He shifted, trying to move blood that wanted to pool in his legs, and coughed into his helmet. He wasn't getting used to the smell of this planet. The air contained sulfur trioxide, which meant it would generate sulfuric acid on contact with moisture. Nevertheless, he'd started trying to figure out how long he could remove his helmet before it would kill him, just to experience the glorious sensation of being free from it. The film would protect his eyes, but he would have to hold his breath, to keep the sulfur trioxide out of his throat and lungs.

Jackson's hand came down on his. "See that?"

He squinted. At the apex of the mountain hung a dark curl of something like smoke. "Shit, it *is* a volcano."

"Could be," Jackson said.

"Then maybe it lets us get at something below the surface. Some mineral we can use in the converter."

They watched awhile longer. The smoke twisted and curled but seemed anchored in place. Its movement defied good sense in a way he couldn't quite figure. Maybe it was the gravity.

"You know what?" he said. "It kind of looks like a tornado. Like it's spinning." But as he watched, it faded away. Within a minute, it was gone. He looked at Jackson, who was still studying the horizon. "What do you think?"

"I think we should get moving," she said, and began to slide down the rock.

12

[Gilly]

THE BENEATH

He cranked the manual release to Eng-1 and, as soon as the door opened wide enough, squeezed through. There were eight core housings, each drenched in soft green light that turned black as the warning glowlights strobed. He moved to the closest. "I'm in," he said. "I have a board."

Jackson: "You have ninety seconds. If what you're doing isn't working by then, you leave."

"Understood."

What he was doing was trying to exert manual control over the ship's combat systems. Which was precisely what he'd said they should never do, because a human being couldn't match the capabilities of an AI. But there was no AI; the AI was recovering from a coma state into which Jackson had plunged it with the kill switch. What they had was Gilly.

"Intel, how are you looking?"

"Good. The AI cold restart is almost complete. It should be fully functional within three or four minutes. I haven't looked at Weapons yet, but I think I can run Armor."

"We enter *huk* range in sixty seconds. You need to be back here before they start landing."

He could see that wasn't going to happen. It would take him at least that long to get to grips with the Armor subsystems, then he would need to run them for the few remaining minutes until the AI could take over. But he said, "I understand."

Armor was primarily a network of interlocking electrostatic fields, which, when sufficiently charged, would seize anything that passed through and tear it into tiny, inert, directionless particles. The challenging part was maintaining that charge, since powering the entire network at once would require more energy than the ship could generate. Instead, the ship normally made it work by charging precise sections right before something hit them, based on its assessment of incoming projectiles. Gilly would need to track every incoming *huk* and key power to an appropriate segment of Armor at the right moment.

It seemed impossible, but as he worked, he felt the stirrings of excitement. He had always enjoyed a challenge, and right now he could set aside any thought of whether this might actually work and simply do the best he could. As he bundled up Armor segments, tying them to commands he could trigger at will, it even began to feel doable. Maybe Anders had been right all along, and they could run this ship like an old-fashioned stagecoach, blasting shotguns out the side.

He deployed a quick test and manually triggered a section of armor. Nothing happened.

"Shit," he said.

"What is it?"

"Minor problem. It's fine." He saw his mistake. The electrostatic field didn't appear from nowhere; it had to flow from generators on particular points on the ship's hull. If he wanted to light up a segment, he needed to create a path to it.

"Hostiles firing. Gilly, you need to come back now."

"It didn't work. I missed something. But I can fix it."

"If we don't move, we'll still be here when the *huk*s start hitting."

"You should detach. You can separate from the ship until it's over. You'll be safe."

"Negative. Not leaving you there."

He got two words into a reply and something far away went *thump*. He turned. The door to Eng-1 was not closed. He'd been in such a hurry, he'd neglected it. He moved to the door. He hesitated and stuck his head out into the corridor.

The warning glowlights were cycling, turning the corridor into a rushing train of shadow. In this strobing chaos, something large and alien moved toward him.

He fell back into Eng-1 and worked the manual release. The door hitched closed one maddening inch at a time. There was scrabbling in the corridor and then the golem face of the creature appeared in the gap, blocky and irregular and thick with translucent resin, and the resin split to reveal jaws and lipless teeth, and he yelled and threw his weight against the crank and the door slid closed.

He stood still, breathing.

Jackson was in his ear. He returned to his board. The salamander in the corridor was silent and he could imagine it probing around. Preparing to *huk*. "You should detach," he said. Jackson began to protest, but he ignored her, studying the board. Sometimes when he was deep in a puzzle, it wasn't until he took a break that he saw the answer, and it had been obvious all along. There was something about the act of stepping back that was revealing. It was immediately clear to him: There were thousands of incoming *huk*s and they were going to strike the ship at the same time. He would be lucky to stop half a dozen of them.

"I've messed this up," he said. "I shouldn't have tried to run systems manually. It can't be done."

"Gilly, come back."

"I should have prioritized getting the AI back. I'm clearing out some subsystem caches. That might help."

"Gilly."

"I can't reach you anyway," he said. "There's a salamander in the corridor. Detach so you don't get hit. I'll stay here and do the best I can."

A calmness stole over him. He listened to Jackson curse and finally ignite and detach the jetpod from the ship. She had a plan to circle around and pick him up from a different location, which wasn't going to work, because the *huk*s would arrive by then.

He worked the board, doing what he should have done in the first place: clear as many obstacles out of the way of the AI as he could, so it could take over as quickly as possible. At last, the display washed clean. "Got it!" he said. "AI is up!"

A section of the door flew inward. He was tossed across the room and landed sprawled on the floor, and when he raised his head, everything was different. Two core housings were shattered. Their boards were in pieces. The air was full of tiny particles of ash like snow. A low wind pulled at him. There was a hole in the door.

The salamander pushed its snout into the hole. It grunted. The door squealed. The salamander forced its way inside, resin falling from its face in chunks, the door bending. Gilly couldn't find his sense of balance. Around the room, the glowlights went out one after another. There was a solid jolt, and then another, a parade of them. The *huk*s were landing.

"*Pak,*" the salamander said. "*Pak.*"

The ship began to growl, a deep, bone-shaking sound that seemed to come from everywhere at once. The door broke. The salamander entered. The floor tipped and Gilly began to slide across it, toward the salamander, helpless to stop. The ceiling burst in a dozen places.

The floor vanished. The salamander staggered, its legs going out, reaching for purchase that wasn't there. It was fantastic and funny but everything was breaking apart. His ears popped. The world filled with tearing metal. The salamander's black eyes fixed on him and its mouth opened and everything disintegrated.

An annoying noise assailed his ears: *blaat blaat blaat*. A dark purple ball hung in his face. When he swiped at it, his arms went everywhere. He swallowed but couldn't get his stomach out of his throat. He was floating. These were problems.

He closed his eyes and swallowed a few times, fighting nausea. His hands were gloved, he could feel that. His breath was loud in his ears. He felt no gravity. This meant his survival core had deployed.

He opened his eyes. He could identify the purple ball now. It was a planet.

There was glittering in the darkness. Stars, but also pieces of ship, everything from dust and debris to a gigantic section he recognized as almost the entire aft quarter, torn and peppered with holes. No way to reach it; he couldn't propel himself. He was, he thought, slowly falling toward the planet. Nothing he could feel. But that would be what was happening.

He closed his eyes again until the urge to vomit passed. When he opened them, the planet was still there. It was hazy at the edges. He was actually looking at atmosphere, he figured. A planet wreathed in cloud. Dark purple cloud.

Some time passed. He had nothing to do but think and so he assessed his situation methodically, checking his logic at each step.

His survival core could keep him alive for roughly five days.

After that, he would asphyxiate.

He probably wouldn't be killed by flying debris: It shared a common origin point with him, and they would move farther apart over time.

He didn't think he would fall to his death, as it would take longer than five days.

He might be rescued. This would depend on what had become of Jackson, Beanfield, and Anders. His ping had a short range; if they were able to, they would search for its signal from the jet. This was a long shot, because it relied on them not only surviving the attack but also managing to return to the same area—as opposed to doing what a jet-pod was designed for, which was aiming homeward and accelerating.

If they were able to return, he figured, it would happen soon. They might delay to let the salamanders disperse, or conduct repairs, and it might take a little while to find him. But after forty hours, he would have to face the likelihood that no one was coming.

He shut down everything nonessential. Broadcasting distress on ping: yes. Scanning for pings: tempting, but no. It wasn't necessary to know rescue was coming a few minutes in advance. He turned down his thermals as far they would go.

He hung in space and watched the cloud planet. It was dark and unfathomable, an arc of light to its left side. He might get to watch a sunrise.

It was a bad situation. But it could have been worse. He had expected to die, and now he had five days and he felt relatively okay about this. It was almost peaceful. Before he'd made crew, a Service psych had told him, "If you're chosen, you will be as far away from the rest of the human race as anyone in history," and peered into his eyes to gauge his reaction. He had been okay with it. She had also asked,

"What do you think you're going to find out there?" This one he struggled with, because he didn't know. But that was the point, he realized. "Answers," he said. "I like finding the answers to questions like that." Her expression had remained carefully neutral, but after the interview was over, she shook his hand and said, "I hope you find your answers."

Maybe not. Maybe he was going to slowly run out of air here, wondering what had become of Jackson, Anders, and Beanfield. Maybe this sun would emerge from behind the cloud planet and cook him alive. Maybe the only answer was that he was an insignificant biological object in a universe of dispassionate physical laws.

He activated his recording function. It would consume a small amount of power, but he wanted to create a record. He wanted to make sure he left something behind, no matter what happened.

"This is Isiah Gilligan. I was ejected from the ship. My core has approximately a hundred twenty hours life capacity. I don't know if the others survived. I hope they did. I'm looking forward to seeing a familiar face."

He paused.

"We lost the ship through a combination of failures. I should have refused to prepare the AI kill switch. Jackson shouldn't have activated it, even to save my life. We underestimated the enemy, who were getting closer to us each time, and overestimated ourselves. We overestimated the ship . . ." He hesitated. "No, that's not right. We underestimated the ship, too. We expected it to behave like a machine, when it's more like . . ." No one listening now, so he might as well say it. ". . . a living creature. Not in all aspects, of course, but in some ways that matter. We have to treat it as such if we're to understand it. And I think we do need to understand it, and can't continue to treat it like a benign black box, or some kind of benevolent deity. Surplex AI is in every Providence.

There's similar software in Freco and many other corporates. We need to improve our understanding of how it thinks, what it wants—we need to find ways to translate its versions of that into concepts we can understand. Because I don't think there's just one alien species out here. I think there are two."

In the void, something winked. He squinted. A minute later, a star disappeared. This time he saw it happen. It could have been anything: spinning debris, the sun catching new objects. But when a third star winked out, he was sure: Something was out there. And getting bigger, or appearing to, because it was approaching.

He fumbled at the suit to toggle his ping. If they were close enough for him to see them, they must know he was here, but he wanted to make sure. A green beacon on his shoulder strobed energetically, singing inaudible frequencies into the night.

More stars vanished. The object had no running lights at all. They might be disabled, but something felt off. It was too large. And the wrong shape: not a simple angular jetpod, but irregular, with gaps, large ones, through which he could glimpse stars. He had the sudden thought that the ship had heard him: He had spoken against it and it had become angry, and was sloughing its way toward him, blackened and burnt but still alive, to punish him. When it drew within a few hundred yards, he could see it wasn't one object at all, but many.

He jerked his limbs, flailing. He yelled and twisted and none of this made any difference as the salamanders came out of the dark. A blocky golem head filled his view. Its jaws opened and vomited resin across his face. His film bleated protests. He felt his limbs stiffening. He was being encased. "Damn it," he said. "Goddamn it!" He struggled until he couldn't any longer.

He knew the salamanders were still there from bumps and dull scraping sounds that resonated through the resin. But he couldn't see and couldn't move. He shouted for a while and that didn't help, either. After enough hours of this, he slept.

His timer ticked over forty hours, the limit he'd set himself for rescue. Over recent hours, the bumping had grown more intense, and he'd felt the stirrings of gravity. This grew until it was stronger than any he'd ever felt. He was dragged and turned over and finally thumped against something solid.

A streak of resin was clawed from his film. In the glow of his suit light was a salamander, its face wide and white, its eyes small and dark, its lipless clown mouth stretching from one earhole to the other. He recognized it as a worker, which he'd always thought of as small, but it wasn't: It was the size of a bear. It pawed at him, stripping away resin in hunks. A smell like cat urine crawled up his nostrils, penetrating the suit filter.

It didn't attack and didn't eat him. When it was done shredding resin, it simply turned and trotted away, moving on all six legs. He breathed. He was alone.

He was in a tight, cavelike space with smooth, curved walls, which he could make out even with his suit light on its lowest setting. He tried to move but found himself bonded to the wall. Not only was resin attached to his limbs and back, it also flowed smoothly into the wall with no visible join. He was welded there.

"They've taken me underground," he told his recorder. This in itself was notable: Salamanders hadn't often been observed on planets, and when they had been, they hadn't burrowed. "From the look of the walls, they carved out these tunnels. Maybe it's a base of some kind. I'll record everything from now. I have"—he checked—"twenty-six hours of power. Maybe this will make its way back to Service somehow."

He fell silent.

"I don't know why they brought me here." He could think of some ideas. Food. Torture. But these were products of fear, not observation. He shouldn't waste the recorder on them. "If I can figure that out, maybe I can learn something about their motivations."

Some time passed. After an hour or two, he heard a noise, warbled through his suit, and a salamander emerged from the tunnel. At first he thought it was the same worker, but it was slightly smaller, with wider eyes and a bluish hue to its skin. Its back was pockmarked with white ridges like scar tissue. At each end of its mouth were parts that might have been whiskers or else thin tentacles. It stopped and rose onto its hind legs. *"Pak!"*

"Crap," he said, because that had scared him.

It dropped to the floor, shifted closer, and reared again. *"Pak. Pak."* Its mouthparts waved.

"Don't hurt me," he said.

"Pak pak."

He tugged uselessly at his bonds. The salamander watched mutely. When he stopped, it shuffled closer.

"No! Go back!"

It seemed to register his intent, retreating a few steps.

"Yes! Yes. Stay there."

It regarded him unblinkingly with pupilless eyes. After a moment, it approached again.

"No!" he said.

Again it shuffled back. A few moments passed. Its head tilted expectantly.

"Yes," Gilly said.

Its neck arched. A sound came out of its throat. *"Nok! Nok! Nok!"* It bent, as if trying to coax the sound from somewhere deeper inside. *"Yek! Yek!"*

He stared.

"Pak pak," said the salamander. When he didn't respond, it moved closer.

"No!"

"Nok." It retreated a few steps. *"Yek. Yek."* And then closer again. *"Nok."*

He checked that the recorder was running. "It's talking. It's learning to talk." The salamander began moving again, so he said, "No!" to send it back. It was definitely testing him. Its movements were inquisitive. Almost playful. He thrust his chin toward his right arm. "Can you let me out? Take off this resin?"

Its head tilted.

"The resin. Yek?" It took some coaxing to approach him. He was refining the meaning of *yek*, he realized, employing it for affirmation, rather than *stop* or *go away*. But finally it reared before him. Its head lowered and it drooled a clear liquid. He felt the resin loosening, and with effort managed to pull his arm free from the wall. "Yes! Yek!"

"Yek."

He gestured to his other arm. "Now this." It didn't move. "This one. Yek. Do it again."

"Nok."

"Yek. This one."

"Nok."

"Yek!" Gilly said, trying a more commanding voice. The salamander was unmoved. "It's not stupid," he said, for his recorder. "It doesn't want to let me free." They watched each other for a few moments. He pointed to his chest. "Gilly."

"Pak pak."

"Gilly." He pointed to the salamander. "Salamander."

"Sssak. Mak mak."

"Salamander."

"*Sak. Mak. Tar.*"

"Yek!" he said. Pointing to himself: "Gilly."

It made several abortive attempts at the noise. He watched muscle ripple beneath its skin, although its face didn't change at all, remaining lizardlike in its lack of expression. Still, he sensed curiosity in its movements. He was dealing with an inquisitive mind, not a hostile one. "*Gik. Kik. Gikky.*"

"Gikky. Yek."

It waited patiently, still as stone, not even appearing to breathe. *What now?* he wondered. He didn't know what you did with an alien after the introductions. "Can you let out my other arm? This?" He pointed. "Yek?"

"*Nok.*"

"But you did it to this one. So now this."

"*Nok.*"

"Shit!" he said. "Yek! Yek!"

"*Nok Gikky.*"

He was silent awhile. "Why am I still alive?"

"*Gikky.*"

"Yes. Gikky. Why is Gikky alive?"

"*Gikky.*"

"I want to know why you brought me here."

But even as he spoke, he realized the answer. He had been absorbed by his own curiosity, thinking only of what he could learn, and forgotten that this was what they did, all the time, and had done from the beginning. From every encounter they'd ever had, the salamanders had learned something, and become more dangerous.

"*Gik-ky ak-live,*" it said.

———

He shut his mouth and closed his eyes and eventually the salamander left. He hung in the orange cave. His film read that fifty-nine hours had elapsed. His core could support him another twenty-two. After that, he would die. There was no question about that anymore. All that remained to be seen was how much damage he would do to his own species first.

Service hadn't advised him on what to do if he were captured by salamanders. He couldn't find it within himself to blame them: He was the first human being to be captured. No one had thought the salamanders did that. There was a lot that the salamanders did that no one had realized, Gilly was figuring out. Service had underestimated their complexity. Even the schema of distinct classes—soldier, worker—was wrong, or at least incomplete, since there were clearly subclasses as well, including an undiscovered one for this blue-hued creature.

He heard dragging salamander movement in the tunnel. These sounds came and went. They barked at each other, sometimes from close by, more often far away. Maybe he would be left alone until he died. He might have been flattering himself, thinking he was a vital military asset. He could be a memento: a curiosity collected from the battlefield and shoved into a drawer. Years from now, young salamanders would sniff his corpse. *This was one of the creatures we fought. It used to move.*

He checked his recorder. "I've realized the salamander may be trying to learn from me. I won't talk to it anymore."

He fell silent.

"I'm going to die here," he said.

He couldn't sleep: The gravity would seize his head and yank it toward the floor. He grew angry. He had nothing to think about except how he'd wound up here, and the more he did, the stupider it seemed. There were twenty-eight billion human beings and none of them had managed to get themselves bound to a wall in a salamander burrow. He mentally traced and retraced the path that had led him here, the precise steps, to establish where he went wrong. One misstep, of course, was his own dumb idea to put himself forward when Surplex asked for interested candidates in a special, secret Service project, but he was starting to think that people had taken advantage of him. People who had implied that crewing a Providence-class battleship was essentially risk-free. He specifically remembered a meeting in which a Surplex engineering lead—or maybe it had been Service— addressed a question about mission risk by saying, "Well, you might be hit by a car crossing the road tonight," and all of them in the room admitted to the underlying point, which was that there was risk in anything and all you could do was minimize it. But Gilly was now thinking that there was an entire dimension to risk that had been seriously fucking understated, because he would happily run into traffic if it meant getting out of this dark place full of salamanders. Also, it was a double bluff: they worked it both ways, because they told the public, *These brave crews risk their lives,* but in private, the implication was: *Not really.*

"Even if it doesn't work out, the exposure you'll get is priceless," a Surplex manager had told him, when Gilly discovered just how intensive the candidate process was, how it required him to live in the arctic wastes for a year, embedded with the military. "The access you'll get working that closely with Service, the managers you'll meet,

Surplex will place a real premium on. Freco will, too. Whether you actually want to go out on a ship or not, by the end of this, you'll be highly sought-after." Yeah. He'd be sought after, all right. He would never be found, was the problem.

He wanted to know why they were at war. Not in generalities. Those had been good enough for him before, but not anymore. He wanted to be in a room with the person who'd made the decision, who'd said, *Go,* and explore whether there had been other options. Because there was dissent. There were protests. There were people who said contractors like Surplex had tentacles all through Service, and manipulated public sentiment in favor of the war, the purpose of which had shifted somehow from driving salamanders back from human territory to absolutely exterminating them as a species, and was that strictly necessary? Was forging into VZ actually the same war that everyone had agreed to after *Coral Beach*? Because back then, there hadn't been corporate AI pouring itself into battleships along with 22 percent of global GDP and making decisions that were literally too sophisticated to question. That part seemed dubious to him now. It felt really dubious.

He knew what was happening. He was inventing a comforting fiction in which it was okay to talk to the salamander because he didn't owe the human race anything. Still, these thoughts grew in his head until he was furious. Everyone but him was home and safe and happy.

He cried a little.

When his core reached sixteen hours remaining, he decided to shut it off. It would stop feeding him oxygen, he would grow dizzy and pass out, and that would be that. It was terrifying, but he couldn't stand waiting around to find out whether he was going to betray his own species.

There was probably no teaching unit on dealing with capture because it was too horrifying to contemplate.

He gave himself an hour to think about it. Then he dipped into his filters and dialed them down to zero.

After a minute, his eyes began to sting. This wasn't an effect he'd expected. He squeezed them shut, but the pain intensified. Something burned in his nostrils. "Ack," he said. As soon as he opened his mouth, someone rammed a flaming fist in there. His tongue sizzled; he heard it. He yelped and brought up the filters and choked and spat until the pain subsided.

When he could speak, he said, "The atmosphere contains a chemical that produces acid on contact with moisture. Sulfur trioxide, perhaps."

His core readout continued to tick. In fifteen hours, he wouldn't asphyxiate. He would dissolve.

The blue salamander returned. It perched on its back legs like a dog and watched him.

"Go away," he said.

Its head tilted. *"Gikky."*

He didn't respond.

"Gikky. Pak pak."

"Gilly doesn't want to pak pak. No pak pak from Gilly."

"Yek," said the salamander.

"No."

"Yek."

It rose. He flinched, but there was nowhere to go. The stench of cat urine intensified. The salamander's head bobbed. Its jaws cracked open. A noise grew in its throat. He felt the stirrings of a force.

"Fuck!" he said. "Okay! Yek!"

The salamander dropped to the floor. *"Pak pak."*

"Yes."

It lowered its head. *"Mak. Tak."*

"I don't know what that means."

"Mak-tak," said the salamander. It took two steps forward and low-ered its head again. *"Gikky."*

"You're Mak Tak? That's your name?"

"Mak. Tak."

"I'm going to call you Martin, because it sounds less like someone throwing up."

"Mak. Tak."

"Yes. Yek. Hello, Martin."

"Hek. Hek."

"Don't bother learning hello. You won't need that."

The salamander fell silent for a few moments. *"Pak pak."* When he didn't respond, it grew agitated, stepping to the left. *"Pak pak."*

"There's nothing to talk about. You killed my ship."

"Kik. Sssik."

"Yes. You know the ship, right?" He used his fist to mimic it flying, opening his fingers to represent the explosion. "Gilly's ship."

"Gikky sik."

"Yes."

"Kik."

"Yes."

"Mak-tak kik Gikky sik."

It was the longest sentence he'd heard from the creature. And it was correct. Martin had killed Gilly's ship. He stared at it. Its eyes were black and unblinking. It had no expressions; none he could discern. "What are we doing here, Martin?"

"Pak pak."

"Talking. Yes. But why? What do you want to learn?"

"*Gikky kik Mak-tak.*"

"Gilly kill Martin?" He felt confused. "No. Gilly not kill Martin."

"*Yek.*"

"No. Nok."

"*Sik,*" it said. "*Gikky sik kik Mak-tak.*"

He hesitated. This ship had killed salamanders. That was correct. "But not Gilly. Gilly was along for the ride. I'm not even a real soldier." The salamander didn't respond. "Nok," Gilly said. "Gikky nok kik Mak-tak. Sik kik Mak-tak."

"*Gikky nok.*"

"Gikky nok," he agreed.

"*Sik.*"

"Yes. Sik."

The salamander made a noise in its throat that he didn't recognize, then twice more.

"I don't understand." Its head bobbed. The sounds were unintelligible but seemed inquisitive. "Are you asking a question?" He mimicked the movement. "You mean, 'What?'"

"*Wak,*" the salamander said. "*Wak sik kik Mak-tak.*"

"What ship kill Martin? I don't know what that means."

"*Wak sik kik Mak-tak.*"

"That doesn't make sense, Martin. You know what ship."

"*Wak. Wak.*"

He hesitated. "Do you mean 'Why?'"

"*Wak.*"

"*Why* ship kill Martin?"

"*Wak,*" said the salamander.

He had been thinking about that himself. "I don't know," he said.

———

"Martin uses words interchangeably to mean either individuals or the species," he told his recorder. "Sometimes when he says 'Gikky,' he's talking about me. But other times, he means the whole human race. In the same way, he seems to use the term 'Mak-tak' to refer both to himself and to all salamanders. This suggests to me that he sees little difference between the two."

Martin was hunched near the far wall. What Martin was up to right now, Gilly had no idea. He had been silent awhile.

"This would make sense, since salamanders are genetic clones, and motivated to prioritize the survival of the hive as a whole over their own lives."

Martin said nothing.

"I'm studying you," Gilly told him. "Maybe one day someone will hear this and use it against you."

Martin didn't answer. Martin didn't know what he was saying. Gilly almost felt guilty, because Martin probably hadn't done anything. As far as Gilly knew, Martin had spent his whole life on this planet, minding his own business. If he had been contributing to the war, it was likely in the same way as Gilly: as a small, replaceable cog in a war machine. If anything, Gilly had done more than Martin, since he'd actively contributed to the Providence program. Although that could have been anyone: If it hadn't been Gilly, it would have been someone else. He imagined this was true for Martin. He remembered telling Beanfield that the real war was between salamander genes and human genes, and this felt true, especially the part where he and Martin were abused pawns in someone else's grand strategy. Whoever that was, genes or Service or some ultimate salamander-brain creature, they should invent a way to go to war with each other directly and leave him and Martin out of it.

When he had nine hours left on his core, another salamander emerged from the tunnel. It was larger than Martin, with thicker, darker skin, and angular where Martin was soft. A soldier, with folded wings. It stopped in front of Gilly and didn't move. He could smell it very strongly. After a minute, it turned toward Martin as if noticing him for the first time. Then back to Gilly. During this time, Gilly kept as still as possible, because it was terrifying.

The soldier moved closer. It rose onto its rear legs. It had no nostrils Gilly could see, but it moved its head as if seeking sensory input. It fell forward, its front legs landing on his arms, and he stifled an exclamation. The salamander's head swung to face him. He saw himself reflected in its dark eyes. Then, slowly, it closed its jaws around his arm.

He screamed. "Martin!" He could see the smaller salamander against the wall. It was doing nothing. The pressure on his arm became unbearable. *"Martin!"*

Eventually, it released him. It turned and departed. Martin remained hunched against the wall.

He wept. His arm was a song of pain.

"Martin," he said. "Hey. Martin."

What was in Martin's eyes, he had no idea. Martin was an alien. Gilly had no way of inferring his thought processes.

"I'm going to kill you," Gilly said.

Of course he couldn't kill Martin. He couldn't even scratch his own nose. But he imagined. He stared at Martin's bulbous head and found things to hate. Tiny hairs. A bulge like a mole. Things beyond the obvious, i.e., that he was a disgusting xenoform with ugly white scars on his back and tentacles around his mouth and skin that smelled like a dead cat. Because that wasn't enough. He wanted to hate Martin on a personal level. As an individual. He wanted to feel that even if Martin were human and they were on the same side, he would still despise him.

His arm precluded sleep but he slipped in and out of consciousness. He dreamed or hallucinated that Service and Surplex were coming for him. Not as a fleet or even as a collection of people but as a god, immense and powerful, and the rock split open and a face appeared above, ancient and ageless, its eyes blazing light. Everything the light touched burst into flames, and he realized too late that it had come not with salvation but with wrath. The light washed over him and he screamed and burned and died.

He came to a place of peace. "Martin," he said. "I know why we're at war."

Martin regarded him with his soulless eyes. Gilly would like to know what Martin did when he didn't have a prisoner of war to interrogate. He seemed to be taking a decent chunk of time off from whatever that was.

"I have human genes. You have salamander genes. That's it. That's the whole explanation."

"*Jek,*" Martin said.

"Genes fight each other, Martin. That's all they do. They're different, so they fight. That's why we kill you. That's why you kill us. It doesn't matter what we think. What we feel. Who's right. That's illusion. Gikky. Mak-tak. Different. War."

Martin said nothing.

"That's why," Gilly said. "You asked."

Martin rose. He shuffled closer and scratched a crude line in the dust. *"Mak-tak."* He made a second line. *"Gikky."*

"Yes. Two alpha species. Can't coexist. You got it."

Martin made a third line. *"Han-hek."*

He squinted. "I don't know what that is."

"Han-hek." Then Martin made a fourth line. *"Pak-tar."*

"What are those two?"

Martin's head lowered toward each line in turn. *"Mak-tak. Gikky. Han-hek. Pak-tar."*

"Are they . . . other races?"

"Han-hek. Pak-tar."

"Have you met other aliens? Not Gillys? Not salamanders?"

"Nok Gikky. Nok Mak-tak."

He checked that his recorder was still running. "That's . . . what do you call them again? What are their names?"

"Han-hek." Martin obliterated the line in the orange dust. *"Nok."*

He blinked. "Gone?"

"Pak-tar." Another line vanished. *"Nok."*

"What happened to them?"

Martin was silent.

"Did you kill them, Martin?"

"Kik."

"Salamanders wiped them out? Two other species?"

"Mak-tak kik Han-hek," Martin said. *"Mak-tak kik Pak-tar."*

"You did." He felt numb.

"Mak-tak kik Gikky," said the salamander.

13

[Jackson]
THE HUNT

They moved through fissures during the day, when their heat signatures would be obscured by sun-warmed rock. At times Anders again carried Beanfield across his shoulders, which was not merely mind-boggling in 1.4G but actively dangerous, since a fall could injure them both. It was also a waste of resources, with Anders sweating out twice as much water. But Jolene wanted to keep moving toward that volcano.

For two days, they made steady progress. In all that time, the tornado at its peak didn't move or dissipate. Sometimes individual tendrils broke away, especially near the top where it disappeared into the cloud, but never for long. She had developed an idea of what it might be, but didn't want to think about it until she was sure.

Every half hour, they rested. Anders checked the lightning gun over and over, as if it might spontaneously charge itself when he wasn't looking. Beanfield sat bent over, looking at the ground. Jolene amused herself by wondering how Service was going to spin this. She was almost sad she wouldn't get to see the enormous snow job that would be required to sell the idea that losing a Providence and its crew was actually some kind of victory. Or, she supposed, an inspirational and valiant loss that nothing could have prevented except perhaps increased military funding. Maybe she didn't need to see that. Maybe she could imagine it.

On the third day, she poked her head out of a fissure to check their surroundings and saw a low depression. It was only a few hundred yards away, and a rare feature in an otherwise empty landscape, so she resolved to investigate. She and Anders left Beanfield, who couldn't move quickly, climbed the fissure wall, and crossed the open rock, Anders carrying the lightning gun, the converter bouncing against the small of her back. The horizon remained clear both of land-bound salamanders and fliers. Now that she was above the heat haze, she was able to confirm something she'd suspected for a few hours: There was a second hill, farther away than the first, also with a twisting tornado at its peak. They slowed as they reached the crater. Anders raised the gun. Whether the thing would even work, they had yet to discover. But there were no salamanders here, either. The depression was full of liquid orange gunk.

"So what's this, now," said Anders.

She stared at it. It was thick, brighter in the center of the pool, darker at the edges, where it seemed to be congealing. It wasn't at all like what they'd swum through as they fled the jetpod. It actually put her in mind of lava, a substance that rose to the surface and formed a hard crust. Which made sense; that was how planets formed. Hot stuff bubbling up from below, then cooling and going hard. But seeing it in glutinous form made it impossible to deny the conclusion that had been forming in her head for days.

"Maybe this is a volcano, too," Anders said. "A baby one, just getting started. It's making rock, see?"

"This isn't rock."

He looked at her. "What?"

She gestured at the landscape. "None of this is rock."

"It looks like rock," he said. "What is it?"

"Resin."

Realization crossed his face. "The whole planet?"

"It's not a planet," she said. "It's a hive." She turned to look at the two hills and their tornadoes. But of course they weren't tornadoes. They were salamanders, coming out of the ground in streams, venting like gas.

Anders followed her gaze. "Ah, fuck it." He turned in a circle as if seeing the landscape for the first time. "Fuck me."

How many salamanders? They had vented at this rate for days. Must be hundreds of thousands. Millions. Which meant that it wasn't even correct to call this a hive, she realized. It was *the* hive. A planet-sized salamander factory.

Her body felt abruptly heavy. She sat. Everything was heavy right now.

"This is what we've been looking for," Anders said. "Since the start of the war. If Service knew . . ."

Every Providence would converge and burn this place to ash. But there was no way to tell them. They were in VZ. She, Anders, and Beanfield wouldn't even survive another twenty-four hours unless they found something to feed the converter.

Anders hunkered down beside her. "So what do we do?"

She didn't want to answer, but there was no other option. "We go there."

He looked, in case something else had appeared on the landscape recently. "What are you talking about? There are a million salamanders."

"We can try to slow them down."

"Come on," he said. "Jackson, that's a Providence job. That's not a three-person, one-rifle job."

She rose to her feet and unstrapped the converter. She doubted the pool would prove more fruitful than resin in its hardened form, but had to try. The pool's edges were smooth and the footing treacherous and she slid in up to her knees. She unfolded the converter and dipped it beneath the surface. There were salamanders below her, she figured. More than she could imagine. They had a smooth breeding operation down there, she bet. A production line of killers.

"Anything?" Anders said.

She waited for the converter to confirm it. She shook her head.

"Well, shit," Anders said.

The goop burped. She froze. A series of small bubbles rose to the surface and popped one after another.

"You should get out of there," Anders said.

She emptied the converter of liquid and tossed it to him. When she tried to move, she discovered that her boots were stuck. She'd been stationary for a while and had sunk into the muck. Anders slung the gun to his back, bent, and offered his hand. She took it. The pool burped again, a larger bubble.

"One," Anders said. "Two. Three."

He pulled. Her boots were dragged free and she sprawled onto the rock like a landed fish. She rolled onto her back. Before her, the surface rose. A salamander heaved itself out of the pool. Its body flopped forward. Its legs reached for purchase. She tried to scramble away but the gravity was hungry and her wet boots had no traction and she slid back into the pool. She went under and orange gunk closed over her head. Panic seized her. She couldn't see. Her feet slipped repeatedly until finally she found purchase. She broke the surface.

The salamander had climbed fully out of the pool. It was a soldier, she saw, with black, leathery skin, folded wings, and a rough, blocky head. It seemed disoriented. Liquid resin ran from its body, spattering the rock. Anders had the lightning gun. One charge, she remembered. Or zero, depending on how it was feeling at that moment.

"Shoot it!" she said.

The air burst and crackled. The salamander screamed. Its body convulsed. Before she could reach it, it heaved to its feet and began to lumber away. Anders simply watched it go.

"Shoot it again!" she screamed.

He blinked and took aim. The gun emitted a short, dispirited tone, red lights lighting along its side.

She grabbed the converter and began to run. The salamander was fifty feet ahead, wounded but moving fast. After a moment, Anders caught up with her.

"Shoot it again," she said.

"No juice."

"Just try," she said. It had unearthed a charge despite reading zero before; maybe it could again.

He raised the gun, stopped running for a moment, and took aim. The warning tone sounded again.

She hadn't paused, and Anders caught up to her again. The salamander was continuing to draw away, and now had a lead of two hundred yards. Ahead lay a plain of baking rock.

"Shit, it's fast," Anders said. "Do we stop?"

Her suit fan began to whine, cooling her skin. "It's hurt. We won't get a better chance than this."

He was silent. They ran. The salamander moved farther ahead until it became a smudge against the rock.

"We're exposed out here," Anders said. "And we should get back to Beanfield."

She didn't reply. He didn't seem to realize it, but the situation had become very simple. They had to catch this salamander and kill it or else die in their suits.

"Jackson. It's got six fucking legs. We're not going to catch it."

For the last few minutes, she had suspected the salamander was drifting to the left. Now it became unmistakable. "It's heading for the volcano. We can cut it off."

They adjusted course. Within a few minutes, they'd made up enough ground for her to make out the salamander's individual limbs again. It was loping painfully, she observed. Then it noticed them and changed direction, beginning to draw away.

"Fuck!" said Anders. "I can't keep this up. How are you doing this?"

"I used to run track. It's practically why I joined Service."

He panted.

"You can do this." She remembered Nettle's painting: the hunter and the gazelle. "Humans are built for running."

"Not this human."

"Whatever you're feeling, it's feeling worse."

They fell into a rhythm. The salamander attempted to veer left again, and again they cut the angle. But it wasn't slowing. Anders's panting became painful in her ears. He started lumbering. Every other moment she expected him to stumble and fall. She expected more dark shapes to appear on the horizon, or fliers overhead.

"I have to stop," he said. "I'm sorry."

"Take the converter, then. I'll keep going."

"You have to stop. You can't . . . kill it. By yourself." He sucked air for a few moments. "We're done."

She shook her head. They couldn't be done. They would die if they were done.

"Shit," Anders said, and began to run straighter. "How did you . . . get like this? Why can't you . . . let shit go?"

"We can't let it go," she said. "It's our only chance."

To his credit, he didn't argue. She was pleasantly surprised at how Anders had performed since the jetpod. She'd often questioned how Service chose crews, both before she shipped out and afterward, and Nettle had assured her that it wasn't just about public relations and feeds: They really were chosen to be an effective team who could perform in high-pressure scenarios. They couldn't always tell why the algorithm believed that, but it did. She was starting to see why it might be true of Anders.

They ran. A while later, the salamander angled right. She thought it was trying to throw her: If she headed right, it would cut left toward the tornado again. But in the distance lay a low mound, some kind of lump, another small hill. *Shit*, she thought. She didn't know what that was. Maybe nothing. But they couldn't afford to encounter anything the salamander could disappear into or receive help from. They had to chase it down across bare rock until it couldn't run anymore.

The suit pulled at her arms and shoulders. Each step, she had to lift feet that felt like rocks and put them down again. "Anders," she said. He had been silent for a while. "You see it?"

"The hill?"

"We can't let it get there."

"I can't run faster, Jackson."

"I know. I can't, either." She panted. "I'm going to take off my core."

His head twisted toward her. "What?"

"I'm faster without it."

"What are you talking about? You're dead without it."

"Not right away. There'll still be air in the suit."

He gave an exhalation like a snort. "Not for long, without the core to refresh it. You can't take it off." She didn't respond. "And even if you manage to catch that thing, if you're by yourself, it'll pull your head off."

Thirty minutes or so until the salamander reached the mound, she estimated. Four hundred yards to close. She had to be fast.

Anders stopped running. The moment he disappeared from her side, she felt a thousand times more alone. But she pushed ahead. "Jackson. Stop." She didn't. "What if there's another Providence?"

His tone suggested embarrassment. He'd been nursing this idea for a while, she realized. He actually thought they might be rescued. It was so ludicrous that she almost laughed.

"We don't know where they are," Anders said. "One could be close. It could find us." She heard him begin to jog after her. "It could send down a jetpod for us."

She found her breath. "A Providence could be in orbit. It would power up its plasma. And kill us all from range." She stumbled on a knob of rock and gasped. "You never understood this. War isn't . . . for us. We're a blip in the AI's cost-benefit calc." She was out of breath but felt the need to ram this point into Anders's skull. "The number of times you've said the word *Service*, and you still don't know what it means."

She slowed and stopped. Every muscle in her body screamed. But it was okay, she thought. They would perform when she needed them. "I can't reach my core. I need you to detach it."

She turned. She felt him fumbling at her back. When the survival core detached, it felt as if he'd removed an iron brick. Her suit gave a brief gasp.

Anders set her core on the rock. At first he wouldn't meet her eyes. Then he said, "Take the gun."

She felt oddly touched. Her first thought was to refuse—it was extra weight and out of charge—but he was right. She would need something, even if it was a club.

Already she felt hotter. No fan. No temperature regulation at all. And no air scrubbing: With every breath, she was filling her suit interior with carbon dioxide. She had to go.

"Thank you," she said. She began to run.

She hadn't sent a letter to David. She'd written hundreds but hadn't managed to find one that felt right, and now she was out of time. He would have nothing but the clips they'd exchanged during sync windows, in which she'd mostly complained. In the back of her mind, she'd had the idea that her letter was coming, this perfect expression of everything she wanted to say, and then he would understand. Without that, it was just two years of her bitching.

He'd basically kept her sane, these last two years, when her crew was testing her faith in her species, when Anders and Gilly were spending their time devising elaborate games and pranks while the ship fought the war for them. *Is this what we're fighting for?* she asked him, rhetorically. *This generation?* Next sync, he replied: *We were the same at that age.* But she didn't think so. She had started to wonder if there was something rotten at the core of these people, who viewed war as a career opportunity. There was a depthless narcissism to them that seemed to go beyond mere youthful self-absorption.

Come home, then, he said. This was their joke. After each rant, his reply: *So come home.* It was a good joke because for a moment it felt possible. Like she could stand up. Tell her dysfunctional crew, *I'm out, people. Best of luck.* Step out of the airlock and into her apartment. Hug her husband.

She closed on the salamander. Her pace was strong; she would catch it before it reached the mound. Her breathing was under control. The heat was bad and she was dripping sweat from every pore, but that didn't matter, not yet. She drew within a hundred yards and then her feet didn't go where they were supposed to and she stumbled and fell and couldn't get up.

Her vision filled with stars. *Carbon dioxide,* she thought. *I am killing myself.* Even this thought was slow and clumsy. There was poison swimming in her brain, dulling her senses. That was the problem, she knew. Not lack of oxygen, but an excess of carbon dioxide. She was enormously tempted to sleep. She wanted to close her eyes and ignore all her problems until they went away.

She grabbed at her throat and peeled back the suit strap. Air rushed past her face, hot and sharp and filled with a million tiny knives, which crawled up her nostrils and swam inside. She gasped and sat up, pulling the suit away from her body in pieces. Everywhere there was sweat, the atmosphere attacked, and that was everywhere, and she tried to wipe herself down with the suit fabric as best she could. She pulled the helmet free so that only her eyes were protected by her film, the rest of her naked except for her underthings. She found the gun and got to her feet.

She inhaled through her nose, keeping her mouth clamped shut. There was oxygen in the atmosphere, enough to sustain her for a short while, and if her sinuses burned, her throat and lungs, that wasn't so different to when she pushed herself on the track. Her bare feet slapped hot rock. She drew closer to the salamander and it turned and saw her.

It didn't stop. She felt furious. She was already working so hard and had to keep going. Blood ran from her nose. It became harder to inhale without choking and then she coughed involuntarily and sucked air through her mouth and pain roared in with it. She spat and what came out left trails of white vapor. She felt terribly afraid that her lungs were filling with blood. She would slow and stumble and stop and be able to do nothing but watch as the salamander slowly pulled away.

She willed strength into her legs. *Just a little farther, please.* She stared at the lumbering salamander and tried to pull it closer with her mind. She was so close that she could see its skin ripple with each step. She could hear sounds it was making: *chuk, chuk.* Its head turned again. She saw it try to increase its pace but it couldn't and her heart leaped at the sight.

David? It's me. There's something I want you to know. I'm sorry this took me so long. But I didn't know how to say it.

I'm sorry you married a happy girl who turned into me.

I'm sorry I let you hope she might ever come back.

I'm sorry I gave you so much less than you deserve.

David, I'm sorry, but I'm not coming home.

The salamander collapsed in front of her, its legs falling over one another. Its head hit rock and slid. It was sudden but also the only thing she'd been thinking about, so she raised the gun over her head and clubbed at the salamander with as much force as she and the gravity could muster. It buckled and kicked. She fell on top of it. Something slapped across her face, thick toes, rough and sharp. She lost the gun. She groped for its head, limbs, anything. But it was too strong and it heaved and sent her sprawling forward. She twisted and rose on legs she could barely control.

The salamander faced her, a few yards away. Shivers ran in waves up and down its skin. Its head dipped and rose. Its breathing was hoarse and erratic. The gun lay on the rock behind it. She took a step to the left. The salamander's head followed, but it didn't shift its footing. She took another step. There was pain in every part of her. But she kept taking steps until she'd circled around to the gun. Instead of turning to face her, the salamander's head dropped. She picked up the gun. She gripped the barrel and raised it above her head and at the last moment the salamander summoned the strength to turn but she struck it solidly and it collapsed. Her momentum carried her to her knees, closer to the thing than she'd intended. She got a good grip on the gun and drove the stock into the salamander's head again and again, until finally it was still.

She stared at it until she was sure it was dead. "Ha," she said. There was more she wanted to add, but even that word was painful. Everything was on fire. She rolled onto her back. She felt okay in a way she hadn't for a long time. Her body was aflame but there was a stillness in her heart. She turned her head so that she could watch the salamander's body until the end. "Ha," she said.

14

[Anders]

THE HIVE

Eventually he made out a dark shape like a sack on the rocky plain ahead. He couldn't tell whether it was one shape or two. His suit fan was running at its limit and his faceplate had fogged. He shuffled on until he was close enough to make out detail.

When he reached them, he sat. He hung his head and breathed.

The light was fading, shadows creeping out of cracks in the rock.

He unslung the converter. He lay on his back and looked up at the cloud. How much he hated that cloud, he had no words. It was the ugliest fucking thing he'd ever seen.

He sat up, unrolled Jackson's suit, and lay it over her body. Beside her, the salamander's head had been eaten away by chemical reaction where Jackson had caved it in. The butt of the lightning gun was corroded, too. The damage seemed superficial, though. He set it aside.

He didn't want Jackson to have to lie beside the creature. He seized the salamander by one leg and dragged it thirty feet away. Afterward he rested. Then he went back and collected the matter converter.

Normally it pulled out into a boxlike shape, into which you would drop whatever you had and close the lid. But it had another configuration for processing oversize material. He detached the lid, set it aside, inverted the converter, set it on top of the dead salamander's body, and closed its retractable grips.

He squatted beside the salamander's head. "Hey. Ugly." He pointed at the converter. "I'm going to feed you to that thing. It'll take a while. But I want you to know. You're going to help me kill more salamanders."

He peered into the dead thing's face. It had no response.

"Let's get started," he said.

The salamander allowed him to fully juice the lightning gun as well as his survival core. The converter could also hold a small charge of its own, so when he made it back to Beanfield, he could buy her EV suit another few days. After that, who knew. It was how they had to live now: a little at a time.

He tried to reach her on ping but her suit came back with basic life readings and nothing else. Most likely, she was sleeping. He considered his options. He wanted to return to Beanfield as quickly as possible. But he was also curious about the mound. If it was some kind of burrow entrance, that would be useful to know. He could scout it and plan his next hunt.

Since he had charge, he opened up his suit's scan range to see what it could find. He had low expectations; it could only sniff the air, and wouldn't map terrain or locate enemies. But any intel would be useful. It flared Beanfield's location, which he already knew, and Jackson's, beside him. Then, six miles away, Gilly's.

Had to be a mistake. But it had life readings, which moved before his eyes. Gilly was here. He was alive.

He opened up comms. "Gilly." There was no response. He worked out that Gilly was on passive ping, which was the kind of thing he might do if he wanted to conserve power but also be rescued.

He turned until he was facing the source of the ping. Ahead of him lay the mound.

He packed up the converter and began to strap it to his back. Then he hesitated. Beanfield needed that. Without power, she wouldn't last another day. But he knew how quickly the gun chewed through power. He needed the gun, too, if there were a lot of salamanders between him and Gilly.

Again he tried Beanfield on comms. While it bleated, he looked at Jackson. "What do you think?" he said. By his reckoning, Gilly's ping was at least half a mile underground. He thought he knew what Jackson's answer would be. She wouldn't hide in a cave while Gilly needed help. While the planet vented salamanders.

He was tempted to wake Beanfield. But he knew he wouldn't be able to explain himself properly. He'd never had those kinds of words. Besides, either he would make it back out or he wouldn't. That was what it came down to. He left her a recorded message anyway, doing the best he could, tightened the converter strap, and looped the lightning gun over his shoulder.

Gilly was trapped in the dark. Anders had to get him out.

The mound was sloped more gently on one side and fell off sharply on the other. He approached the sloped side and when he neared the top, he pressed himself to the rock and inched forward until he could peer over its edge. Below waddled a procession of salamanders. Fat white ones, a long line of the little fuckers, emerging from a hole in the ground to vomit resin at the base of the mound and then file back inside. No soldiers, as far as he could see. He watched until he was sure. Then he slid down the slope and prepared the gun.

When he stepped out, they barely reacted. The nearest raised its head and sniffed the air, or so it looked like. It had tiny black salamander eyes and a face like the inside of a cow and he slotted the butt of the lightning gun into his shoulder. It was maybe smarter not to do this, to instead get down into the hole and make as much progress as he could before doing anything to alert the soldiers. But he had the gun and Jackson was dead and this salamander was here.

He squeezed the trigger. The gun spat electricity in brilliant jagged lines. The rocky ground between them cracked and coughed dust. The worker split into two sections, three if you wanted to be generous. He would call it three; its legs were barely attached. Its body caught fire. It made a thin mewling sound. Its front legs pawed at the ground. It crawled forward a short distance and stopped to burn in peace.

The worker ahead in the procession turned to see what had happened. Anders pointed the rifle at it but it didn't seem to care one way or the other. Its head weaved left and right and then it turned and continued toward the vomit hill. Behind the burning salamander, other workers milled, confused. He watched them explore around the flaming corpse, seeking the ant-trail of their colleagues. One came within thirty feet of him and didn't so much as glance in his direction.

"You dumb shits," he said.

The gun's charge remained at 100 percent, he was glad to see. He had been reckless on the ship, he thought, hosing down corridors like he was pressure-washing them. He didn't need to do that. He just had to point and give it a little pop. He was tempted to stay and burn workers all day long, but Gilly was a thousand yards away, so he made himself approach the hole. It was large enough to accommodate him and the workers, as far as he could see, but that was the problem: He couldn't see a hell of a long way before it got dark, and then who knew. He tasted the familiar fear, tickling the back of his throat, feathering across in his brain.

Hey, Pauly.

He turned on his suit's exterior illumination. It extended only twenty or thirty feet but was, he had to say, a hell of a lot better than a glowstick. He made his way down sloping rock to the entrance. A little circle of white light danced before him like a friendly spirit. The ground grew rougher, less weather-polished rock and more newly dried resin, a little easier to stumble over in the dark and be swarmed by monsters. But he walked on and let the hole envelop him. The tunnel walls drew closer and he decided he was getting a little too up close and personal with the workers after all—who knew what they did if they were startled, or if a manager salamander turned up—so he raised the barrel and popped one in the tunnel ahead of him. It cried and burst into flame and he hadn't even thought about this but the firelight immediately improved the lighting situation a thousand times over.

He advanced past it, flames licking around his suit, and popped another one. He continued like this for a few hundred feet, following the tunnel as it turned, until the parade of workers stopped. Then he paused, listening. He'd passed a few forks and side tunnels but hadn't noticed any salamanders in them. He was still on the highway, as far as he could tell. Which made the lack of traffic suspicious. He checked behind and ahead. Nothing. Gilly was fifteen hundred feet away. Anders resumed walking.

It came at him faster than he expected. He was being careful with the light, keeping his spirit guide light trained on the floor at its maximum distance, and still the thing was on top of him almost before he could react, glinting teeth and thick limbs, and he hadn't expected them to *run* at him. He'd been waiting for the sound, *huk*. But instead it charged at him like a horse and he squeezed the trigger and splashed ignited ozone. It lunged and fell apart and the pieces hit him and knocked him down. There was fire in his face. He struggled free of the dismembered salamander and rose to one knee. Thirty feet was not enough, clearly. Not nearly enough. He pointed his little spirit guide down the center of the tunnel and saw something else there, a bowl of worms at the bottom of a well, and he sighted the gun, shifted the mode from auto to ranged, squeezed the trigger. The tunnel filled with light. There were salamanders in a heaving mass. The VX-10 was not ideal for this kind of thing, losing a lot of power over distance, but it was a con-fined space, a very, very confined space, and it barked and scoured the rock with light and flame. More were coming already, squeezing through the flames and bodies like they couldn't wait to greet him, like it was the day before launch and there wasn't a person alive who didn't want to stop and shake his hand or grab a picture, and a little pop here and there was no longer enough, it seemed, despite his best intentions to preserve charge, so he held down the trigger for a full second, two, three, and made them split and char until he was certain they were dead.

There were so many that their bodies blocked the tunnel. But the flames guttered quickly, which allowed him to force his way between them. He still wasn't sure why there had been no *huk*. It was all they fucking did in space. Even the one he'd killed on the ship had spat a *huk* at him. But here, so far, nothing. He devised two theories: They were different salamanders, a kind of soldier that didn't *huk* but did like to run through tunnels like out-of-control trains, or they were reluctant to punch holes in their own burrow. It was the kind of ques-tion Gilly would have enjoyed, and been able to solve, but Gilly was still twelve hundred feet away, in the dark, so Anders guessed he would find out when he found out.

The gun displayed 72 percent charge. He was still wearing the converter; if he could find a good location, somewhere to set his back against a wall, he could put the converter to work on salamander bodies. The only problem would be transferring that charge to the gun, which would take a minute or two, during which time he couldn't use it. That part he would have to figure out when he came to it.

They came again a minute later. He gave them a burst from the lightning gun but this time it didn't stop them: more and more scrabbled through the burning corpses, forcing him to stop and feed a continuous stream of energy into the tunnel until the gun began to bleat in protest. When he released the trigger, flame was everywhere in great pools. The walls dripped and glowed red. He could feel the heat through his suit. He tried to advance and a salamander clambered over the top of a flaming corpse and he popped it. Behind that was another and he repeated the process and it was the only way he could advance: a step, a bark from the gun, over and over. Their numbers seemed endless. When he next glanced at the gun, its charge had dropped to 44 percent. White smoke curled continuously from its barrel. He'd carried a small hope of making it to Gilly and back without needing to recharge, but that was gone now.

Ahead of him, a salamander backed away, its movement unusually calculated, and he recognized that, the kind of shit his brothers would pull before he was old enough not to be fooled by it, and he turned and spat fire into the tunnel behind him. The air forked and ignited and cleaved three salamanders. There were more behind those. He heard: *huk*.

He dropped. The *huk* passed by and threw him into the wall. His vision flared. His suit wailed. But he didn't let go of the lightning gun and used it to hose both directions, ahead and behind. He broiled salamanders until there were no more.

He got to his feet. The *huk* had torn away hunks of rock and resin and salamander and strewn them about. But the path ahead seemed clear. He checked the gun. Eighteen percent. Not good. Not good at all.

So they could *huk*. He didn't know why now and not before. They could have made mincemeat out of him if they'd stayed back and done that earlier.

He unstrapped the converter. This wasn't the cul-de-sac he'd been hoping for, but it was a lull, and he needed juice. Before he could set it to work, though, he caught a hint of movement in the tunnel behind him. Not a salamander: There was something funny about the wall. He'd passed it by without noticing, but now that the place was helpfully illuminated by flame, he could make out a dripping, like the rock was some kind of slow, gelatinous waterfall. He re-slung the converter and approached. It didn't look like much besides a wall of goo, but he was interested in anything that might get him out of this tunnel, so he poked it. His hand went through.

He moved forward. The goo admitted him. Resin covered his suit and helmet. He felt his arm emerge into air on the other side, so he forged ahead and wiped the faceplate and saw his little white spirit guide flitting around a cavernous space.

From the floor rose a gigantic slab of smooth resin. Beside it stood another, and more, side by side in neat rows. They rose fifty feet high and were longer still, running off into the dark, farther than his spirit guide would travel. To put some distance between him and anything that might follow through the waterfall of goo, he moved into the aisle between two slabs. The sides that faced each other were divided into hundreds of compartments only a few feet across, like honeycomb. Inside each compartment was a sac made of something soft and white.

He peered at the nearest. Its surface was translucent. Beneath that, something dark and indistinct. He had a feeling he knew what it was, and it was the reason the soldiers had been reluctant to *huk* him until he'd passed this area by. He poked the sac with the end of the lightning gun. The dark form twitched. He pushed the barrel in farther, until the sac popped and gushed fluid. A dark, twisting shape flopped from the compartment onto the ground. He watched it in the white light. It was long, glistening orange and black, with curving pincers at each end and a segmented body. Six stubby legs. A tiny head, a mouth surrounded by pincers and wet waving hairs. Even in this form, he could recognize the salamander it would one day become. It swung toward him and made a high, thin sound: *hik.*

He glanced around, in case there was a mama bear. But his spirit guide found no movement in the dark.

He left it. If he could, he would deal with it later. The slab continued another two hundred feet, but it wasn't taking him toward Gilly; he was going sideways. He saw a honeycomb compartment with no bulging sac and stopped to examine it. It was rough-hewn and empty except for a few dry white fragments. As he continued, he encountered more of these empty chambers. From ahead, wet noises.

At the end of the slabs lay a dark pool of thin brownish fluid. Around it crawled dozens of salamander larvae. There were two adults, workers, he assumed, although they were large, and their backs were grotesquely distorted, bulging with weeping blisters or cysts. He watched the larvae's pincers grip and pull the blisters' flesh, their round mouths press to the hole and suck.

In the pool, a faint shape bobbed to the surface. Brown fluid drained from it. A sac. A worker emerged from the gloom and stepped almost daintily into the pool to retrieve it. Using its middle legs, it pressed the sac to its belly, retreated clumsily from the pool, and made for the slabs.

All right, he thought. *All right.*

He dropped the converter to the floor. He turned in a circle, sweeping the rock with the little light. If there were any secret tunnels, he couldn't see them. The chamber seemed fully enclosed. He turned back to the nearest nurse. The correct move here was probably to leave as many of them alive as he could, as a waystation for the return journey. But he couldn't allow this place to survive. He slotted the corroded butt of the lightning gun into his shoulder and began to wash the place clean.

It took the converter eight minutes to process the first batch of larvae. He had to refill it twice, watching its power dial upward. Once it was pushing maximum, he unslung the gun, squatted beside the converter, and hooked the two together. This was the dangerous part, where he wouldn't be able to fire the weapon. He crouched, waiting, listening.

The pool burped. He eyed it. Where did that go, he wondered. Or where did it start, was maybe the question.

He checked Gilly's ping location and committed it to memory. Once he left this nursery, he suspected that he would encounter a lot of salamanders. He might not have time to check his bearings again.

Were there more nurseries? If the planet was a hive, like Jackson said, there would be, perhaps thousands of them. He would need more. Gilly was now only a thousand feet away, but Anders had lost the element of surprise, so he expected more resistance, which would consume more power. He should pay attention to any area where the soldiers were reluctant to *huk.*

The gun blinked green along its glowlights. He detached it from the converter and looped its strap over his head, where it belonged. The converter was still processing larvae. He waited until it was full, then packed it up.

When he reached the resin waterfall, he stuck the gun through and let it do its thing. After that, he pushed through and emerged into a smoking hellscape of flame and charred flesh. They were everywhere. They filled the tunnel, packed tight, scrabbling over each other to reach him. He fired the gun in tight bursts and it was like carving a hole in the ocean, the tide rushing back the moment he released the trigger. He forged ahead, using the gun to wash clear his path. How many salamanders on this planet, he wondered. How many coming at him right now. How long in the box.

The gun was growing hot. He could do this for another few minutes, he reckoned. Gilly was close. He wasn't sure he could make it. If he didn't, it wasn't the worst way to go out, he supposed. He'd come out here to kill salamanders. Anyway. No sense in overthinking it. No point in looking back. He picked up his pace until he was running.

15

[Gilly]
THE SOURCE

Sometimes Martin was still for long periods. He stayed in the exact same position, so that Gilly couldn't even tell whether he was conscious. But when Gilly didn't move for a while, Martin became restless and would move closer or bark at him.

"*Gikky,*" Martin said.

"What," he said.

This seemed to content Martin, and he returned to his position by the wall and went still again. For a while, Gilly had been developing the theory that Martin was some kind of officer: a high-intelligence subclass whose aptitude for language was paired with a talent for coordinating hives and destroying Providences. But now this felt less plausible. He didn't think Martin was smart enough to command troops. Also, the idea of a commander ran against everything he knew about salamander behavior. It was a human way of thinking. Salamanders weren't coordinated. They didn't follow orders. They were like ten million separate pieces of the same thing. Martin was just one more, soaking up everything he could learn from Gilly because that was what salamanders did.

"Gik. Kee," Martin said.

He must have not moved for a while. "Still here," he said wearily. He had kind of gotten used to Martin. He didn't really hate him anymore. He understood him too well, had found too many things in common. The curve of Martin's wide face was almost doglike. The thick white scars on his back, Gilly imagined, were from punishment, when Martin had been bullied or tortured by other salamanders.

"Martin," he said. "Let me go."

Martin didn't respond.

"You know what I want. Let me go, Martin, please. I have less than two hours left on my core. I just want to sit down."

Martin regarded him without expression.

"No one will know. I won't tell anyone, Martin."

Martin trotted toward him. *"Gik. Kee."*

He gestured at the arm that was bonded to the wall. "Please, Martin. This one. Please."

"Plek," Martin said. *"Plek."*

"Plek, Martin."

Martin took a step forward and hesitated.

"Plek," Gilly said. "Plek, plek."

Martin's head tilted. After a moment, Gilly detected a faint noise. A kind of thrumming, which he could feel as well as hear. Martin turned to face the tunnel entrance. The noise came again. Martin's head swung back toward Gilly.

"Don't look at me," he said.

Martin trotted out of the cave. Gilly hung, listening. The sound continued, stopping occasionally, then resuming, louder and more defined. There was something mechanical about it, something very Service, very human. The wild thought leaped into his brain: *rescue.* Service had sent a team and they were burning their way down to him. It was ridiculous but too amazing not to imagine and he couldn't think what else it might be. His active ping was disabled to save power, but now he brought it up and toggled it on.

After a second, his film pinged with a blue dot and the word: ANDERS.

He gasped. His heart began to bang painfully in his chest. The sounds resumed, closer than before. They had a rhythm, a kind of beat like a fast drum, drawing closer, until it became a pounding. There was silence for ten seconds, twenty, thirty, and then rock burst from the wall near where Martin sometimes rested. There was dust and a ragged hole and a suited figure climbing from it.

"Anders," Gilly said. "Anders. Anders." The figure came toward him. It had a helmet and a shining light and he couldn't see who it was.

Comms, he realized. He'd disabled those, too. He toggled the subsystem and there was breathing in his ear, which he recognized at once.

"Don't get too excited," Anders said. "There's no one else."

"Anders. Anders."

He came closer until Gilly could see his face. "Can you walk? Why are you standing like that?"

"I'm stuck to the wall."

Anders began to inspect him. "So you are." He checked his surroundings and saw the tunnel. "Let me know if salamanders come out of there."

"Thank you, Anders. Thank you." He began to cry. "I thought I was going to die."

Anders tugged at Gilly's shoulder. "You still might. Am I reading your core power right? You have eighty minutes?"

He nodded.

"I have a converter," Anders said, and Gilly began to shake, because that was something he hadn't even dared to imagine. He'd been preparing for death. "There's a safe place to use it back there. How did you get stuck like that? We need to get you off there."

"Yes," he said. "Yes."

Anders glanced back at the tunnel, slinging the lightning gun.

"Where are Jackson and Beanfield?"

"Jackson's dead. Beanfield's topside but in bad shape. Like I said, this is it."

He felt stunned. "How did you . . . What about the jetpod?"

"Sunk."

"The suits are good at depths of up to—"

Anders shook his head. "Jet's gone, Gilly. It was busted up even before it sank."

"But . . ." There had to be something. He couldn't be rescued only to be trapped on the planet. It was a puzzle. He just had to figure out the solution.

Anders shook his head. "I'll tell you when we get out of here." He strained and grunted. "You're really stuck there. I think I have to shoot it."

"What? No."

"The wall. Not you."

"It's a VX-10. It's like a firehose. You can't control where it goes."

"If I put any more pressure on your suit, it's going to rip."

"It won't." Anders looked doubtful. "Just try."

Anders turned the gun around and wedged the butt into Gilly's back. "Salamanders ever come out of there?"

"Yes."

"Seriously?"

"One of them visits me."

"How are you not dead?"

"It's . . . we've been trying to understand each other."

Anders peered at him. "A salamander?"

He nodded.

"What are you talking about?"

"I'm telling you they use this tunnel," Gilly said.

Anders pulled on the barrel of the lightning gun, straining for leverage. Gilly felt pressure building on his back. "Keep watching it."

"I'm watching."

"Unh," Anders said. He adjusted his grip. "So what did you learn?"

"What?"

"The salamander. Could you communicate?"

Now that he was being rescued, talking with Martin seemed very foolish. He shouldn't have done that. He shouldn't have engaged with the alien at all. "A little. I called him Martin. He learned very quickly."

"'He'?" Anders said.

"I mean 'it,'" Gilly said. "I was studying it. It's like a worker, but different. A new class, I think. Something we've never seen before. If we made it back to Service, it would be critical intel."

Anders strained against the rifle. "I don't think Service is taking our calls, Gilly."

"I know," he said.

"This is the source. We saw them venting. Millions coming out of the ground. At first, we thought it was a tornado. This is where they come from. The whole planet is a hive."

"What?" But it made sense to him immediately. One of the puzzles of salamander biology had always been that they weren't adapted for any known planetary environment, but seemed perfectly at home in space-faring hives. But this thinking rested on the assumption that hives were something like spaceships, temporary accommodation. The truth was, the salamanders were literally at home in hives. "We have to tell Service."

"Yeah," Anders said. "Shame about that. Goddamn, this resin. It moves but doesn't break."

"If they're venting, they must be breeding."

"Saw it myself. They have nurseries. They're safe for us, because the soldiers won't enter."

"Nurseries?"

"Slabs full of babies. In eggs."

"Eggs?"

"Sacs," Anders said, and began to describe a brown pool, which delivered translucent white jellies, to be cared for by nurses.

"How deep was this pool?"

"I didn't go in. Deep, I think. From how it bubbled, seemed it was coming from a long way down."

"So the breeders are deeper?"

"I guess."

"Why would that be? They physically isolate the breeders? Don't they trust the soldiers around them?" He shook his head. That couldn't be it. "You said the soldiers stay out of the nurseries. So they do obey physical limits."

"Beats me, Gilly."

"They must have special requirements," he said. "Or else . . ."

"Watch that fucking tunnel," Anders said.

His eyes had drifted. "Sorry."

"I don't give a shit about breeders, Gilly. I just want you and me to get out of here."

But he'd had a thought and couldn't keep it in. "Or else there aren't many. They have more nurseries than breeders. So they have to transport embryos in sacs from one to the other. Through liquid-filled tunnels. Tubes, which come up in pools."

"Watch that fucking tunnel. I've got this gun stuck halfway in the wall. It's going to take me a second to pull it out."

"Understood." Anders strained again. "If there aren't many breeders, they're valuable," Gilly said. "That could be another reason to separate them: for their protection. There might be only a small number." He licked his lips. "There might be one."

Anders looked at him.

"A queen."

"Gilly—"

"They have identical DNA. They're all produced by a single animal. It's a common hierarchy in colony species. It's been hypothesized. We just never had any evidence for it." Anders opened his mouth. "Anders, if there's a queen, and we kill it . . ."

Anders sighed.

"They'd have a way to replace her, but that would take time. Years, potentially. And until then, no new salamanders. It would end the war."

Anders shook his head. "All that money on the ships and you want to go face-to-face."

He snickered. "The ship got us here. And it chose us. AI selected the crew."

"Yeah, I'm sure it was imagining this situation. Gilly, I have to shoot this wall."

He couldn't argue any longer. "Not here. Farther over. You don't have to disintegrate the rock. Just warm it up enough to soften."

Anders positioned the barrel of the lightning gun against the rock a few feet away. "Here?"

"How much energy will that put out?" He couldn't remember the specs. He had skipped all the small-arms sessions, because he thought he'd never use one.

"Shitloads," Anders said.

"Farther," Gilly said.

Anders shifted. "I'll give it the smallest kick I can."

"Uh . . . all right." He turned away.

"Don't look away! I've got my back to a tunnel. I don't want to get jumped."

"I don't want to get shot in the face."

"You'll be fine," Anders said, and pulled the trigger.

There was a flash. The wall cracked. He strained and something tore. He felt himself falling. He tried to balance but his legs were useless.

Anders pulled him to his feet. "Now move." Gilly stumbled to the hole on wet-noodle legs and followed Anders through. There were a few feet of rock and then open space. It was dark and he brightened the small light on his helmet, which did nothing in the gloom. The pool that Anders had described lay a short distance away. When he moved toward it, he felt something soft underfoot. There was a centipedelike creature, black and sticky, with long pincers and a segmented body. A larva. He stared. It was larger than he'd imagined. He squatted beside it while Anders moved around the chamber, sweeping with his light.

"Is this an older one?" Gilly said. "A juvenile?"

Anders returned and began to set up the converter. He scooped up larvae and placed them inside. "No. They come out of the eggs like that."

"Sacs. This size?"

"Yep." The converter's lights glowed on, revealing more of the chamber. There were giant slabs of rock or resin just as Anders had described. Again, the spaces were disconcertingly large. "Problem?"

"If there's a queen producing millions of these, she must be huge."

"It's a big hive."

"Yeah." He began to explore the math on how much mass would be involved. It seemed like the answer was a lot. He poked at the burned larvae.

"There's the pool," Anders said. "Check it out while I feed these little shitholes to the converter."

He rose. The pool was filled with briny brown fluid, its edges laced with stringy froth. In theory, beneath it was a liquid-filled tunnel that served as an express elevator to a breeder. If it were large enough, they could traverse it in their suits. Which, he figured, it had to be, since the larvae were big.

Beside the pool lay two slumped forms. As he drew closer, he saw they were fully grown salamanders.

"Eyes open," Anders said. Gilly saw him bent over, fixing the lightning gun to the converter. "We have no gun while it does this."

"Didn't you say adults don't come in here?" Gilly said.

"Right."

"Then what am I looking at?"

Anders's light swung onto the creatures. "Nurses. The babies eat them. It's disgusting."

Gilly moved closer. He let his light play over them. The bodies were disfigured by the effects of the lightning gun; he could barely tell which way they were facing. He'd never heard anyone propose that salamanders might have nurses. "The larvae *eat* them?"

"Or drink. I don't know. The nurses have bulges on their backs. See them? Like blisters. The little ones suck on those."

He squinted. He didn't see any blisters. Most had popped and shriveled under fire, and hung in loose flaps. Some, toward the front of the creature, seemed older. Remnants of past feedings, maybe. These had dried to thick white ridges, like scars.

"Oh, no," he said.

"What is it?"

"Martin is a nurse."

He looked at the hole. He couldn't tell how long Martin had been there. When the light struck her face, she launched herself and landed heavily on the floor. Anders yelped. He ripped the lightning gun free from the converter. Gilly saw two glowlights along its barrel blink on. Anders rose to his feet and Martin collided with him with enough force to jerk it from his grip. She galloped across the floor and drove Anders into the end of the slab.

Gilly ran to the gun and snatched it up. He didn't know how to fire it. But he'd seen Anders hold it and raised it in the same way.

Martin was slumped to the floor, moving slowly. Gilly advanced, keeping the gun trained on her. Her hind legs twitched. She began to rise. She took a few unsteady steps and that was when he saw that Anders was crushed against the rock.

"No," he said. "Anders. No."

"*Gik. Kee,*" Martin said.

He sank to his haunches. He couldn't look at Anders but also couldn't look away. There was a wild grief in his chest, pressing against his lungs.

Martin tottered toward the pool. She made no move to attack him. She lowered her head and nosed at the burned larvae.

Beside her, the converter lay in pieces. Martin had stepped on it during the attack. Even from here, he could see that it was destroyed.

He breathed. He looked at Anders. Then away.

According to his film, he had approximately an hour of life remaining.

Martin hunched over the larvae, her middle legs scooping at the pieces.

He stared at her. It was as if a veil had been ripped from his vision. Martin wasn't his friend. She wasn't like him. She wasn't like anything he had created in his imagination.

His core battery reading flipped below sixty minutes.

He explored the gun. It didn't seem complicated. There was a thumb latch, a trigger. He thought he could figure this one out.

He forced himself to his feet. "Martin," he said.

She turned. What was in her features, he had no idea. He couldn't intuit her thinking. Martin might have understood what he was doing, or not.

He squeezed the trigger. The gun kicked. The afterimage of lightning crawled across his eyeballs. He sat and cried for a while.

He spent some time inspecting the converter piece by piece, just in case. But there was no miracle: It had been destroyed.

He sat with Anders. He squeezed shut his eyes. He didn't think he could do this without Anders. Anders was the one who made impossible things happen. "I'm sorry," he croaked.

Anders's core, too, was unusable.

So that was that. There was no chance of escape. This was not a carefully designed puzzle with a tricky solution he had to work hard to find. It was simpler than that. It was the logical result of forces beyond his control.

He enabled his suit's ping sweep, and within a minute it flared Beanfield's location. She was on the edge of his range, her little blip flitting in and out of existence. He tried to hail her but received no response. He was able to transmit asynchronous data at a low rate, though, so, for what it was worth, he sent the recordings he'd made, everything from the beginning. Then he recorded a clip, describing what had happened and what had become of Anders, and sent that, too.

When that was done, he shut down all comms and ping. It meant that Beanfield couldn't reply, even if she moved closer. His core read forty-two minutes. For what he wanted to do next, he couldn't spare the power.

"I'm going after the queen," he said. He was still recording, but realistically, this was just for him. It had probably been like that for a while. "I might be able to make a difference."

He moved to the edge of the pool. He wound the lightning gun's strap around his body and waded in.

The sides quickly grew steep. When he reached the point where his next step would take him out of his depth, he gave the chamber a last glance, then let the liquid close over his faceplate.

Gravity tugged him downward. His helmet light illuminated thick brown muck to a distance of ten inches. He put out a hand and felt rock sliding by.

After a few minutes, his boots hit something solid. He jerked. He wasn't sure of the effect of discharging the lightning gun underwater and didn't especially want to find out, but he thrust the weapon in that direction. A shape loomed, amorphous and indistinct, a sac: a translucent blob congealed around a dark larva. He let it float by.

He tried to control his breathing. His thermals were rising. None of this was good for his core battery. He had thirty-five minutes.

Soon he encountered another sac, then more. The fourth was smaller and less well formed, and frayed apart as he maneuvered by.

For most of his descent, he had periodically scraped the sides, as the tunnel fell at an angle, but now it widened to the point where he couldn't feel the walls. He found this disconcerting. He'd been prepared for a long tube, but expected it to be narrow: one end connected to the nursery, the other to something he could shoot.

"Where are you?" he said.

He began to swim and still couldn't find anything solid. Soon every sac he encountered was little more than sticky clumps of gossamer. He feared he'd taken a wrong turn, becoming lost in the muck and winding up in a place for discards and genetic failures. This tube might have side tunnels. It might be a network. He sank through soup.

Eventually his boots found the floor. He used his light and saw round boulders. There was nowhere else to go, so he struck upward at an angle.

Unexpectedly, he broke the surface. He bobbed, casting about with the light. He was on a lake. There was a high rocky roof. To his right, it curved down to meet the soup. The rock was different: rough and irregular, gray rather than orange. He swam until he found a natural shelf on which he could rest.

He breathed, exhausted. He had been avoiding looking at his core, afraid of what it would say.

Six minutes.

He had to move. The queen, or whatever there was, could be a hundred miles away. Or it could be around the next turn of rock.

He couldn't resist activating his ping sweep one more time, searching for Beanfield. Now she was outside his range. When his light played against the rock wall, he saw a twist of something that appeared organic, almost like ancient tree roots. He wondered: Had the salamanders encased a planet in resin? Perhaps there was a whole world down here that they'd slowly drowned.

The soup flowed gently by, lapping at him. When he raised a leg, it was filmed with a sticky substance. Sacs. Remnants of sacs. The lake was thick with the stuff. He couldn't figure out why there was so much of it. It didn't make sense to him that they would float around here until half of them disintegrated.

Also: How were there so many?

He hadn't finished his train of thought from before. It was conceivable that all salamanders came from a single breeder; there were animals that bred in those kinds of numbers, fish that spawned thousands of eggs at a time. But tiny eggs, because the fish didn't have much mass to give.

If there were a queen, she would have to be the size of a city. Larger than he could imagine, spawning salamanders in an endless flowing tide. How would that work? What would she eat?

What do you think you're going to find out there?

Answers. I like finding the answers to questions like that.

Even if he couldn't kill the thing, he wanted to see it. He at least wanted to answer that question to his own satisfaction.

His suit was losing the ability to replace carbon dioxide with oxygen. It had been complaining for a while with low, insistent tones. He should move. But first, he closed his eyes.

When he opened them, he saw the truth.

The sticky film; the disintegrating sacs. They weren't old. They weren't broken. They were new. They were forming.

He dialed up his suit light. Illumination spread across the surface of the lake. The edges of the light ran farther and farther back and found no end.

There was no queen. Of course not. There was only soup.

He laughed despite himself. "Oh," he said. "Wow."

His core was beginning to list off imminent systems failures, thermals, filters, pressure. He shut off the display. He didn't need to see that.

"The salamander reproductive element is an amorphous fluid," he said. "It appears to consume resources from the planet and create eggs via an exogenic chemical process. It's too big for me to do anything about."

He stared at the gentle flow of soup. It didn't even have a brain. There was no intent. No malice. They were at war with a blind string of DNA. He was glad he'd found the truth.

His head nodded; he caught himself. He had run out of air.

"Wow," he said again.

16

[Beanfield]

THE SURVIVOR

She sat up. She was surrounded by rock. She turned her head and there was no Anders and no Jackson.

Her throat was dry. "Anders," she croaked. There was no sound but her own breathing.

There was a low rocky overhang and she banged her helmet on it. She stopped and tried to think. Anders and Jackson had left her to go explore some kind of hole they'd spotted. She had lain down and exhaustion had fallen over her like a blanket and now this.

She hobbled along the ravine. "Anders?" she said again. She fumbled at her film but couldn't bring him up on it, for some reason. She couldn't find either of them. "Jackson?"

You wake up on an alien planet. There is no one and nothing. Go.

She began to climb the side of the ravine. This was a lot harder than it looked, because she had a hot mess of an ankle and the gravity was relentless, but she fought her way up it a toehold at a time. There was a lip, and more rock after that. This would make a good Talia feed, it occurred to her: There was plenty of really identifiable Feed Talia behavior right here. Those were her most popular clips, the ones with vulnerability, and she was feeling pretty vulnerable at the moment, pretty goddamn vulnerable, because no one was here. She was starting to freak out a little, which people liked, too, watching Talia losing her mind over something silly. There had been a clip where she couldn't find her white socks and it had sparked a set of memes and references that she hadn't completely understood, but people dug it, was the point. There were so many people who would stand beside her in this moment, if only they knew. If she ever got out of here, she would tell how it had happened for her feed, and it would be amazing, and people would love her. She focused on that. When she gained enough height to turn and scour the landscape, there was rocky plain, split and sundered, as far as she could see and nothing else.

You have been abandoned. Your home is fifty trillion miles away. Go. It was really unfathomable that she could be alone right now.

She checked ping again. She didn't know if she was doing something wrong or her survival core was preserving power or Anders and Jackson had decided to play a hilarious practical joke, but she was not loving this. She picked her way back down into the ravine and sat. She waited. That was what you were supposed to do when you were lost. That was what everyone said. *Stay where you are and we'll come find you.* You definitely shouldn't wander off, because you might get *really* lost, and never found.

Time passed. She tried to clear her mind. She wasn't terrific when left to her own thoughts, to be honest. She was better when she had other people to bounce off. When it was just her, all alone, she would return to old fears and inflate them. Like thinking she was the only person alive on an empty world.

She tried to remember her roleplays. But she couldn't think of one that applied to the situation, and was there any point to a roleplay if no one was watching? She might as well drop the facade. She might as well go ahead and give in to the bubbling terror that the worst thing she could imagine had come to pass.

She couldn't stay still any longer and rose and began to walk. She would go a short distance only. It wasn't like a maze; she could find her way back. Once she got moving, she felt better. She was accomplishing something, putting one foot in front of the other. She walked for a while before realizing there had been a tiny red dot in the corner of her film this whole time.

A notification. Messages. People. *Oh, thank you.* She activated it and found two clips awaiting her attention: one from Anders and one from Gilly.

She was so awash with relief that it took her a moment to remember that Gilly was supposed to be dead. He had died on the ship. Then Anders was filling her view, standing on a landscape of blasted rock.

"Beanfield," he said. "I've got a ping on Gilly. He's alive." He pointed at something in the distance, a smudge like a low hill. "There's an entrance to a burrow. I'm going to try to get him out."

She blinked. First, that didn't sound like a good idea. Anders hated confined spaces. She wondered if it was too late to do something. Get Jackson on the line, tell her: *Do not let Anders enter a burrow.* Second, could she get some elaboration on the part about Gilly? Because as far as she knew—

"Jackson's dead."

Her heart jumped. Anders kept talking. Something about a salamander, a chase, the gun. She couldn't get past the first two words. How could Jackson be dead? She was bigger than that.

"I have to take the matter converter. I'm sorry. It's our only chance. Stay put. If Gilly and I make it out, we'll find you. If we don't . . . well, I'm sorry I was such a shit to you, Beanfield. I always liked you."

The recording ended.

She felt like: *Excuse me?* That couldn't be it. You couldn't abandon someone on an alien planet and leave them a message like that.

She swept her ping again. Nothing.

It occurred to her to check the timestamp, to establish when Anders had sent this message. When the number came up, it was six hours ago.

Time distortion. Her suit was confused. The days were longer. It was the time zone. Did they do daylight savings here?

If Anders had sent that message six hours ago, he wasn't coming back.

A trembling began in her legs. She flipped to Gilly's message. It was enormous, with multiple parts and what seemed to be days of video. She couldn't make sense of it. She skipped ahead, but that was even worse, so she rewound to the beginning.

"Hi, Beanfield." Gilly. Definitely alive. Somewhere dark. Not on the ship. Behind him was shadowy orange rock. "I've been trying to ping you, but we're too far apart for a synchronous connection." He glanced at something in the background. A slumped form. She already knew what he was going to say and turned away but of course the projection followed. "Anders found me. But he didn't make it."

The timestamp. She backgrounded the vision so she could expand the message details. Five hours ago.

"I've been documenting what I've seen. It's useful intel, if you can get it home. I guess that's impossible. But I figure you've got a better shot than me. I don't have enough time on my core to get out of here, Beanfield. But Anders and I might have figured out how salamanders breed, and I'm going to see if I can stop them."

She shut off the recording. She wrapped her arms around her head and keened.

Everyone is dead but you.

Go.

In the ravine, something scraped against rock. She raised her head. She rose and hobbled ahead to the next turn of rock. At first there was nothing. Then a salamander appeared, picking its way through the fissure toward her.

She began to retreat. A soldier, she thought, an enormous black salamander as big as a bear, and she moved as quickly as she could but her legs were shaking and if she put her foot in the wrong place, she would slip and fall and that would be the end of her. She could hear it behind her, its hard skin on rock, and she forced her eyes to stay focused on what lay ahead. Only when she reached a turn did she glance back, and it was there, thirty feet behind.

She shrieked and stumbled forward and heard the salamander start after her. It was going to catch her and she scrambled up the ravine wall, which was possibly idiotic, because it could almost certainly scale the rock faster than she could. The salamander galloped toward her and its jaws opened and she pulled herself upward onto the lip of the ravine and rolled away.

This was not a good feed. This was not amusing, relatable vulnerability. This was horrible. It was Feed Talia being torn to pieces by an alien. She found her feet and began to stumble across the rock on her bad ankle. She should have stayed where she was. She shouldn't be here at all. When she looked back, the salamander was clawing its way out of the fissure, its black wings spreading, beating for lift, and then they folded down and it began to gallop after her. Its jaws cracked open and it issued a sound: *"Pak! Pak! Pak!"* The sound cut through her. There was a pressure, a feeling like the clouds were coming down on her like a vise. More salamanders began to emerge from the fissure, one by one, as if there were a procession of them down there and she'd encountered the band leader. They echoed its cry, *"Pak! Pak!"* which, she now knew, meant, *Quick, come eat this human!* She stopped running and they swept toward her.

I'm sorry. I don't think I can continue with this roleplay.

I think that's scene.

The first salamander was twenty feet away when its front half disappeared. She was looking at its insides, at thick twitching meat. Its legs jerked and it fell over. She didn't know what had happened. She wasn't sure where the rest of it had gone. There were sharp kicks in the soles of her feet and she didn't know what they were, either, but the salamanders jerked and split and became dark stains on the rock. In moments, they were dead.

She looked around. From farther away, more salamanders began to emerge from the fissure.

The pressure in her head was unbearable. She felt as if the air had compressed, as if the sky was falling in a solid slab.

There was a noise like the wail of dying angels. Above, the roiling cloud split open. From it, the ship emerged.

Its hull was almost entirely the burnished yellow of new skin. Wind tore at her. The ships' mass projectors were rotated onto its belly, flashing. They pounded the rock and obliterated salamanders. After a minute, it fell silent. There was only her and the ship. The wail sounded again.

A white disc glowed hotly at the center of the ship's belly. She'd never seen that particular weapon powered. It was the plasma cannon, the one they called the planet-killer.

Oh, she thought. *Of course.*

The ship hadn't come for her. It had come for the salamanders.

She'd known her relationship with the ship was largely invented. She had just forgotten that for a minute. The wail came a third time. It was the warning siren that meant imminent discharge. The white disc was enormous, like the blind eye of a god. Gilly had been right all along: She was insignificant in the scheme of this war, which would be won by forces larger than any of them, and go on even then, in new and unpredictable forms. She was a bystander. She stood on the rock against the buffeting wind and waited for the ship to destroy everything.

A few hundred feet away, rock burst open. A black torrent of salamanders sprayed forth. A second place exploded, then a third, until the air was thick with them. The rock beneath her feet jolted and she stumbled. Everywhere the ground opened up and black salamanders flew out. In the distance, she saw a swarm like a black cloud swinging toward it from a mountain. As she clung to the rock, they came as if there was no end to their numbers, as if the planet were made of them. One thumped against her, its wings warm and heavy, and did not stop but flew on toward the ship. Even the salamanders realized she was meaningless. The ship's mass projectors began to cycle again. Salamander bodies plunged around her. But there were so many. As they rose, they filled the air with sound: *Huk. Huk.*

Through a torrent of salamander bodies she saw the ship's foredecks split through by a thousand little gluon-quark balls until the structure could no longer support its own weight and broke off toward the rock. Everywhere the ship was punctured and breaking. "Shoot!" she screamed. The planet-killer was primed. It could end this. It would kill her and maybe itself but it would take the salamanders with it.

Although now that she thought about it: Why was it so close? It didn't need to breach atmosphere to use the weapon. It was better not to. It should have stayed clear to avoid the incredible amount of flying debris that would exist after it put a lightning bolt through a quintillion tons of planet. She knew she wasn't supposed to try to read the mind of an AI, but this was insanity.

A dark shape fell toward her, a maimed salamander, perhaps. There was an engine roar and a flaring of hot thrusters. The bull-nosed shape of a jetpod set down. Salamanders flew by, ignoring it. She stared dumbly and then scrambled toward it. When she slapped the tactile panel, the door opened. "Gilly?" she said, but there was no answer, and no occupants. Before she could process this, the door closed behind her. The engines kicked. She felt herself began to lift off. The viewports were thick with dark salamander bodies. The acceleration drove her toward the floor but she was able to crawl to a harness and work the straps. Salamander bodies thumped against the hull. As she rose higher, they began to thin, and she could see more of the ship and the terrible damage it was sustaining. Its engines began to crumble. "No," she said, because it was dying. It wouldn't survive long enough for her to reach it. Then she realized the jetpod was arcing away. It wasn't taking her to the ship.

The accelerative force increased. There were charts and numbers on the viewports but they were shaking too much to read. She saw the ship falling to pieces and then the viewports fogged and were enveloped by cloud.

She fought the darkness creeping in from the edges of her vision. When the shaking stopped and the viewports filled with inky starfield, she saw the path the ship had plotted for her: a hard burn and a skip to take her all the way out of VZ and then to home.

"Wait," she said. She twisted until she could see what she was leaving behind. The ship was invisible, submerged in a balled mass of cloud. The numbers on the viewports blanked. A word appeared:

GOODBYE

The planet heaved and went white. The jetpod began to skip ahead even faster. A minute later, a wave of turbulence passed through so violently that she thought it would pull the teeth from her head. She fought to stay awake but this time could not.

Eventually she raised her head. It had been three hours, according to the viewport numbers. She had traveled forty thousand miles. A little under fifty trillion to go. The jetpod continued to accelerate, making movement difficult, but she managed to free herself from the harness and grab a support bar. She was approximately ten months from home. There was no food, no water, no anything. The only way to survive this trip was to crawl into a medbag and let it put her into a coma.

She wasn't ready for that. She brought up her comms and rewatched the message from Anders. Then she played the one from Gilly, the one she hadn't gotten to the end of, not even to the parts he'd apparently recorded as an exposé of his captivity in a salamander hive.

"One more thing," Gilly said. "This isn't on any of the recordings, because it's not about the mission, but I wanted to say, I don't think I ever told you I think you're good at your job. It took me a while to figure out what you really did. I didn't appreciate that for a long time."

Her teeth chattered. The jetpod was cold. She couldn't postpone the next part much longer.

"Anyway," he said. "I should go. I hope you get this."

She dragged herself to a locker. She pulled free a medbag and forced herself into it. She peeled the film from her face. She had to zip the bag all the way up, which was not the greatest sensation, being basically suffocated by a bag, but as it pressed around her body it gave a kind of comfort. She could feel them with her, Gilly and Anders and Jackson and the ship. She closed her eyes and let the engines carry her home.

THE RETURN

When the escort fighters break out of the cloud, people clap and cheer. They're tightly packed all around you, crackling with excitement, these people who were drawn together like they've congregated all over the world, in New York and London, São Paulo and Bombay, every town large enough to erect big screens in an open space. Like you, they've come to watch with as many fellow human beings as possible, because that's what you're celebrating today, the thing that unites you. For the last few hours the screens have been playing backstories, feed clips, and mission highlights. But now it's happening. She's here.

The fighters bank and turn in opposite directions. From the cloud behind, the jetpod emerges. People start yelling. You're struck by how small it is: a toilet paper tube with a rounded nose. It moves slowly, with no visible engine exhaust, and a moment later you see why, as a big helicraft comes out of the cloud, four rotors blasting. It's lowering the jetpod to the ground. Because, of course, that little ship isn't well designed to land by itself; that's not its main job. Its job is to bring her home.

A man to your left throws out an arm. Suddenly you're hugging. Together you watch the jetpod descend until the helicraft's rotors are blasting dust across the Vandenberg tarmac. Cables detach, fall to the ground. The helicraft peels away.

Now there's a minute where the jetpod is just lying there. The crowd quietens.

The thought crosses your mind: *Something's gone wrong*. After all this, there's been a fatal mistake. But that can't be right. You know this moment must have been engineered down to the smallest detail—that Talia Beanfield returned eight days ago, and since then has been in low orbit, being cared for, debriefed, and, you assume, told how to act once she makes it down. You know she was packed back into the jetpod for show, even though a shuttle would have made more sense. You know that a lot of what you're told isn't the plain truth—and not lies, either, but rather satisfying stories wrapped around cold facts. Everyone understands that you only get to see the best side of these things: that Providence crews aren't really that noble; the ships not as infallible; Service and its corporate partners not as uncompromised.

But so what? People don't care about the cold facts. If the salamanders weren't really driven by a hatred of humanity; if Jackson, Anders, Gilly, and Beanfield didn't have quite as much agency in the destruction of the hive planet as has been suggested—hell, if the whole thing really was providence, and once the ships were built, nothing any mere human did at any stage made the slightest difference to the ultimate outcome at all—that doesn't matter. You don't want a universe of absent gods. You want meaning and purpose. What happened to those people matters because that's the part of the story you care about. And so when Talia Beanfield comes home, it's because she deserved to.

There's a puff of white smoke on the jetpod. A hatch shifts, opens. The screens zoom in.

She pulls herself out. You've seen her image more times than you can count but in this moment she's unearthly. Her eyes are calm and clear and take in the wide ring of people and equipment around her. Then she looks straight into the camera. It could be planned, but it doesn't matter: It feels as if she's looking right back at you. You know her. The journey she's been on, it's been your journey, too. In that way, you make each other matter.

The man beside you jumps up and down. He's screaming something. The crowd noise is incredible but you can make out his words. *It's over,* he's saying. *We won.*

ACKNOWLEDGMENTS

A long time ago, in high school, I wrote a story about two people on a spaceship who encountered this other ship, which was all abandoned and spooky, and one of the people went in to see what was going on, and when he came back, he was infected with something. It was a short story, only a few pages, and most of it was concerned with a stand-off in a corridor between these two people, only one of whom was still human.

I shared this story with my best friend, Freddy, who had a major problem with it. "They don't fire the guns," he said. "At the start of the story you say their ship has these huge guns, but they never use them."

This was true. I did describe huge guns. I was thinking it was clever, because in the end, weapons couldn't save them. It was ironic. Freddy disagreed. "You can't have a spaceship with *huge guns*," he said, "and *not fire them*."

This was my introduction to a storytelling principle known as Chekhov's Gun, which was a good thing to learn. But it was also an early experience with a reader who disliked a story not because it was implausible, or badly written, or made no sense—the usual reasons—but because it didn't go right. Freddy was totally on board for a story of infected astronauts. He just felt short-changed about the guns.

I'm endlessly grateful to the people who let me into their minds a little bit and help me figure out what happens when I put different words there. They have been doing it forever, and without them, I would still be writing stories with huge guns that no one fires. I have a lot to learn, but at least I'm not doing that.

For reading early, incoherent *Providence* drafts, thank you to the usual suspects, especially Kassy Humphreys and Charles Thiesen. For pouncing on later ones and championing them with passion and insight, all my thank-yous to Luke Janklow and Claire Dippel.

For believing in me and this story, and giving me the most wonderfully useful analysis of it, thank you to my editors, Mark Tavani at Putnam and Ruth Tross at Mulholland. Thank you also to Ivan Held, who, before he became my publisher, was on the very first cover of my very first novel, which just goes to show that some people never get punished for anything.

Thank you, you who picked up this book and read it all the way through. There are so many distractions now, so many forms of entertainment that are quicker and easier and only a tap and a swipe away. But nothing beats a good novel, if you can find one. I hope you did.

Thank you, Jen, for everything. You and me to the end.

Freddy—thank you for waiting. I know it took a while. Let me know what I screwed up this time.

PROVIDENCE

MAX BARRY

Discussion Guide

Excerpt from **The 22 Murders of Madison May**

BOOK
ENDS

PUTNAM
— EST. 1838 —

DISCUSSION GUIDE

1. *Providence* is told from the point of view of four very different characters—Anders, Gilly, Jackson, and Talia. Did reading the novel from these multiple perspectives change your reading experience? How did the three perspectives inform one another?

2. Discuss the different motivations presented for conducting the war on the aliens. Do you think the war is justified? Why or why not?

3. Gilly says that human beings are "throwaway survival machines" for genes, and Talia suggests that the ship is the same thing for them. Do you think this is correct?

4. Talia believes that her position as Life Officer is the most important on the ship. Do you agree or disagree? What role did each crew member serve, both within and outside of their assigned jobs?

5. Discuss the way that isolation impacts each member of the crew, comparing and contrasting their different reactions to being cut off from the world.

6. What role does social media and propaganda play in the Providence mission? Do the characters and the mission change after access to social media is lost?

7. The characters have different opinions about the nature of the salamanders and the ship. How reliable are these? What do they say about the characters themselves?

8. Discuss the ways that artificial intelligence and humanity are intertwined in the novel. Look specifically at moments when both human relationships and technology break down.

9. *Providence* is set in the future but has many parallels to our life on Earth today. What are the lessons or warnings that you took away from your reading that may apply to the present?

10. Discuss the final actions of the ship—why do you think it sacrificed itself to rescue Talia? Does this imply that there was something "human" about the ship? Do you think that technology can ultimately be trusted?

11. What did you make of the final scene in the novel after Talia's return to Earth? Have the humans really "won"? If so, what exactly does winning mean in this context?

12. Was the crew necessary? The final chapter asks: "If the whole thing really was providence, and once the ships were built, nothing any mere human did at any stage made the slightest difference to the ultimate outcome at all. . . ." Was this the case?

13. What genre do you think that *Providence* falls into? Is it science fiction, a social novel, a thriller, a dystopian tale, or something else entirely?

TURN THE PAGE FOR AN EXCERPT

In *The 22 Murders of Madison May,* a serial killer stalks the same woman across parallel lives.

Felicity Staples hates reporting on murders, but as a journalist for a New York City paper, she must investigate the shocking death of real estate agent Madison May. At the scene of the crime, she sees something utterly unexpected: scratched madly into the drywall, a mysterious insignia and the word STOP.

Pursuing the story, Felicity has a violent encounter with a suspect—after which, she finds her life strangely altered. Then Madison May is murdered again—in a different place, at a different time, now as a struggling actress. Swept up in a deadly game, Felicity must attempt to put a stop to the next killing while also trying to put back together the broken pieces of her own what-if lives.

1

She pulled to the curb and peered through her car window at the house she had to sell. The mailbox was lying across the lawn in pieces, as if someone had taken a baseball bat to it. "Oh, come on," Maddie said. The house was a dump. The mailbox had been one of the best things about it.

She retrieved her bag from the passenger seat, climbed out, and tugged down her dress. It was ninety degrees and humid. Her house's best feature was spread across the earth. But she had brought her sneakers, which meant she wouldn't have to do this in heels. She carried broken mailbox shards around to the side of the house and dumped them beside a pile of old wood and a deflated football. While she was picking clean the small lawn, she noticed two boys of about fourteen loitering on bikes outside the fence, so she straightened and waved to them.

"Bend over again," said one of the boys. The other laughed.

She went into the house. It was dark. The walls leaned close. There was a fusty, hard-to-mistake, neglected grandma smell. But it was hers to sell, so she drew the curtains, drained the sink, and opened the back door. She set candles in strategic locations: hallway, bedroom, and a weird L-shaped space that she'd decided to call a study. These were her special candles, which she'd found after an online search for *conceal stench*. She checked her watch. The candles were good, but for emergencies, she had another secret weapon: a spray can labeled *Just Like Cookies*. It was less convincing than the candles, closer to *Just Like Burnt Dirt*, but it worked faster. She moved from room to room, spraying in controlled bursts.

She was staring at a dark stain in the corner of the living room when a car eased into the cracked concrete driveway. "Shit," she said. She yanked off her sneakers, stuffed them into her bag, and squeezed her feet into stilettos. She swiped open her phone and keyed a playlist, SELL MUSIC, which was pianos and swelling strings, a little brass: classy, but also motivational. The car door thumped. She used her hand mirror to verify that nothing had gone horribly wrong with her face, then focused on reaching the front door without driving a heel through the floorboards.

The buyer was approaching the concrete front steps, removing his sunglasses, craning his neck to peer at something higher up. The drainpipe, she guessed. It wasn't actually attached to anything. She had meant to do something about that.

"Hi!" she said, and smiled, like: BZZZT. The saying went *Location, Location, Location*, but at Henshaw Realty, it was *Teeth, Tits, Hair*—at least according to Maddie's mentor, Susie, who'd been selling houses for thirty years and presumably knew what she was talking about. BZZZT: Head up, teeth out, shoulders back, little head tilt, hair falling to the side. She had long hair, red edging into auburn, which so far she had resisted blondifying. "I'm Maddie!" she said. "Thanks so much for coming."

The buyer shook her hand. He was about her age, early twenties, dimples, thin, but somewhat cute. Despite the heat, he was wearing a long-sleeved collared shirt over chinos. "I'm Clay," he said. "Wow, you're tall."

"It's the shoes."

He looked down, so she took the opportunity to turn one leg and do a little pose. When he met her eyes again, she went: BZZZT.

"You're really pretty," he said.

She laughed and turned to let him follow her into the hallway. Too much BZZZT. She would tone that down. "You're lucky," she called over her shoulder, as they entered the kitchen's chemical embrace of cookies-slash-burnt-dirt. "We've had a lot of calls about this house. You're the first to see it." Lies. Terrible lies.

"Is that right?" He had removed his sunglasses. Strong eyebrows. His hair was a little shaggy, not really her thing, but she liked the implication, that he had his own style. Went his own way. Was possibly uniquely into falling-down unrenovated 1960s clapboard two-bedrooms in Jamaica, Queens.

She collected her phone, which was tinkling piano noises. "Do you mind if I take your photo?"

"What for?"

"It's a security thing."

He seemed confused.

"It's silly, but we're meeting people alone, so they like us to—"

"Oh, of course. I get it."

She raised the phone. He straightened and smiled, a little BZZZT of his own. He was kind of awkward. Beneath the dimples and the shaggy hair, she sensed a guy who wasn't comfortable with people.

She snapped. "Done," she said. "That goes to our office." Where they had his details from when he'd made the appointment. He was Clayton Hors, of Ulysses, Pennsylvania. Currently living with his parents, after dropping out of Carnegie Mellon, looking to start a new life with a move to the city, thanks to, Maddie was guessing, a push from the folks. She put down the phone. "Thanks."

"No problem. There are some bad people out there. You have to take precautions."

"I also know jujitsu." She did not. "So," she said, "I really love this window. You get so much light."

He nodded. "How long have you been selling houses?"

"About a year." He wasn't looking at the window. Although maybe that was a good thing: The backyard was thigh-high weeds and a quietly rotting shed.

"Is real estate your"—he searched for words—"long-term ambition?"

"Oh, I love houses." Technically the truth. Houses, she loved. Real estate, which, it turned out, was mostly about pressuring people into making decisions, not so much. She had been wondering lately whether she'd chosen the wrong career. For a long time, she'd dreamed about acting—never seriously committed to it, of course, because it was so impractical, like saying you wanted to be an astronaut, but if she was still thinking about it, did that mean something? That she should have been braver?

"You love this house?" he said, looking at the crooked cupboards, the blotchy curtains.

"Every house has something to love. You just have to look for it."

He smiled. A genuine smile. He had warmed up. "Well, good for you." He headed into the living room and she followed. "Although I'm a little surprised you're not an actress."

She stopped, startled.

He glanced back. "Sorry. I blurt out whatever I'm thinking. Is it okay if I look around by myself? I'll let you know if I have questions."

"Sure," she said, recovering. "Knock yourself out."

He moved off. She peered at a cupboard door that was hanging by one hinge, wondering if she could fix it. Susie, her mentor, would say: *Maddie, leave it. The house is shit. You can't make it not shit. Try to dress it up and all buyers will see is that you're lying to them.* It was true, Maddie supposed. But this kind of thing wasn't even about the buyers. It bothered her on a personal level to see something that needed fixing and not fix it.

The *Just Like Cookies* was wearing off, so she moved about the house to deploy a few more tactical sprays. On a pass through the kitchen, she checked her phone, because she had a boyfriend, Trent, who was supposedly going to let her know whether he would be home tonight or out with friends. Nothing.

Clay appeared in the doorway. "I'm just gonna grab something from my car."

"Sure," she said.

He'd pushed up his sleeves. On his right forearm was a discoloration, a patch of purple, red, and yellow all mixed together, like an injury that wasn't healing right.

He caught her looking. "I have a dog. Goes kind of crazy sometimes."

"Oh," she said. What was she doing? Staring like an idiot. "I'm sorry."

"She has a good heart. Just doesn't always know it. I'll be right back."

He disappeared. She felt mad at herself. She moved to the living room and watched him open the trunk of his car. A nice one, a new black Chevrolet SUV. Rental sticker, so she couldn't infer anything about his finances. She returned to the kitchen and her musical phone.

He clomped back inside the house. After a few minutes, she called: "Everything okay?"

There was no answer, so she put down her phone and set out to find him. He wasn't in the hallway, nor the laundry—"laundry," with air quotes—a tight cupboard of rusted steel and water stains. He wasn't in the room she was calling a second bedroom, even though the only way you were getting a bed in there was upright. The hallway ran down the middle of the house; possibly they were circling each other. But if so, he was being very quiet. She didn't think it was possible to move around this house without making a sound unless you were very intent on doing so.

When she entered the master bedroom, she found the curtains were closed. She had definitely opened those earlier. She reached to toggle the light switch, but of course there was no power; it had been disconnected months ago. In the gloom, she could make out a silver lump on the carpet: a case of some kind, possibly a toolbox. The lid was open, but it was facing the other way, so she couldn't see what was inside.

Her phone in the kitchen fell silent.

She turned. "Hello?"

The front door was ten feet to her right. It was open. Outside was a clear, bright day. Concrete path, low chain-link fence. The road was a cul-de-sac—rare in New York, a real jewel in this house's cardboard crown—so there was no passing traffic, but she could hear kids calling to one another, most likely the two who'd been out front when she arrived.

She had sent Clay's photo to her office. They had his details, which had been verified before she'd even come out here. Clay knew this. The security process was on her side.

She headed to the kitchen.

He wasn't there. Neither was her phone. That was less cool. "Hello?" she said again, more aggressively. "Can I help you?"

The outside noise fell away until she was standing in a closed-in bubble of quiet. The front door had closed, she realized.

The wind. You opened all the doors and the breeze can be strong, can blow right through, slam a door—

Only the back door wasn't open. None of the doors were open. And none of them had slammed. They had closed so softly she hadn't heard the click.

No breeze had blown her phone away, either.

She called: "Clay, my office has your information. They know who you are."

She was in an empty kitchen. The drawers were empty: no knives, nothing she could see to use as a weapon. Outside, though, were those kids. The house was clapboard; if she screamed, they might hear.

She bent down and unstrapped her stilettos. Whatever might happen next, she didn't want to face it on heels.

"Sorry." His voice floated toward her. "Sorry, Madison, I'm here."

She stayed where she was. "Do you have my phone?"

"I'm sorry, I needed it for a second."

"Why do you have my phone?"

Silence.

She opened her mouth to repeat the question. He appeared in the living room doorway. She tensed. She could be hitting the back door in about three seconds. Would it be locked? Would it stick? If so, he would catch her before she got out.

"I'm super-apologetic about this. I really didn't mean to freak you out." His palms were up to indicate his complete lack of threat. But he was moving toward her, one slow step at a time, which she did not like at all. She could see that discoloration on his forearm: the dog bites that weren't healing. A mix of old and new wounds, she realized suddenly. He'd been bitten over and over. By that dog he said he owned, who had a good heart but didn't always know it.

"Can you stop?" she said. "I am actually freaked out."

He stopped. "I'm really sorry to do it like this. I know how it looks. But I'm out of time."

"Can I have my phone back?"

He looked pained. "Unfortunately, no."

"Why not?"

"Madison, you have to trust me. I don't want to hurt you. I'm here for you." He began to edge toward her again.

"Stop. I want you to leave this house."

"I can't do that. I'm sorry. I need you to come to the bedroom."

The bedroom. Where the curtains were closed. Where a silver box sat in the gloom, facing the wrong way. She was not going to the bedroom.

He ran his hand through his hair. "This isn't going well. I'm sorry. I don't have time to explain."

She took a half-step to her right, just shifting her weight, and he leaned in the same direction. He was prepared to chase her, she saw. If she ran. If she tried to scream.

He said, "Please, please, just come to the bedroom."

She began to act. Not in the way she'd been thinking about before, for a stage, or a camera—the ordinary way, like when she met clients, or buyers, and had to be a slightly different version of herself for a while. For them, she was a sparkly, chatty Maddie, who was very interested in whatever you had to say and however long you wanted to take to say it. For Clay, she would be a person who did not need to be chased. She would be that person as completely as she could, until she saw the opportunity to be a person running for her life.

She nodded.

He exhaled. "Thank you. Thank you." He gestured, indicating for her to go past him. But that was a bridge too far, even for a person who did not need to be chased, and she hesitated. He nodded and backed away, making space. That was good. They were establishing trust. He was granting concessions, which she could abuse.

In the hallway, though, he stood with his back to the door. He gestured to the dark bedroom and she stared into his face but saw no other option. "Madison," he said, and pressed his hands together like a prayer. "I promise, I promise you can trust me."

She screams. Outside, the kids hear. Their heads turn in unison. Moments pass. Then they shrug and return to their bikes. It's a bad neighborhood; there are screams, sometimes.

No. Not this. She does not scream.

But she couldn't make herself enter that room. "Why?" she said, even though it was moot; he was close enough to seize her if he chose.

"I only want to talk. I swear to God."

She was terrified and possibly only seeing what she hoped for, but there was honesty in his face. She was a reasonable judge of character, from the acting: You learned what emotions looked like, which parts of the face moved when a person was envious, or sympathetic, or angry. Or lying.

She walked into the bedroom. Clay closed the door behind her. A thin shaft of light split the curtains and slashed across the carpet. The silver case sat in shadow, its mouth open to the far wall.

He moved to the curtain, opened it two fingers' worth, and peered out. Looking for . . . what? People, she guessed. Making sure no one was around. She reached behind her, seeking the door handle. She was only two closed doors to freedom. All she had to do was open this door, get out, fling it closed—this part was important!—so that it actually shut, and Clay would have to navigate the handle, and by then she could be pulling open the front door, and she would be outside, running, and, yes, it was a bad neighborhood, a terrible neighborhood, where there was every chance that no one would come to help, no matter how much noise she made, but it was her best option, she felt; it was far, far better than staying and finding out what was in the box.

Clay let the curtain fall closed. She tucked her hand into the small of her back before he could see. No one reaching for the door handle here. No, sir. No one who needed to be chased.

"I think we have a few minutes," Clay said. "I can tell you what's going on. But it won't be easy for you to hear. I need us to give each other a chance. All right?"

She nodded.

"Can you give me that chance?"

"Yes," she said, although she didn't like that: the push for affirmation.

"Like you said, your office knows who I am. They have my name, my photo." He held up his hands. "I've left fingerprints everywhere. Right?"

She nodded. Yes! These were excellent points. They could all agree that it would be crazy for Clay to do anything. There were security measures. Yes.

"So you can relax."

"Okay," she said. She was not relaxed. This situation had a long way to go before she would be anywhere near relaxed. But she was being agreeable.

He rubbed his hands together, a nervous gesture. He was still near the curtains. It was not completely impossible that she could get out the door before he reached her. "I'm just going to tell you. Madison, I'm not from this world."

Oh, God, she thought.

He came toward her. At first she thought he meant to take her hands, and that jolted her to her senses, because for a moment there she'd been snagged on the preposterousness of what he'd said: *I'm not from this world*—like, what did that mean, exactly, in what sense? But now she realized: the crazy sense.

The photo at the office didn't matter. The fingerprints didn't matter. He believed he was from another world.

"I've traveled here for you. Only for you, Madison." He hesitated. "How do you feel about that?"

She felt like vomiting from terror. But she said, "I'm . . . confused." Her tone was level, almost curious, and that was good; that was exactly what she wanted.

He glanced at the curtain again. When he next moved to the window, she was gone. She should have run the first time. "Of course you are. And scared, I bet. But you can trust me."

His face was hangdog, and here it was again, this weird insistence on her approval, even though he had all the power. It might be something she could use. For whatever reason, he cared what she thought, and if she were smart—if she didn't push too hard—she might be able to find a way to turn that against him. *I need us to give each other a chance,* he'd said. Maybe she could make him give her a chance.

"I . . . do feel like I can trust you," she said. "I don't know why."

His reaction was bigger than she'd expected: His loud eyebrows shot up and his mouth dropped open. "Really?"

"Yes," she said, rowing hard. "I felt that when we met. Maybe you remind me of someone I know?" No reaction. That was a swing and a miss. But he was waiting, his expression expectant, offering her another pitch. "Or . . . maybe we've met before."

Whack. A solid hit. His face lit up. "When do you think we've met?"

Oh, Christ. "I don't know. There's just . . . something."

"When?" he said again.

"College? High school?" But these were bad guesses, she saw. Not even close. She did something very brave and took a step toward him, *i.e.*, away from the door. A small deposit toward the hope of a future return. "Or something deeper. More spiritual."

He exhaled shakily. "You're right. We have met before. But not on this world."

She nodded. *Yes, of course, that's probably it.*

"All this . . ." He gestured to . . . the room, the curtains? No, no: the world, of course. "It's a drop in the ocean. There are more worlds. More than you can count. They look the same but they're not, not if you pay attention. And you're in all of them. Everywhere I go, you're doing different things. Every time I leave, it's to find you again."

He gazed at her. She felt required to ask a question. He'd just told her there were a bunch of worlds; of course, of course, she would have questions, if she took that seriously, and was not devoting most of her brain toward figuring out the location of the door handle. She said: "Why?" He didn't answer, and she thought maybe that had been a bad question, but no, it wasn't that: He just wanted her to figure out the answer. "In these . . . other worlds . . . are we . . . together?"

He gave a rueful smile and shook his head. But that was the right answer, she thought. That was what he'd wanted her to say. "Sometimes I can't even get to see you. Sometimes I can get to you but it doesn't work out. There are people trying to keep us apart. People who move, like me." He glanced at the curtains again. "They're getting close."

She was interested in that: in people who wanted to keep them apart. She would like to meet them now, if that was at all practical. "Why do they want to keep us apart?"

"It's complicated. I'll explain on the way."

On the way. For a long moment she tried and failed to imagine what on earth that could mean. Then it hit her: His box was a portal. Inside would be a car battery or a dead opossum that he'd convinced himself was a transdimensional travel device, and he would hold her hands and ask her to close her eyes. Then: *Kazam!* They would be in another world. Which would look the same, according to him. So, very conveniently, there would be no evidence of whether they'd traveled or not. But all this was fine, Maddie realized, completely fine, because after that, he would want to leave the house, and then she could run.

"On the way to where?" she said, widening her eyes, like: *Interdimensional travel, how amazing.*

"I have a hotel room," he said.

Ah.

They said never let yourself be taken to a secondary location. That was where you got murdered. But she had to get out of this house. She would go with him, but not get in his car. "All right," she said.

He smiled. "I still can't believe you recognized me. That never happens."

She smiled back.

"I mean, never," he said.

She felt a touch of ice in her throat. Her smile felt welded to her face.

"You know, I love you, Madison. In every world. Even when you don't love me back."

"We should go," she said, "before those people arrive."

"Can I ask you something?"

She nodded mutely.

"Can I hug you?"

She said nothing.

"It's just, it's been so long. It kills me to get this close to you and not touch you." He spread his arms.

She reviled at the idea. She could shove him, she thought. He was standing in front of the silver box; she could move in for the hug, then push him over the box.

She moved toward him. She didn't know if she could really shove him. It was fine in theory, but dudes were always a little faster and stronger than you expected. It was easy to forget, but occasionally there was a situation, a game of mixed basketball, a guy getting out of hand at a party, which made you realize: *Oh, shit, they are quick.*

He spread his arms. His disfigured forearm caught the shaft of light and she saw it clearly: a mess of older scar tissue and newer bruising, a red scab that couldn't be more than a week old. None of it looked like it was made by a dog.

She stopped, unable to make herself approach any closer. He stepped forward and gently put his arms around her. She let it happen. He exhaled noisily. His cheek rested on her head. "This is nice," he said.

She could see over the lid of the case. She had been right earlier: It was a toolbox. It had levels. On each was a different kind of knife. It was a box of gleaming metal and pain. She saw a space, as if something belonged there but was missing.

She began to tremble. "Shh," Clay said. "Shh." But she couldn't stop. His hands moved to her shoulders and pushed her back until he was holding her at arms' length. She couldn't help throwing fear-stricken glances at the box, and a smile crept along his lips. "Oh, Madison. You don't need to worry about that. That's only for if it doesn't work out. This time is different. Because this time you know me, don't you?"

She nodded.

"You felt a connection, right? As soon as we met?"

"Yes."

"Or," he said, "you were messing with me. Stringing me along." His fingers tightened on her shoulders. "Is that what you were doing?"

"No."

He gave a short, dismissive exhalation. "You know what I find crazy? There are so many of you. You're as common as dirt. I can find another tomorrow. But you always think you're so special. You're a real estate agent, for God's sake. But I gave you a chance, like I always do. I was honest with you and you lied to me."

She seized on this. "You said you didn't want to hurt me. You promised."

"I *don't* want to hurt you. But this . . ." His eyes ran down her body. "This isn't you. I can't stand to see you like this. I honestly can't."

She couldn't stop thinking about the space in the box. There was a missing tool and he had it somewhere.

She fled. Tried to. He had her before she'd so much as twitched, and she opened her mouth to scream and he jammed his forearm into it. Then his bulk followed, forcing her to the floor, knocking the breath out of her. She couldn't breathe, choked by his forearm, by the horrible puckered wound. When she tried to bite him, her teeth perfectly filled the indentations of his scar tissue.

He was reaching behind for whatever he had in his back pocket. "I hate that you make me do this," he said, and even as she struggled, she could see that he did indeed look regretful, like a man forced to put down a pet dog, one he'd loved that had turned rabid. The knife loomed, fat and wide and evil. "I really hate it."